LYING FOR LOST GIRLS

BOBBI DENZER

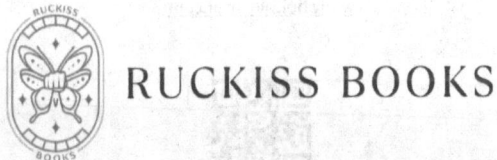

RUCKISS BOOKS

www.bobbidenzer.com

For my amazing family
who listened to "I'm a writer" for a good fifteen years
before this debut book was published.
Sorry about that.
Writing is hard.
(They heard that even more often)

Content Warnings

AT HEART, LYING FOR Lost Girls is a mystery romance between a strong young woman and the boy she is desperate not to fall for. However, this story deals with some difficult themes, both on and off the page, including but not limited to the following:

Physical Abuse, Violence toward a Child, Emotional Abuse of a Child, Racial Prejudice, Class Prejudice, Hate Speech/Slurs, Underage Drinking, Underage Drug Use, Car Accident, Death (not of the main character), Pregnancy (not of the main character), Miscarriage due to trauma (not of the main character), Missing Children, Medical Descriptions.

Please read with your personal and mental wellbeing in mind.

If there is a topic which is not listed above that you believe should be noted, please feel free to contact me either through the contact form on my website here, or by email to bobbi@bobbidenzer.com

ONE

now

I F THEY WOULD JUST handcuff her, Evyn would have something to push against. She'd twist and pull until her wrists reddened and bruised, blue and purple marks she could press at long after they release her.

But they never do.

They guide her gently, pressing the top of her head so it doesn't hit the cop car's door frame. At the station, they bring her water when she vomits stolen rum into the white, plastic bags that are always on hand or toss her packets of crackers when she smokes too much of Daire's weed. They sit her in a bare, sick-green room with bolted furniture, sometimes for hours, with her hands twisting useless in her lap.

Evyn waits on the bench with her chin in her hand, inhaling the stale, herby smoke that still clings to her fingers. Absently, she reaches into her shirt and pulls out her necklace. When she flicks open the lid of the broken compass pendant, pressing it against her lower lip, a flash of Daire hits fast and sharp: his mouth dropping open in surprise and then the sudden sureness of his hand on her bare arm. The skin where he touched her tingles.

"So stupid," she mutters, smudging the pendant to her mouth.

Detective Calver arrives and Evyn tucks the necklace away fast. Her cheeks burn and she presses at them with the back of her hand, scowling as he opens the door wide and pushes a plastic wedge into place with the toe of his boot. The file tucked under his arm is a familiar, coffee-ringed beige. He places it on the table, leans against the edge, and crosses his legs at the ankle. He's silent, as always, and Evyn is high enough that the bright light over his head makes him seem monstrous and dark. She leans forward, elbows on knees.

Calver's face is passive, but there's a twinge of satisfaction in seeing that the heatwave has gotten to him too. His shirt sleeves are rolled up, his usually-crisp collar is open and drooping on one side. He's wearing his standard issue baseball cap and the scars on his face are blurred, shadowed by its peak.

When the silence stretches, Evyn purses her lips and meets his eyes with a hard stare, refusing to speak.

It's a thing he does, waiting for her to talk first. She doesn't know if it's a tactic he learned in the city or if he'd formed it here in Blackditch Bay, just for small-town, pissed-off teenagers. Either way, it's effective.

The detective tilts his head and the light from the fluorescent strip pours over his cheek, an open invitation to stare at the thin, white scarring that runs over his jaw. There's a part of his neck that is clear and tan, but then it's there again, twisted skin that snakes under his shirt.

Everyone knows his chest is ruined, a jump-scare in a horror movie. Someone at school had once seen him swimming in the bay at 5am, had gotten nightmares from the sight of it. Evyn keeps her face as blank as she can. There's nothing worse than pity so she won't show it, not even to him. But still, she wonders, how could anyone survive that kind of pain?

When she can't take the silence anymore, when it's wrapped around her, squeezing until she wants to throw her arms out and spin, she huffs a short, angry breath and leans back against the wall.

"So, am I under arrest?"

Calver sighs and puts the file on the table next to his hip, taps it twice.

"What do you think?"

She doesn't answer, just shrugs and pulls up one knee with exaggerated swagger, as if it doesn't matter whether she's kept here overnight or dropped home in the back of his luminous Land Rover at the end of his shift.

"I've called your father. He's on his way."

Evyn stiffens and works to keep her face as neutral as Calver's. She's not successful. Calver leans toward her a little, eyes searching her face.

"This is your fourth time in two months," he tells her, fingers pressing into the file, "I need to know if you're okay. If you need help."

The room sways a bit, the last lingering effects of Daire's joint swirling in her bloodstream, stinging at her eyes. She catches herself. Planting her feet on the floor, Evyn reaches out toward the detective and raises her middle finger.

Calver is unaffected, sighing as he opens the file.

"Officer Obasi found you on the gallery roof this time. Was anyone with you? Anyone who might have gotten hurt running from the scene?"

Evyn blinks rapidly, chasing the image of Daire's face from her mind, as if Calver could see her thoughts.

"I was on my own."

"Sure you were, Evelyn," he says with a raised eyebrow.

Her reaction is lightning fast and violent.

"Don't call me that!" She spits the words at him through bared teeth, "My name is Evyn."

Calver straightens, the only sign of shock she's ever managed to pull from him. There's a moment where she teeters, thinks that maybe she should leave it at that. But she can't.

"It's what Stella called me." She's quieter now, tilting her head to watch his reaction carefully. "She couldn't pronounce Evelyn. You remember Stella, right? Or have you forgotten her too?"

It shouldn't feel this good, digging at him this way. But it does.

Calver closes the file, calm and gentle, and tucks it under his arm. He straightens his cap and nods at the floor. "I remember your sister, Evyn," he says, so low that Evyn has to strain to hear him, "I remember her."

It's there again, that lump in her throat, that burning urge to burst into tears she always feels in Calver's presence. Every time, no matter how she tries to shore herself against it. She swallows hard, swipes angrily at dry cheeks, and stares up at the open slit windows that line the very top of the wall, as if she could float right through them, out into the too-hot night.

This time, she wins the stand-off. The door knocks against the wall as Calver pulls the wedge from beneath it. He taps the doorframe, a light thud sounding until she throws him an irritated glance.

"You dad will be here in fifteen minutes. Is there anything you need while you're waiting?

She sneers at him.

"The door's not locked. If you want anything just yell down the hall. My office is on the left."

"I remember," Evyn says before she can stop herself. It has to be the weed. Daire must have overstuffed the smokes like he's always telling her not to. That's the only reason her voice wobbles, it would be rock steady otherwise. Evyn drags her knees up as the door closes with a soft click. As always, he doesn't lock it.

The heat in the room doubles instantly, sweat pricking along her arms. Her t-shirt sticks to her back and wisps of hair dampen and glue to her forehead and cheeks. There's no clock in the room, no way for Evyn to tell how long she's been here, and time moves differently when she's high.

Calver's wife had once told Evyn that life is short and she should take every opportunity she could. But Evyn knows that time is anything but reliable. A forty-minute class can feel like forever, an afternoon with Daire can whip by in just a few minutes, and then there are times like this, when she's waiting for her father to pick her up from the station. These minutes feel like hours and seconds all at once.

"Where is she?"

Her father's voice, deep and over-accented, comes like an echo. There's a thin sound she recognizes as he slaps the counter in the reception area. The station is pathetically small, an old, converted feed store with damp-stained ceiling tiles and thin partition walls. Evyn can hear the inner doors opening and closing as he approaches.

Her fingers start to shake. She clamps her hands together, tries to stop it, but that never works. The trembling spreads to her arms and legs like a virus. She focuses on the long, reinforced window that runs the length of the door, watching the empty hallway beyond it, pushing her lips against her clasped fingers. It might look like she's praying but there's no-one to ask for mercy, even if she could.

His arm bursts into view, overly-thick fingers reaching for the door handle, and Evyn sucks a deep breath. Before her father can open the door, Calver's hand lands on his shoulder. His fingers tighten, rippling the faded plaid shirt, stopping him. When Calver leans forward, his broad back blocks Evyn's view, but she can still hear the low rumble of his voice, too quiet to make out the words.

"You've some nerve telling me what to do with my own kid." Her father's voice is loud and clear. "When you have your own, you can talk to me, John. Till then, just open the door."

"It's not locked." Calver says, harder than Evyn has ever heard his speak. There's a chill down her spine as the door swings wide and her father fills the frame.

"Get up," he tells her and turns away before she can respond. Evyn bounds to her feet, following as quickly as she can, ducking past Calver with her eyes trained on the tile floor. Her father waits at the reception doors, watching her approach like he's pulling her to him with the steel wire of his temper. His shirt is damp all over, sticking transparent to his skin, and it's buttoned wrong in two places. His jaw is hard. Evyn can't meet his eyes. That will only make it worse. But the anger coming from him is so strong she's afraid she'll run if she meets the full force of it. He grasps her elbow and pulls her into reception.

At the counter, a woman is screaming.

"Of course, I looked in her bedroom! I told you she's gone! I've looked everywhere and I can't find her! For God's sake, she's only four years old! You have to help me!"

Her father pulls to a stop. The panic in the woman's voice is so familiar that Evyn feels limp. Calver swiftly brushes by them and strides toward the counter.

The woman, in silky blue pajamas and bare feet, turns toward him like he's a lifebuoy she's been thrown, clutching at his arm. The relief is so clear Evyn feels it in her shoulders.

"Miss Gilbride," he says, standing even taller, "What seems to be the problem?"

"Aimee's missing." She reaches forward, hand pressed flat in the center of Calver's chest, "I went to check on her at midnight and she wasn't in her bed."

Calver takes her wrist and gently removes her hand from his shirt with an almost imperceptible step backward. He holds her hand in both his instead, a gesture of comfort that keeps his body at a distance.

The conversation is so familiar that Evyn drifts involuntarily back against her father. He's unmoving behind her, stiff as a board, and Evyn feels lightheaded again, an odd buzzing in her ears that dampens the sound in the room. She brings her hands to her ears, batting away the noise as if it's coming from outside herself.

Evyn knows Rachel Gilbride. Everyone does. Blackditch Bay is packed with tourists during the summer, but the real people, the locals who batten down for harsh winter storms and electricity black-outs, who see each other in the supermarkets and bars when money gets Spring-tight, the ones who *live* here, all know each other. Rachel Gilbride was the girl who came home from college with a rounded belly and whispers following her every step. She was the shake-fisted warning her father had given Evyn before she even had her first period.

It's after midnight and Rachel's little girl, Aimee, is missing.

Stella had been in bed too, tucked up right beside Evyn, in her usual spot. And then she was gone. Evyn had searched for her through the dirty rooms of their run-down home. Shouting her name. Then, screaming it.

Sound rushes back as her father clears his throat behind her, a raking cough that catches everyone's attention. Rachel's eyes widen, recognizing them, holding Detective Calver's forearm as if she might fall to her knees at the sight.

"Calver never found my little girl," her father says, his voice rumbling, his words like a freight train, ploughing through the bright reception room, "What makes you think he'll find yours?"

"Oh, God."

Evyn isn't sure which of them has spoken but Rachel is looking right at her, eyes impossibly round, like there's no-one in the room but the two of them.

Evyn had stood right where Rachel is, with Daire's upper arm touching her shoulder in a way that had made her feel like he was holding her up. She'd felt that same panic, that same desperate fear, when her little sister went missing two years ago. And now Rachel is here in this same place, with a thousand agonizing possibilities darting over her face like a horror movie reel.

"Oh, God," she says.

"Pass me Miss Donovan's things," Calver orders the officer behind the counter, and takes the plastic bag with her phone and lip-balm to toss it at her father. He catches it, his arms snaking out so lightning-fast that Evyn flinches hard.

"Take her home, Mattie," Calver says flatly, barely glancing at them before he turns back to Rachel.

Her father pulls her out through the double doors. The stifling night air stinks of seaweed and harvested lavender. He drags her to where his rusted, pock-marked truck is parked in the closest disabled spot despite the empty lot around it.

"Get in." He opens the door and shoves her toward the seat. Evyn catches herself against the door frame and climbs in, her eyes following her father as he stomps to the driver's side. She risks a quick glance at the station while he fishes in his pocket for his keys. Detective Calver is still there, Rachel disappearing through the back door with officer

Obasi's arm around her shoulders. Calver is watching them, and the scar on his face is red-tinged and raw, like a warning. He's frowning in that unnerving way of his, where his whole face darkens but his eyebrows never quite draw together. It's not anger. Evyn has seen enough of that to know it in all its forms.

She watches him stare as her father pulls away and knows, without doubt, that what she sees on Calver's face is guilt.

Good.

Two

Then

Most of the tourists left the Fair when the wind picked up, fluttering the row of canopies that ran down the center of Pier Street. They held their bags over their heads against the misting rain and jogged, laughing, into the cafés and bars that lined the street.

The heavy, rolling sky made it seem later than it was but Stella tugged on Evyn's wrist, her painted face pleading as she pointed at the last stand they had yet to visit.

"Just trinkets, Stell," she warned her sister, as they wandered over "No more candy."

"What if I save them for tomorrow?" Stella grinned up at her, her teeth stained blue from the popsicle she'd just finished, and Evyn laughed louder than she meant to, an immediate approval for forbidden sweet-buying. She already knew she didn't have the heart to say no, "We'll see."

Evyn had been face-painting for most of the afternoon. She was still dressed in the fairy costume Alanna had loaned her. Her wrists and fingers ached from holding the brush and her cheeks were sore from smiling at tiny faces held so still as she drew superhero masks and princess flowers.

"That squall is gonna hit soon so choose quick," she warned Stella as they came up to a table filled with jugs of lavender. Sprigs tied in bunches hung from the canopy bar, bursts of purple flowers artfully dried and arranged against small canvases, two tattered-looking cupcakes on a crumb-strewn purple stand, and the remains of homemade mallows and fudge flavored with lavender and blueberry in foil trays that lined the front of the table. She stepped back to peer between the stands at the horizon over the bay as Stella chose her last treats of the day.

The cloud cover was charcoal thick and the sea was storm-green and dark. They'd be drenched by the time they walked home.

"Don't you go to Evyn's school?" Stella piped up as she held her hands out, her palms filled to capacity with purple-tinged gummies and flower-shaped chocolates.

Daire Silva-Doyle, wearing a frilly apron over a too-tight t-shirt, smiled a lopsided grin as he took the treats from Stella's hand.

"I do," he told Stella, then looked up, still smiling, "Hi, Evyn."

"I'm manning the stand for my aunt," he told Stella conspiratorially, as he bagged the sweets and then raised his arms wide to better show off the delicate, flower-printed apron, "Don't I look manly?"

Evyn smiled as Stella giggled and took the purple bag of candy.

When Evyn held out the money, Daire put his hands behind his back, "Just take it, half this stuff won't sell now." He jutted his chin toward the harbor, "Season's over."

Evyn shook her head, smile fading, and kept the money raised, "Wouldn't want you to get in trouble," she said, trying to keep her voice light.

"That's alright." Daire's face was briefly confused before he grinned again, "I should teach Aunt Val a lesson on unpaid labor. I'm sure my mom will represent me if she sues."

Stella laughed, though Evyn was certain she didn't understand the joke. She kept her hand out, her cheeks pricking hot, "Really, Daire, just take the money."

He stopped smiling, reached forward, and hesitantly plucked the bill from her fingers. "Yeah, no problem," he said as he turned to the till box. Evyn shuffled Stella away from the stand and down toward the harbor, walking fast, the coming rain already misting her face. Her feet were cold in the ballet slippers she'd taken from the lost and found bin at school and she absently checked Stella's laces as she trotted along beside her.

"Evyn!" Daire's voice called out as they reached the harbor wall, "Your change!"

She stopped and turned with an irritated sigh, pulling Stella into her hip as he jogged up, his apron discarded. He held a bill in his hand, far more than she should be getting back for the hefty bag that Stella had clasped in her fist. Townies always got a discount on Fair days. Evyn had paid half-price at most of the stands that day but it was different coming from someone her own age. Daire was only a year older, and it grated, having him run out in the rain, drawing attention.

"Daire! You coming?"

Over the harbor wall, halfway down the pier, a girl Evyn didn't recognize stood waving one arm in a long, graceful arc. Behind her, in a small packing alcove, six summer kids sat in a small circle, huddled under the stone roof, a small gas camping fire in the center. He waved back and shouted at the group, "Yeah, two minutes!" before turning back to Evyn with a frown.

"Are you walking in this?" he asked, raising the change toward the darkening sky.

Evyn snapped the money from him with a brightly-voiced 'thanks' and turned toward Main Street. She nodded at Stella to press the crosswalk button.

"My brother's picking me up in an hour if you want to wait with us?" Daire called after them, "It's just some kids from the camping ground. It's their last night and..."

He trailed off as Evyn waved him off and crossed the street. At the halfway point, a streak of lightning flickered out beyond the bay, flashing in the pink-curtained windows of the tearooms on the opposite side. The rumble of thunder sounded almost instantly and the rain poured down like an open faucet a moment later. Stella shrieked and laughed, pulling on Evyn's hand until she turned back to Daire. He was smiling at them as if he'd specifically ordered the skies to open, his face dimpled. Evyn couldn't help but laugh back. She shrugged, allowing Stella to pull her back toward the harbor. The rain was already seeping through her costume.

"Want a boost?" Daire helped Stella up onto the wall so she could clamber onto his back. They jogged down to the dock, avoiding the small lip of Hangman's Beach that remained in high tide, Stella giggling and shouting to go faster.

"This is Evyn," he told the group as they huddled into the small space, the summer kids shuffling to make room in their circle, "And the small one is..."

"I'm Stella," her sister shouted far too loudly, high on sugar and the thought of getting to sit with the older kids. There was a small ripple of laughter and Evyn relaxed, smiling at everyone as she sat.

One of the boys opened a takeout bag, took out a sandwich so greasy that the paper dripped slick droplets down his wrist, and passed the bag around the group. The smell of salty fries made Evyn's mouth water well before it reached their side of the circle. Stella shivered, her shorts and t-shirt now far too light for the weather, and Evyn tucked her under her arm as the group finalised their plans for their last night in Blackditch Bay.

"There's a party on the beach later," one of the girls leaned forward to ask, holding her pink-tinted braids with both hands to keep them back from the gas fire, and dropped her voice to a whisper, eyeing Stella, "Wanna come?"

Evyn shook her head, smiling, "I'd love to but I have track in the morning."

"Evyn's a runner but she plays volleyball too," Daire said, taking two fries from the bag and handing them to Stella with a grin, "Better than Vince anyway."

"Hey!" called a tall blond boy on the opposite side of the circle. Daire dodged a flying fry and laughed off the low competitive rumble. It was an easy conversation, quieter than she had expected from summer kids, who usually hung out in loud groups that Evyn only interacted with when she was serving from behind the counter in the small ice-cream parlor.

Stella was half asleep by the time Daire's brother arrived. Daire's t-shirt was still damp at the shoulders and Evyn's borrowed fairy wings felt heavy on her back. She lifted her sister onto her hip and waved an awkward goodbye to the group as the car honked insistently from the packing factory's small lot at the top of the dock.

Daire lagged behind, one hand on the hip of the girl who'd invited Evyn to the party. As he leaned down to kiss her goodbye, a current of something uneasy ran through Evyn's stomach and she turned away from them, walking slow.

"I can take her if she's heavy," Daire said quietly when he caught up.

Evyn shook her head, smiling tight, and took note of the shiny new car his brother was driving. She remembered Jake Silva-Doyle from school, the easy way he took up too much space in the hallways, but he'd been in college for two years now. Daire and he were similar, the same golden-brown skin and dark hair they got from their Venezuelan mother, though Daire was taller and broader, like his father.

She sat in the back seat and Stella laid her head heavily on Evyn's thigh. It was past her sister's usual bedtime and she was having trouble staying awake. The drive back was quiet, Jake asking low, good-natured questions to Daire in the front, laughing about Aunt Val's latest business, while Evyn looked out the window and tried to work out the best place drop them.

"Here's fine," she said eventually, leaning forward as Jake turned onto the Lake Drive.

"Don't you live out by the woods?" Daire asked. The rain was still coming down hard but Evyn shook her head, plastering a bright smile onto her face. "Here's perfect."

Jake pulled the car over and Daire turned in his seat as she opened the door. "You sure you don't wanna come to the party tonight? We won't be out too late. It's their last night..." he trailed off again and his brother snorted beside him and then covered it with a cough. Daire elbowed him and turned even further, taking up all the space between the seats, "It'll be fun."

"No, but thanks." Evyn pulled Stella into her lap and struggled out of the car, bending down to thank Jake quickly before shutting the door. It would take a while to get home from here and she walked as fast as she could, the rain soaking her fairy-glittered hair.

Both car doors opened behind her, Jake's voice full of laughter as he called out, "If you crash dad's car, I'm not covering for you."

She glanced back as Daire took the driver's seat, lifting his fingers in a small wave. The indicator light flashed as he ten-point-turned in the small road.

At home, she pulled Stella into her threadbare pajamas and settled her into her cot bed, tucking her favorite soft doll under her arm before she grabbed a drink from the kitchen and went to her own room. Dragging her sketch-pad from beneath her bed, she drew familiar lines and soft indents, trying to get that uneasy feeling out of her belly.

Re-creating a private moment that wasn't hers felt wrong, but she drew it over and over, all the same. Daire, leaning down, mouth slightly open. The girl he'd kissed, just the outline of her braids and the curve of her jaw, tipped up and waiting.

It didn't help. Drawing after drawing, Evyn still felt that strangeness in her stomach, wishing it away until she fell asleep.

HER LEGS STILL KICKED, though she was already sitting up, fully awake, clutching her sleep-shirt in her fist. The nightmare was so vivid that she reached down to pat Stella's head, in case she had shouted in her sleep and woken her. The bed beside her was empty, a stained mattress and twisted sheets snaking around her calves. Evyn leaned over to see if Stella had somehow ended up on the floor but it was bare too.

"Stella?" she called, catching her breath.

There was no response. Pure silence except for the birdsong coming from the scraggy woods at the back of the yard and the light patter of soft rain against the windowpane. No sound of cartoons from the living room or sloppy strikes of a spoon against a cereal bowl from the kitchen. She grabbed her phone to check the time. It was after eight, past when her father would usually leave for work. Safe.

Evyn stood and stretched, freeing up her muscles after the tension of the dream. She gathered up her sketches from last night and tucked them into the box under her bed. In the hallway, her foot hit a stray beer bottle, dropped by her father at some point in the night. She picked it up and stepped into the bathroom, tossing it into the little basket under the sink.

"Stella," she called as she spread toothpaste on her brush, "I have to go out for a couple of hours. Come clean up before I make breakfast."

She listened hard, trying to hear what her sister was up to. It wasn't usual for Stella to wake before her. It only happened when she'd been up late the night before, reading or drawing. Stella would creep in once Evyn was asleep, all sharp elbows and determination as she crawled over Evyn's legs to curl up in her spot between Evyn and the wall. Every morning, Evyn woke to a small pointer finger in her side and her little sister's increasingly annoying requests for food. Stella never managed to get up without waking Evyn too.

She paused, toothpaste mint-stinging against her tongue. Had she even felt Stella sneak into her bed last night?

"Stella?" she peeked around the door frame, looking down the dingy hall toward the kitchen. The visible side of the table was empty, the packet of sweets from the fair sitting neatly by the sink, unopened. The fear from her dream reared up, a weighted sensation, like Evyn was being chased but couldn't run. She shook herself, trying to brush it off, but the silence in the house felt thicker and she couldn't hear the birds anymore.

"I have new glitter slime for you," she called, forcing her voice to turn sweet and tempting, "If you come right now, I'll let you play with it while I'm gone."

No response.

Evyn stepped across the hall to Stella's tiny room. Her sunshine-yellow sheets were tangled on the mattress.

"Stella?"

She jogged to the kitchen and found it exactly as she had left it last night. Even her father's breakfast bowl, which she had laid out for him on the table, was untouched. She could feel the rushing quiver of her heartbeat at the base of her thumbs. She checked the moldy shower cubicle, behind the ripped, chintz couch in the TV room where her father smoked and drank every night until he stumbled to bed. She looked under their rusted cot-beds and in their tiny closets. No sign of a hiding child.

A missing sister, for the average girl, would mean an anxious phone call to a parent, asking for help. That's where her friend's responsibilities would have ended. But not hers. Instead, Evyn ran back to her room, sat on her bed, and texted the girls from track.

Can't make it today. Daire asked me to his parent's harvest BBQ and I gotta scrub up!

She even added smiley faces, as if there was nothing wrong, as if her stomach wasn't cramping and her breath short and sharp in her chest. Years later, she would ask herself why she'd given Daire as her excuse. Why was it, out of everyone she could have turned to, his name was the first that had come to her? Was there a part of her that had already worked out the worst thing that could happen and tried to construct a plan?

"Stella!" she called, loud and angry, "This is not funny. You need to come out here right now."

Nothing but the slow tick of the clock in the kitchen. She followed it, deliberate steps through the dim hallway and into the shabby room. "If I catch you hiding, this slime is going back to the store and I'm buying myself new mascara. You hear me?"

But she already knew what the response would be. Silence. Grey light through warped, grimy windows, untouched plates on an oilcloth-covered table, and the familiar, skittering sounds from behind the fraying curtain under the kitchen sink. Somewhere, deep under her ribs, the panic was already bubbling.

The front door was locked so she turned and headed back to the kitchen door. Also locked.

Evyn stopped with her fingers on the handle. She pulled her hair back from her face, frowning at the dark hallway. If both doors were locked, Stella had to be inside. Most of the windows in the house were nailed shut and the warped wood of the two that actually did open, only allowed them to be pushed out a crack, certainly not enough to climb through. There was no other way out of the house.

"Stella! You better answer me right now! Where are you? I mean it!"

The only answer was the muffled sound of bird-call from the woods at the back of their yard.

"Stella, please!" Her voice was shaking.

Evyn opened the back door and ran out into the yard. There were so many places to hide out here. Once, when Stella was only three, they played hide-and-seek and Evyn couldn't find her for almost an hour. She'd felt this same fear then, until she found her sleeping, curled up in an old truck tire. She ran there now. Stringy weeds had grown up through the empty center.

She called out, over and over, upturning old planters and peering into their bug-lined depths. She pulled apart a pile of broken furniture, even though it would have been impossible for Stella to have crawled into it. She peered under rusted car carcasses, half-crawled beneath the broken oil tank, and searched the listing shed with its one remaining shelf of empty anti-freeze bottles and discarded tools.

Though she avoided the overturned fridge at the back fence, the peeling green paint kept drawing her eye. It called to her as if it was the thing from her nightmare, reaching out dark fingertips to claw at her. Evyn kept searching the yard until there was nowhere else to look.

She bent down in front of the fridge, her hands pushing into her knees. There was something in her throat, like the lump she got there when she was about to cry, as if all the air in her lungs had condensed right there in her neck, stoppering her screams. It took effort to straighten and walk toward the hulking frame.

The handle was rusted chrome. It didn't budge when Evyn tugged on it. She pulled harder, dug her heels into the ground, and wrenched until her shoulders popped. Finally, it jolted open, sending her sprawling backwards into the rain-soaked earth, the door falling heavy on her feet and ankles. She lay there for a full minute, as the mud seeped cold into her back, unwilling to look away from the sky, unable to breathe.

Haltingly, she forced her legs to move, pulling them from under the door, and willed her arms to push her upright, eyes closed tight until the last moment.

The inside of the fridge was bright, white plastic. Chrome racks tangled in a metallic mesh, half out of the base with the force of her opening it.

There was no little girl inside.

The few seconds of immense relief were immediately replaced with a renewed panic. Where was she?

"STELLA!!!!"

She had meant only to shout, but her name came out in a stuttering, high-pitched scream. The birds in the trees that lined the chain-link fence at the back of the property made a raucous noise as they startled and took flight.

There was lavender on the breeze, a calming, earthy scent that drifted from the farms on the other side of the woods. She breathed it in, trying to work out a plan, trying to think of someone who would help her without judgement. The only name Evyn could think of was one she had already given. Daire.

THREE

THEN

EVYN SWERVED HER BIKE to avoid the group of tourists bursting through the Grand Hotel doors. Her legs were burning and she could barely hear Mrs. Garcia's worried call as she raced by the tearooms. She crossed at the intersection, ignoring the hesitant wave from her biology teacher, sitting behind the wheel of his station wagon with a vape pen between his knuckles.

The harbor was a wintry green but there was already a line outside the Creamery, the chilly morning air doing nothing to deter the summer people from over-priced ice cream at 9am on a Thursday. She stood on the pedals to push herself up Pen's Hill toward Daire's tree-lined street, planted on either side with houses of increasing grandeur. Misty rain slipped beneath the collar of her raincoat and pooled between her fingers as she gripped the cracked handlebars. She was panting and her chest felt tight and hot.

The bike wobbled over the last few meters of the steepest part of the hill. Evyn was certain she'd career off the road before the incline eased out enough to sit back down. It was the fastest she'd ever cycled and now that she was nearing the decorative stone walls of Daire's home, her mind raced faster still. Had she checked everywhere? Should she have dragged a chair from the kitchen and tried to climb into the eaves, where their meager Christmas decorations and winter clothes were stored? Maybe she should have walked their property line before leaving? How was it possible for Stella to get out of the house with both doors locked?

The rough wall scraped her arm as she pulled up alongside it, dismounting beneath the neatly inset intercom. There were so many back-lit buttons she wasn't sure which to press. She opted for the largest, holding it down for longer than she meant while her heart beat franticly.

"Yeah?"

Daire's voice, slurred and gritty with mild irritation, came from the panel.

"It's Evyn," she said, and the pause was so long that she felt the need to clarify "From school?"

She fiddled awkwardly with the end of her t-shirt. What was she doing here?

"Yeah, Evyn, I know who you are. Sorry," he said, and the gates buzzed, starting a slow slide behind the hydrangeas, "Come on up, front door's open."

The pale-paved driveway curved down toward the house, profusions of greenery with tropical-looking orange flowers on either side. Jake's car was parked to the side of the huge glass entryway. As she walked her bike to the front door, Evyn could see straight through the house, to the massive glass panels of their patio and out to the horizon beyond. She paused at the door, dropping her bike on the path instead of leaning it against the house.

It felt wrong, testing the door handle, and she opened it only so far as her head and shoulders would fit.

"Um, hello?"

The sound of her voice echoed in the massive open plan space. She stared at the pale leather couches with soft throws and cushions piled haphazard, the clean, marble kitchen island with masses of white hydrangea and willow in glass vases, and beyond the glass wall to the outdoor seating area. The house seemed empty.

She stepped inside and closed the door behind her to stop the cold air from getting in and stood gingerly on the pretty rug. There was artwork on the walls, alongside black and white photos. She recognized Daire's face, a side-angle shot too close to see more than the long, straight line of his nose buried in a book. The staircase was nothing more than thick, bleached wood planks attached to the wall at one end. Evyn immediately thought of falling.

Daire's voice floated down from somewhere upstairs, "Come on up Evyn, first door on the right."

She hesitated, carefully positioning herself close to the wall and refusing to look down as she climbed. Through Daire's half-open door, she caught a whirl of motion as he pulled on a t-shirt and simultaneously kicked a drawer closed. She'd forgotten how early it was, how he'd been out late at the party the night before. His hair was sticking out in all directions and he spun in a quick circle, shunting discarded clothes towards a rattan basket.

"Where's my shoe?" he muttered to himself and rubbed at his hair before spotting her in the doorway, "Hey, Evyn. What's going on?"

He kept searching, a satisfied *ah* coming from him as he spotted his bright blue sneaker under his desk and tugged it on, hopping on one leg.

Evyn leaned into the door frame. The sudden urge to run was over-whelming, as if telling Daire why she was here would somehow make it more real. She tightened her abdominal muscles, trying to squeeze some of the shake from her stomach. When she didn't answer, Daire stopped hopping and stood tall, looking hard at her.

"Jesus, are you alright?" He came toward her and Evyn froze. If he was kind to her now, if he tried to comfort her, she would fall to pieces.

"You have your license, right?" Her voice was so hard that Daire pulled up short, dropping his hands awkwardly to his sides.

"To drive? Yeah."

"I can't find Stella."

The moment she said it, Evyn's body betrayed her. Her knees weak-ened and her lip trembled and suddenly the door frame felt like the only thing keeping her standing. She took a deep breath and clenched her fists. "She's too young to be out on her own and I need someone to help me find her. Can you drive me to a few of her favorite places?"

She couldn't keep the demand from her voice, her only substitute for pleading. Daire's mouth dropped open, a worried frown creasing tight lines in his forehead as he shook his head. He asked the one thing she had hoped he wouldn't think of.

"Shouldn't we go to the police?"

"I can find her," she responded and it was only pleading now, her voice high and tight with it.

"OK," he raised his hands immediately, placating her, "Alright, Evyn."

He turned back to his desk and rifled through it until he found a pen and paper. Pushing his desk chair out, he motioned her to sit.

"Write down her friends' houses, all the places she likes to play, any-where you can think of that she might go. The sat nav will find the quickest route."

He dragged a sleek black guitar amp away from the wall and used it as a seat, pulling the cable so the dusty bass attached to it fell on its side. It was quiet until she finished the list, Daire plugging in the addresses as she wrote them so the map on his large phone screen showed circuitous rings around the town. Once she'd vetted it, making sure he'd caught every area she needed to check, he set the phone down and crossed his forearms on the desk.

"Evyn," he said, slow and hesitant, "If we don't find her by this afternoon, I'm driving you to the station, okay?"

It wasn't a question, Evyn could tell by the tense set of his mouth. He was giving her a provision, bartering for an agreement. She nodded despite herself.

Lying wouldn't matter, she was certain, they would find Stella long before it became an issue.

Daire tapped the table-top, looking at her for a little longer than was comfortable, as if he knew her sudden willingness wasn't the whole truth. But then he stood, grabbed a raincoat, and tilted his head toward the door. "OK, let's go find her."

Relief. It was an odd feeling, having him take the lead. It wasn't something she was used to. But right now, it felt like the easiest thing in the world to follow Daire down his pristine staircase and into Jake's expensive car.

Noticing her slight shiver, Daire pressed a button so the seat began to warm up.

"We'll start with her friends' houses," Evyn told him, trying to take back some of the control that seemed to come so easily to him. Daire tapped his phone and re-adjusted the map before slinging one arm over the back of her seat and reversing into the turning spot in his driveway.

BY LUNCHTIME, THEY'D VISITED every house Stella had ever had a playdate in, combed the playground and the water park and the candy shops, double-backed and searched through the woods around her house. Evyn had asked Daire to wait outside as she searched through every room again, just to make sure. His face had stayed steady as he took in the peeling paint, a tarnished shade of seventies peach, and the large cracks in the windows. It was the first time anyone from school had seen her house and Evyn felt the horrified embarrassment she had always known she would. But she couldn't focus on it, instead searching through the dusty attic space and emerging dirt-streaked and empty-handed, calling Daire away from the listing pile of old tires.

"There's only one place left I can think of," she told him. Her voice shook. She hadn't put it on the map and it was getting late. Daire might insist on going to the police before Evyn could find her. "The lavender field has a willow tree she loves. She makes it her pirate ship or her underwater castle, depending on the weather." She tried to smile, bolstering her certainty that Stella would be there.

There was nowhere else to look.

Daire nodded, gave her a quick, subdued grin. He was quieter on the drive to the farms. The lavender harvest was a popular attraction and the garden center was surrounded by tourists, sitting under purple umbrellas holding cups of steaming hot chocolate and coffee. They drove into the packed car park, pulling up so tight against the wall that Evyn had to scramble over the seats to climb out the driver's side door. They headed away from the main area, trekking through rows of flower-hewn lavender plants, green and sharp-twigged, with spatters of fallen lilac flowers on the compacted walkways between them. The scent was earthy and heady and Stella loved that smell so much that Evyn had once bought her an over-priced bottle of pillow spray, hoping she'd stay in her own bed for once.

She *had* to be here.

They raced to the far end of the second field, the willow tree drooped thick trailing vines toward the ground. It was so profuse at this time of year that the trunk wasn't visible. That was Stella's favorite part. She could have picnics beneath the bows, pretend to be a superhero, or a princess, or a mermaid, and no one in the outside would ever know she was there. They hadn't come much this summer, Evyn's job at the tea-rooms had kept her busy most days and she worked the Creamery's evening shift. Once she found her hiding in there, Evyn would take her back every single lunchtime until Stella was so sick of it that she would never think of running away to play there again.

Daire pulled back a shaft of willows leaves. Glancing up at the huge boughs, Evyn took a deep breath and ducked beneath his arm into the dim, green-filtered light at the center. Here, the noise from the garden center was muted, and the trill of birds above was eerily urgent.

"Stella?" Evyn's voice was quiet, timid, "I know you're here, and you're not in trouble. Come on out now."

Daire went to the other side of the huge trunk and disappeared from view. After a quick scan of the branches, Evyn lifted trailing leaves, cascading raindrops as she checked beneath them for a little girl tuckered out after playing too long.

"Stella!" she called, louder, and even *she* could hear the desperation behind it.

Daire came back into view, circling the trunk and then raising his hands to the side, solemn and helpless. "It's clear back there."

Evyn shook her head, sprinting to the other side of the tree, tearing through the leaves until they tangled in her clothes and hair.

"Stella, come on!"

Daire jogged up behind her, his cautious voice low and soothing. But Evyn couldn't hear the words. Something was cracking open inside her, a pit that threatened to swallow her whole. Where was her little sister? Her vision dulled and then brightened and she was on her knees without realizing she had dropped to the ground. She couldn't catch her breath, every exhale coming out with half-finished, panicked words, "Where? How could she even... Nothing makes any..."

And then Daire was there, kneeling on the ground with her, arms wrapping tight. Evyn blindly grasped, found his thumb, and curled around his arm while the awful truth sank in.

Stella was gone. Really gone.

She felt the joint of Daire's thumb pop against her palm, and he pulled her closer, half into his lap. Time softened and wavered, Grey midday morphing to bright afternoon, and Daire was talking to her, words soft and blurry until she forced herself to focus on them. "Evyn, it's time to go to the station."

She should have felt embarrassed, tear-damp cheeks and dirty palms on his expensive t-shirt, her listless body resting on his outstretched legs. She should've moved away and pulled herself together. But her limbs felt heavy and dull, unresponsive when she tried to get up. He had to help her, and she let him, mute as he hugged her into his side and pulled her through the branches.

Outside the tree's dense cocoon, the ordinary sounds of people talking seemed out of place. Slowly, she pulled away from Daire and trudged forward, her back too straight as she followed the trail back to the garden center.

A large group of people milled about in the parking lot and an odd trail of cars backed up onto the road. Daire cursed quietly and jogged away from her, heading downhill at speed. A blue SUV, unfamiliar and enormous, had pulled in behind Daire's car, unable to squeeze past it despite how tightly Daire had parked against the wall. Officer Obasi, her arm raised to talk into her radio, was directing a tow truck in the wrong direction around the lot, trying to clear irritated tourists out of the way.

Daire jumped the wall one-handed and Evyn watched him apologizing as the cop leaned in to listen. His face told her what Evyn needed to know, even before he pointed back toward her, signaling. He was reporting Stella missing. Evyn's climb over the low wall was slow and ungainly. A woman with a small child on her hip raised her arm in annoyance and rolled her eyes but Officer Obasi motioned her away and Evyn could hear the ripple of irritation through the group of tourists.

Officer Obasi quieted them and pointed at Daire. "Move your car out of the way," she said, her lilting accent and low voice soothing, "While I talk to your friend."

Daire hesitated for a brief moment, eyes flicking to Evyn's.

"Can I borrow your phone?" Evyn asked, so quietly that both the cop and Daire leaned in to hear her better, "I have to call my father."

FOUR

now

THE TRUCK'S SUSPENSION RATTLES as her father drives through the rusted-open gates of their home, bumping over the ancient cattle grid. He pulls up on the baked mud and turns off the engine. It ticks a moment, cooling down. Evyn twists her hands together in her lap. Now that the car is still, the air wafting in through the open car windows stinks of exhaust and diesel.

Her father says nothing. She knows he's staring at her, can feel the chill of it even through the stifling warmth of the cab. When he opens the door and hauls himself out, slamming it so hard the car rocks, he doesn't have to tell her to follow.

Evyn takes a breath to settle her stomach and hops down onto uneven divots of dried earth. The darkness is thicker on her side of the truck. It's difficult not to twist her ankles before she reaches the opposite side, where the dim television flickers from the living room window, throwing dappled light on the sparse gravel. She can't help but slow her walk, though she knows that will only prolong the inevitable.

By the time she steps inside, her father already has a beer in his hand and is settled in his battered armchair, one foot on the ancient coffee table. He swirls the bottle as she stands limp in the doorway.

"D'you think I need this shit?" he asks, voice clipped and biting.

"No, Dad." Evyn doesn't flinch, willing herself to stay calm and still.

He seems not to hear and Evyn recognizes the tone of his voice, gearing up slowly like a valve releasing rage into the room.

"You think I need Scarface Calver calling me at two in the morning telling me I'm no good because of you?"

Evyn shakes her head, stares at the ground.

"Do you?" he gets louder, a decibel away from a shout.

"No, Dad." She flinches despite herself.

He stands, drains the beer in three long gulps, and sets the bottle down on the table. From beside his chair, he pulls another bottle, whiskey this time, and takes a slug.

"You with that Mexican again?"

"He's not Mexican." Evyn doesn't know where it comes from. Usually, she just says no. But she can't this time. Not after what happened on the gallery roof. "His mom's from Venezuela." As if it matters. As if anything but middling poverty and whiteness would sway him.

"I don't give a shit where he's from!" Her father skips past the shouting stage entirely and roars, grabbing the empty beer bottle off the table and lobbing it at her.

Evyn ducks quickly enough that it flies past her shoulder. The bottle ricochets off the wall and hits the middle of her back with a soft thud, spilling dregs of warm liquid on her leg as it falls to the floor.

"Sorry, Dad," she says and, the moment the words leave her mouth she knows, it's too soon. He smiles, a mean slit in his clouded face, and takes a another quiet sip of whiskey.

"You're sorry? How many times am I gonna hear that, huh?"

Evyn doesn't reply, waiting for what comes next. Even though she knows it's coming, this time, everything feels different. She'd slipped up tonight, lost her hard-won control. Now there will be a shred of truth to what he's going to say and it slithers over her, burning in her cheeks.

"Running round with some rich, uppity immigrant," he starts, pointing the neck of the whiskey bottle at her so the liquid inside sloshes and glugs, "You come home pregnant and you can pack your things, you hear me?"

"It's not like that," she tries but it doesn't sound right, even to her. It's the truth, but there's more to it now. She can feel Daire's surprised breath ghosting over her neck and she's so exhausted her knees feel weak. "I swear, Dad, we're just friends."

He strides forward so fast that Evyn doesn't have time to prepare. Her father grasps her chin, looming over her to stare into her face and Evyn's hands tighten into fists by her sides.

"Filthy liar," he spits and she forces her fingers to uncurl, "Just the sight of you makes me sick." He gives her chin a harsh squeeze before shoving her face away so hard that her back knocks against the door frame. She takes her cue, whispering another apology as she turns to leave.

It happens fast, as it always does.

Her father growls and reaches for her, pulling her back into the room. He's saying something but Evyn can't hear him. Her ankles twist together as he turns her and she loses her balance. Evyn stumbles, arms wide, upending the coffee table as she falls to the floor.

There's a blinding pain in her ribs where she hit the corner of the cheap wood. Another empty beer bottle rolls away from her as she lies still, trying to catch her breath. It's impossible. She's trying to breathe into lungs that have closed tight against her. The room seems brighter, flashing along with the throbbing pain.

"Get up," her father says, kicking at the sole of her shoe. She can't answer, still trying to take in a breath. She tries to push her hands into the floor, to get to her knees, but they won't take her weight.

He grasps the back of her t-shirt, yanking at her, lifting her from the floor.

Evyn's breath rushes in loud tearing gasps. Her father curses, dragging her upright. Her legs barely holding her weight. He tosses her onto the couch and leans over her sniffing.

"Jesus, you stink of weed," he tells her, "You're so out of it you can't even stand up. Get the hell outta my sight."

He rears back and goes to the kitchen without another word. Bottle clink as he roots through the fridge. The pain is raw and sparking. She can't stand. But her father had told her to leave so Evyn has no option. She uses the sofas' wooden arm to climb to her feet, hugging her midsection even though it hurts to touch. The walk to the door is nothing more than five swaying steps but she is almost certain she will fall again until the door frame is in her grip. She slides along the hallway to her room, closing the door as softly as she can.

Her father thunders back down the corridor and Evyn's whole body shakes, her fingers clutching the door handle to hold it closed. She presses her forehead to the plywood, her warm breath curling back to hit her cheek softly as she waits for the tell-tale sound of his chair creaking. Once she hears it, she sags to the floor and crawls to her cot-bed, the mattress springs hard against her thighs as she sits.

If she could lie down, she would, but Evyn knows she will feel worse in the morning if she doesn't try to fix herself up. She pulls her phone from her pocket, gasps at the flash of pain in her center when she bends to plug in the charger, then sets about wrapping her ribs with the thinnest scarf she can find. Her skin is clammy and cold, despite the heat in her stuffy room. The warped window means she can never open it and, in the second week of the heatwave, she should be sweltering now. Instead, she's freezing.

She pulls on her thinnest nightdress, a satiny slip she found at the thrift shop this summer. Its smoothness lets her turn more easily and she'll be warm again once the shock wears off. Her phone beeps as she lies back against her pillow, angling her ribs so they don't touch the mattress. Even at this awkward angle, she can see the black and white sketch she drew that he uses as his profile picture; Daire, studying, a pen in one hand and his notes in the other. She can't make out the words in the text he's sent her and she's too sore to reach for the phone. Exhausted, she closes her eyes. Her phone pings again as she falls asleep.

IT FEELS LIKE PULLING herself from a warm, dark pool when Evyn wakes. It's early morning, she can tell by the pinkish light that wavers on the far wall. The room is boiling already and her skin sticks to her nightdress as she shifts on the bed. The pain in her ribs has become a dull throb overnight but it flares high and fast with her movement. She almost shrieks, biting her lip hard so she won't cry out.

There's a spring pressing into her shoulder. Instinctively, Evyn leans into it, diverting her attention away from her midsection. It works. She lets her breath out slowly, controlled, then reaches for her phone. There are five texts from Daire. The first is angry, accusing.

I would have come back for you.

It's so rare from him - a short snapping text, and the guilt runs through her. She shouldn't have done what she did. She should have gone home when that first shard of emotion slipped through. She should have run when he told her to.

The next three texts apologize for the first, soft words and soothing talk of how nothing will change when he leaves for college. She only has one more year and she can visit him whenever she wants. He tells her she might like the city. Evyn can almost hear him say it. The tone of his voice always hints at more, closer than ever to slipping over that line they never cross. It's her fault, she knows. She slipped first.

Evyn reads every message several times before she deletes them all, one by one.

The last message is different, sent this morning at five a.m., a short, clipped note.

Evyn, call me when you wake up. Something's happened. It's important.

She knows what he wants to tell her. Aimee Gilbride is missing.

Evyn isn't sure if she can talk about it, not when she'd been in the room where Aimee's mother had begged for help. Not when her own presence had made it so much worse. Evyn is a walking reminder that bad things can happen, even in a small town like Blackditch Bay.

She sets the phone down and turns gingerly toward the wall, pulling her knees up. Sometimes, if she lies still for long enough and breathes as shallow and slow as she can, she'll start to feel warmth on her belly, as if her sister were right there in her usual spot. Once, when she held her breath for so long that her lungs had tugged hard in her chest, she'd felt the soft brush of baby-blonde hair on her chin. Her eyes had flown open as she gasped for the air she'd denied herself, but there was nothing there but a mattress so old that the springs pressed through the fabric and the faint scent of lavender.

Gently, she untangles her legs from the sheet. Skin sticky, she longs for a shower but her father would wake at the sound of running water so early in the morning. Instead, Evyn tiptoes to the bathroom and gently washes her skin with a moth-holed towel, avoiding her ribs until she can't anymore, until the thin, muslin scarf that wraps her middle is all she has left to clean.

This is the worst bit, assessing the damage, how to cover it, how to work around the broken parts so no-one will see them. She unwraps the scarf slowly, eyes trained on the mirror, as if the reflection isn't as real, or as painful. Her ribs are red, skin puffy with dark streaks spidering out over her skin. She tests the bones, pressing different parts with the cool cloth. They're not broken, she's almost certain, but she re-wraps the scarf all the same.

There are finger-shaped bruises on her upper arms too. Those will be more difficult to hide. In this weather, it will be hard to justify long-sleeved tops.

Back in her room, Evyn riffles through the piles of clothing stacked in her broken closet. She'll need new shirts for the next couple of days but her savings are drastically low. In the two weeks since she lost her job at the hardware store, she's had no luck finding another.

She had begged Mr. Murphy for another chance. She'd explained that she'd only taken the flashlight so she could search the woods at night. It was broken anyway, a cracked display model that could never be sold. But he'd squeezed her upper arm and told her gently that he couldn't trust her anymore. He'd promised not to press charges, as his hand slid to her shoulder, in light of the 'trouble' with her sister. Evyn had suppressed the urge to push him away and left without her last week's pay.

But word had gotten out. Evyn was a thief. And even the tea-rooms had politely turned her away, one-page resume still in her hand.

She sighs hard, slips on her polyester robe, and quietly makes her way to the kitchen, tiptoeing so as not to wake her father. His shift doesn't start until later and she decides to make him pancakes. Evyn is still chilled at the words he'd used, how quick the thought of kicking her out of the house had come to him. With nowhere else to go, Evyn pours a tub of wilted blueberries into a pot, hoping that the syrup will sweeten him. She works slowly and quietly, gently whipping milk into the eggs, folding in flour and sugar and cinnamon. She concentrates on her facial muscles, steadying them. By the time a stack of pancakes sits steaming on the small Formica table, Evyn has mastered her expression. She can move without a hint of pain crossing her features. It's a relief, this control she has over her body, but the purple syrup is the same color as her ribs and the pain is still there, throbbing.

It hits her hard and sudden, a flick of anger that tightens her fingers on the pot handle. She leans forward, spits into the thick liquid, and pours it slowly into a chipped glass jug. The surge of vindication only lasts for a moment before it freezes, dropping like lead, at the familiar purr of Daire's car crossing the cattle grid.

It must be punishment. Seconds after she'd tried for revenge, her father is snorting awake at the sound of those expensive tires on his dirt.

Daire knows never to come here when her father is home. He never has before. He's never even stepped inside this house, except for the one day she'd begged for his help. But now, he's here, and her father is cursing and stomping around his room. With stone-cold terror, Evyn hears the feathering clicks of the old gun case he stores in his closet, and she flies through the hallway, ignoring the pain.

She skids over threadbare carpet, soles dirtied by stubbed cigarette butts, and crashes into the front door. It's unlocked and Evyn throws herself through it. Behind her, her father's bedroom door tears open. The cinder blocks that serve as the front step wobble as she jumps and the pain in her ribs grows wilder with every jolt of her feet on the ground.

Daire pushes the car door open, stands, and raises his hand in a hesitant wave, a dazed frown as he takes in the thin robe flaring around her.

There's an incoherent roar behind her, somehow slurred despite the lack of words. Evyn stops dead in her tracks, mid-step, three feet away from her best friend. Daire jogs round to the front of the car, as if to help her steady herself. She holds out her palms to stop him, straightening up with her back to her father, trying to place herself between them.

Daire doesn't stop. He sets his jaw and takes another step, looking past her, up to where her father teeters on the makeshift step. He doesn't flinch, not even when she tries to signal to him to get back in his car. He doesn't move a muscle.

Not even when he sees the gun.

FIVE

THEN

"I JUST WANT TO make sure you're okay."

The hallway stopped around them, kids standing stock still with their eyes on stalks as Alanna rubbed at her shoulder. It was as if Evyn had punched her oldest friend, instead of just shoving her away.

"I'm wonderful!" Evyn's voice was too high. She sneered, making her face as hard and nasty as she could, "I'm having the time of my life, can't you tell?"

"You won't talk to anyone so, no, I can't tell," Alanna's voice was soft and filled with concern, "I just want to help you."

"Of course you do," Evyn practically spat, holding her books tight against her chest like a shield, "Like you have any idea—"

She cut herself off because, if she kept going, she would show too much. Instead, she let loose the meanest thing she could think of. Where did it come from, this new ability to nip at the thing her friends were most sensitive about?

"Makes *you* more interesting though, doesn't it? Bet everybody wants to talk to you now, right?"

Alanna blinked, her mouth slack and shocked. "What do you mean?"

"Forget it," Evyn said, already turning away.

"No!" Alanna called out, "What are you talking about, Evyn?"

There was nothing for it but to sweep back around, ignoring the crowd. Alanna was tougher than the rest of Evyn's friends. They'd been easier to deter, pushing them away with short responses and rudeness that seemed so insignificant and small. But Alanna wouldn't stop trying.

Evyn wheeled, finding the sharpest barb to use, her stomach churning.

"'I'm so devastated!'" she parroted one of Alanna's posts she'd seen the week after Stella had gone missing, "Two *thousand* likes." Evyn held up two fingers, two vicious jabs, as she continued. 'Stella was the sweetest girl.' That one had a photo for good measure. Must have been worth at least a few re-posts, right? A sympathetic comment or two?"

Alanna backed away but Evyn followed her, shuffling steps that she forced her feet to take. "You know, if you keep using Stella the way you are, you'll be an influencer in no time."

Alanna's eyes widened so much that Evyn could see the whites all around them. She tried to respond, a stuttering half-cry that seemed pathetically small after Evyn's speech. With a snap of her mouth, Alanna turned and ran to the girls' toilets.

Evyn was left in a pool of people, all staring like rabbits caught in her ominous light.

"What?" she shouted at them. The younger ones moved fast, skittering away. The older kids were slower, eyeing her with downturned mouths.

The doors at the far end of the hallway opened and the basketball team tumbled in from the courts. Daire was head and shoulders above most of them, spotting her almost immediately. He frowned. When opened his mouth to call out, Evyn turned on her heel and pushed through the crowd, disappearing into the science lab as if she couldn't hear him say her name. She hid in the supply room, and pushed his face from her mind.

No-one from school had asked her about their search. None of the texts she actually managed to read had mentioned it and no-one she followed online had posted it. Which meant Daire hadn't told anyone what they did the day Stella went missing. No-one even knew she'd gone to him for help. Or knew how, under the willow tree, she'd cried and screamed and checked out of reality in his lap. How she had never even thanked him.

Hours later, after she'd back-talked a teacher and skipped two classes, she was finally sent to the principal's office, a more and more regular occurrence in the three months she'd been back at school. She sat and listened to the same formalities; Everyone understood this was a difficult time, the teachers empathized with what Evyn was going through, they wanted her to talk to them and ask for help. But that wasn't what they *really* wanted.

Evyn could see the gleam of interest in everyone she met, even the friends who didn't know what to say. It was fascinating, being so close to tragedy. They wanted to pry at it, lift the lid and look at all her broken, tear-stained insides. It made her sick how much they wheedled at her to open up.

She pulled one leg up on the plastic seat, stared out the window while Mrs. Ottomeyer sighed and counted off today's transgressions.

"Evyn, this isn't like you. You're not participating in classes or sports. Miss Enright says you didn't audition for the musical and Mr. Paleckis says you've not even signed up for the soup kitchen's food drive," she tapped her desk with manicured nails, hammering home her point, "You *organized* it for the last two years."

Evyn sighed and shrugged, refusing to expand on why she didn't have time for extracurricular activities, and Mrs. Ottomeyer continued, softer voiced, "You've always been such a good girl, Evyn. I know you're going through a lot right now but this withdrawal and anger won't help you," she picked up a wad of papers from her desk and ordered them, "And we can't allow fighting in the hallways, no matter the circumstances."

Their goodwill wouldn't last any longer.

Evyn nodded and grabbed her bag, already retreating from her principal's worried eyes.

"Yeah, thanks, I'll try harder," she said, her voice dull and listless as she backed out the door.

In the empty corridor, she stopped at her locker and put away her books. There were only a few minutes left in the school day and she couldn't bring herself to walk into a full classroom. Instead, she made her way outside and across the lacrosse field to where she'd stored her bike.

Typical, she thought as she rummaged through the side pocket of her bag for the keys to her bike lock, that she would meet Daire now. He was leaning against the wall, scrolling through his phone. The tinny music of whatever game he was playing was accompanied by the tiniest purse of his mouth. His schoolbag was enormous, a rucksack littered with tattered travel stickers, dropped careless at his feet.

He looked up as her keys jangled. Squinting and tucking his phone away, he pushed himself off the wall.

"Hey," he said, as if it hadn't been months since they'd spoken. As if Evyn hadn't ignored his calls and texts and turned away every time she saw him, "So, I'm reading this book, I think you'll like it."

For a moment, Evyn was stunned. She paused with the bike lock in one hand, gaping at him. Daire came closer, setting picking up his rucksack and rifling through it, chatting as if she'd asked him to tell her all about it.

"I found it in my dad's office. Technically, I'm not supposed to be in there. He built it underneath the deck for his drones and stuff. He'd murder me if he knew I sneak in whenever he's away on business—"

"I gotta go," Evyn swung her leg over her bike and turned her back to him. Moving easily, Daire side-stepped in front of her bike, holding out a curled up graphic novel in his fist, leaving just enough room for her to get by him with the smallest turn.

"Here, you should read it," he said, waving the book slightly, "It's kinda old but futuristic in a clockwork kinda way—"

"Steampunk" Evyn couldn't help but interrupt him, giving him the word for the giant motorised weapon she could see in the curve of the cover.

"That's it!" he smiled like she'd given him an award, "It's about this guy who wants to rebuild his community but his people are used for labor and have no real power so he tries to seduce the queen's daughter to broker a deal... I'm not making this sound very good...." He broke off, thumping the rolled-up book off his forehead.

"Yeah, you're really not," Evyn told him, softer than she meant. It would be easier to say something mean if he asked her how she was doing, tried to pry into that deep pit that had opened inside her since Stella disappeared. But Daire wasn't asking anything. He just wanted her to read a book.

"I'm not a big reader."

He glanced pointedly at her schoolbag, where an impossibly large fantasy novel jutted from the front pocket. "Okay. But there's lots of other stuff I found in my dad's man-cave too," he said, unmoving from his spot in front of her bike, "I guess that's why he's so protective of that place, I mean, I would be too if I had—"

"Daire," Evyn was determined to be rude this time, pushing down on the pedal to float passed him, "That's a great story but I've got to go. See ya."

"He has a huge stash of weed."

She jammed on the brake, gaping up at him.

"What?"

Evyn had seen Daire's dad a couple of times. He was on the board at the school, always there at big events. He gave the lecture on architecture during career week, dressed in a sharp suit, with a slide show that was actually interesting. He was passionate about design, showing building after building that he'd constructed all over the world. Evyn couldn't imagine him smoking a joint.

Daire smiled, a huge grin that dimpled more deeply on one side of his mouth.

"Wanna try it?"

Evyn rocked her bike back and forth as she spluttered indecisively. Before she could respond, he held out the book again, practically putting it into her hand. Her fingers gripped it before she could think it through and she arched her spine to tuck it between her schoolbag and her back.

"Read that first," Daire told her, "I'll steal a couple of joints and we can meet up Friday night. You can tell me what you thought of it."

"I can't," she said, suddenly, "The library opens late on a Friday. I print Stella's missing flyers there after work so I can put them up at the weekend."

She expected one of two responses, the only ways anyone ever reacted if she mentioned her sister. He would either back off straight away and find the fastest way to leave her presence, as if tragedy was contagious, or he would try to console her with slit-eyed pity and overly-personal touches.

But Daire did neither. He took his phone from his back pocket.

"What's your number?"

"Why?"

"I have a printer at home. Send me the file and I'll knock out a few copies for you. I'll bring them with me on Friday. I can even help put them up, if you like?"

She should say no, shake her head and hand his book back, pedal away before he could get her to agree to anything else. Instead, she found herself nodding, scowling at him as she gave him her number.

"Alright then." He slung his bag onto his shoulders and started to walk back toward the school instead of out the gates like she'd assumed he would. Evyn watched him for a few moments, turning away fast when he looked back at her with a small wave.

"You know the gallery on Main Street?" he called out as she rolled her bike away.

"Yeah," she shouted, refusing to look back at him, "I'll be there at eight."

Evyn didn't wait for him to respond, just cycled fast over the pock-marked road, ignoring the jittery feeling spreading rapidly through her, pushing it down so it wouldn't feel like excitement.

Stella was missing. There wasn't room for excitement. No time for fun.

In the months since Stella disappeared, Evyn had never stopped searching. She'd signed up for every local paper's newsletter, read article after article, sometimes not even knowing what she was looking for. Some sign of her sister had to be out there somewhere.

But this night with Daire wouldn't be fun exactly. It was an opportunity to save money on printing, for one. But it was more than that. Of all the ways she'd lost her old life, all her responsibilities and her friendships and her reputation, smoking a spliff seemed like the easiest. She could lose herself for a few hours. Feel nothing for a few brief moments.

For just a little while, Evyn could disappear too.

SIX

now

"M R. DONOVAN," DAIRE'S VOICE is calm and easy, as if he had run into her father in the grocery store. But his hands are raised to shoulder height all the same.

Evyn angles her body so she can see them both in her peripheral vision. Her father looms, gun held over his shoulder like he's woken up in an old western movie, though he looks nothing like a cowboy. His hair is mussed, his pants creased and hastily tied, the pockets tufting out over his hip bones. He's shirtless and the tan lines around his pale upper arms are a comical red.

If she wasn't so terrified, Evyn is certain she would say something now, try to diffuse the situation. But she's frozen solid, bare feet pricking on the sparse gravel.

"So you're the Silva boy, huh?" Her father's sneering tone is so clear that Evyn doesn't need to check the awful tilt of his mouth.

"Silva-Doyle, sir," Daire answers without an emphasis on either part of his name.

"You're a big lad, for a Mexican."

Daire blinks, eyebrows high, but his response is only slightly hard-voiced. "That must be the Doyle part."

Her father snorts, an ugly, surprised sound of amusement, and then spits a glob of green-tinged phlegm onto the ground by Evyn's bare feet. "Evyn, get in the house."

She backs up like a puppet reeled in. Her foot hits the concrete block hard and she tips forward. Daire reaches to catch her but her father is faster. He grasps the collar of her robe, hauls her up the step and tosses her against the door. Her ribs roar in response, the pain shooting down to her thighs. Daire's outraged shout sounds subdued, like she's listening to it underwater.

"Take your fancy car and get the fuck off my property," her father yells.

Daire's hands raise again, but this time, it's as if he's reaching for her. She does the only thing she can think of. She lets him see her fear, doesn't try to mask it. It's a silent form of communication she'd only ever used with Stella but it has the opposite effect on him. She wants him to turn around and run, but instead, his fingers move and his whole face softens, forming the expression she's always dreaded seeing.

Pity.

In the two years she's known him, he's never once looked at her this way. She can't stand it.

"Stay away from my daughter, you hear me?" Her father is still raging, the gun slipping from his shoulder and over his arm. The barrel is pointed down at the ground but the movement is enough to startle Daire. He drags his hands higher, takes a small step back.

"Evyn," he says, but she can't listen. She wants to turn to stone, to melt away and hide where no-one can see her. She mouths the word at him, filled with rage and betrayal.

Go.

Daire drops his hands, backs up until his spine hits the passenger door of his car, and she can see the hurt in his eyes.

He's going to leave. Evyn can tell by the way he shakes his head slowly, giving up, but her father isn't finished. He tilts the barrel of the shotgun, opening it to check the chamber. It's so old that Evyn isn't even sure if it works anymore. He's cleaned the thing a hundred times, but she's never once seen him fire it. He hasn't needed it since the last of the chickens died when she was a little girl. But the chilling click of him closing it freezes her in place.

"You better move, boy!" He roars, then quietens, and that's somehow worse, "I know who you are, who your parents are, but I've got this and," he waves his free hand around in manic demonstration, "not much left to lose. So, I better not see your smug face around here again."

Daire walks to the driver's side, one hand on the chrome inlay like his car is a safe zone. Her dad follows him, gun pointed at the ground. Once he gets behind the wheel, her father trains the shotgun on the hood and follows for a few steps as Daire backs out of the dirt track of their driveway.

When the yard is clear, her father doesn't speak to her, just elbows her aside and goes back to his room. The ancient gun safe whirrs and Evyn slips into her bedroom, her arms wrapped around her middle, face twisted. The pancakes will be cold by now but she can't find enough energy in her body to go reheat them. She should be on her best behavior. Her father has reached his limit. This time of year is always bad, when people around town randomly tell him they're sorry for his loss, and the heatwave has made it worse. He's drinking more and it's getting harder to tell what will set him off.

Daire's face is imprinted on the red-black backs of her eyelids. That look she had always feared seems wrong now. Her mind, unfrozen from a state of terror, picks out details she hadn't seen in the moment.

He had raised his hand toward her. His fingers had moved. He'd said her name. His eyebrows had come together and turned up, in question. Had that look been pity or pleading? Had he really been asking her to come with him, to get in his car despite the shotgun trained on him?

Since Daire had gotten his first choice of college, the university his mother and father had met in, things had started to shift between them. At first, Evyn hadn't noticed. They huddled under the harbor wall or climbed to the gallery roof and smoked and drank like they'd always done, but there was a tremor of something urgent that Evyn worked hard to ignore. He'd changed, but he was still the only person she spoke to, the only person left who understood anything about her. And she'd felt like she knew him too, until now.

She pulls on a pair of her shortest shorts, drawing attention to her unblemished legs so the oversized shirt won't look conspicuous. The covering up is the part she hates the most but she does her make-up like she's putting on armor, reshaping herself so the world will only see what she allows.

She's tying her hair up when she spots her phone, propped up on her pillow. There's a text from Daire she can read without unlocking it.

You OK?

Immediately, her cheeks flood. She swipes the phone and deletes the message without thinking. Still, she stares at his profile picture, when another text comes in.

I came to tell you Aimee Gilbride went missing last night. I'm sorry, I know it's fucked up. There's a search down at the harbor.

I'm going there now. Can you text me, let me know you're
alright? Please?

Her father is bumping around his room, she can hear him cursing
as he pulls on his clothes and suddenly, Evyn can't take another
second in this house. She texts back so furiously she's not sure Daire
will even understand her.

Cn i com?

Daire's response is almost immediate.

I'm still here. Meet me at the gate.

There's a trick to leaving the house when her father is awake. She
knows every one of the hallway floorboards that will creak if stepped
on, knows exactly how to close the front door without a sound.
Her footsteps are light as she crosses over the gravel to the pile of
parts-stripped farm machinery and she makes it through the patch of
underbrush to the main road without missing a step. He's waiting,
windows closed, staring at the opposite side of the road where the
scrub brush turns into structured rows of orderly pine trees. His face
is intent, staring hard at a gap between the trunks. Dappled morning
light catches on something reflective, flickering, and Evyn squints at
it, shielding her eyes from the sun before she taps on the window.

Daire jolts in the seat, so hard the car rocks a little. At any other
time, Evyn would laugh and tease him the moment he unlocked the
doors. Now, she says nothing, raising her battered red sneakers onto
the dash and hunkering in the seat. The last time she'd been this close
to him, his aftershave was a faded wisp. Now it's everywhere, subtle
woodsy scent with something sweet at the edges. It's heady and she
twists her hands in her lap, trying not to think of his strong fingers
pulling steady on the back of her knee.

It hits her all at once. Her father had pointed a gun at him, called him names, and insulted his family. He'd stayed, waiting to hear from her despite all of that. She doesn't know what to do with it. He could call the cops, he *should* call them, but he won't. It's overwhelming, owing someone so much, and it thins her voice.

"You okay?" she asks.

Daire sits with one hand on the wheel. His t-shirt is, as usual, too tight, and artfully faded in the way only expensive clothes are. He's not moving, watching her twist her fingers in her lap so hard her knuckles pop. And her tone is too harsh, like she's asking him why he hasn't started the engine already.

He sighs and twists in his seat, waiting until she looks up at him. She's almost afraid to. Another reel of last night is running through her head: him leaning down with his palms cupped to boost her into the tree, the back of his head tipping over the roof's low guard wall to blow smoke straight up at the sky, the slow bob of his Adam's apple before he turned to look at her.

"Are *you* okay?" he flips her question back on her, with all the venom taken out. His voice is soft, filled with concern, and Evyn deflates.

"I'm sorry," she tells him, hating how she sounds, "About my dad. This time of year is really hard on him—"

Daire cuts her off, covering both her hands with his, stopping her twisting fingers, and instantly Evyn flips her palm up. It's instinct and she stares at their entwined hands like she's not fully certain of what has happened. Her skin is zinging and the hair rises on both their forearms, prickling goosebumps in the heat of the car.

She tugs out of his light grip and crosses her arms, shifting uncomfortably until he takes his hand away and puts it back on the wheel.

He doesn't start the engine, staring out at the empty road, morning light falling over the lower half of his face, shadowing the sharp dip of his jawline. His mouth is pursed in thought.

"Are we gonna talk about this, Evyn?"

She stares out the window until her silence is enough of a response. After a few moments, he sighs and presses the button so the electric engine purrs to life. The air con sends a blast of cool air toward her and Evyn leans back and presses her burning cheeks.

"Calver came to my house this morning," Daire tells her, watching the road as he speaks, "He wanted Dad's help to search the shoreline. Dad and Jake went down with the drone. Even some of the summer people are helping search. It's all over the internet already."

"I was in the station when Rachel came in," Evyn tells him, voice tight with the memory.

Daire swears under his breath, bringing the car to a full stop at the intersection. She can see it in his face, the urge to ask her why she had stopped running last night and let herself be caught. Why she had pushed him away when they were so close to escape. But he points to the supermarket across the street instead.

"We should get some water. We'll be out for a few hours."

He leaves the engine running while he jogs into the shop and Evyn digs her phone out of her pocket and checks through her feed. Pictures of Aimee's face race through her timeline, upturned and smiling, her hair almost white where the sun hits it. She scrolls through well-wishes and prayers until she finds what she's looking for. It's a small post, but it already has more than fifty likes. She doesn't recognise the name of the account:

Didn't another girl go missing there last year?

Someone from her school had already commented.

That was two years ago. Stella Donovan. She was never found.

There's an accompanying picture, posted like evidence. Her sister's missing poster, almost exactly the same pose as Aimee's but with dark, curling hair. It's enough to make Evyn nauseous and she quickly closes the app and shuts off her phone, deciding she won't open social media again until this is done.

When Daire throws himself back into the driver's seat, he hands her two bottles of water and four protein bars.

"Eat," he tells her, and her stomach grumbles before she can tell him she's not hungry. He's smiling easier, teasing, but he's probably overthought his way around every aisle. She gives him a practiced eye-roll and tears open a packet, splitting it with him.

As he drives, they devour two bars and Daire has to brush the crumbs from his lap when they pull into the harbor parking lot. It's familiar, coming here with him, like the last two years never happened, like they're looking for Stella again. There's hope in her belly, a determination that it will be different this time. When she opens the door, the overpowering smell of lavender reminds her that the harvest has started and the Fair will already be gearing up, though the stands are not yet set up.

Pier Street is pedestrianized for the summer but now, two police cars are idling, facing each other to block the entrance. Detective Calver and Rachel Gilbride are leaning over the hood of the furthest car, a few people milling around behind them, obviously waiting.

Evyn walks behind Daire as they approach, using his wide frame to hide herself.

As they join the group, there's a small gasp. Mrs. Garcia, the owner of the tea-rooms where Evyn once worked the summer, quickly looks away. It's a brutal reminder; the way everyone turns to look at her and then immediately finds something more interesting a moment later. The sudden quiet is not lost on Calver.

He looks up, finding them by following the crowd's stare, and puts his hands on his hips. Murmuring to Rachel, they both turn, and Calver motions for her to stay by the car as he comes toward them. Daire crosses his arms over his chest, further blocking her.

"Over eighteen only, kids, I'm sorry." Calver pulls the cap lower on his forehead as Evyn moves to Daire's side. There's that same horrible burning in her throat but she pushes past it to speak.

"You can't stop us looking."

Daire grasps her wrist, gently holding it by her side, and she's so stunned by the gesture that she looks up at him. He's pulled himself tall and he's not looking at Calver, but at Rachel, standing behind him with blank, red-rimmed eyes.

"I'm eighteen. And Evyn will be in a few weeks," Daire's voice is different, calm and confident as always, but subtly deeper. Was this how he speaks to everyone except her? "Please, Detective, you could use the help and you know why this is important to her."

Rachel tips her head to the side, "Let them help, John." Her voice is dull and Evyn wonders if she's taken anything to make her seem so unnaturally calm, but her tone still holds authority.

Calver sighs and squints at the road, rising up past the bars and gift shops, toward the pretty cottages that line the cliffside. He's reasoning a way to say no, working out how best to get rid of them without causing a scene. Daire tightens his fingers, holding her still as Calver speaks again.

"Alright," he tells them, "From Miss Gilbride's house to the Welcome sign at the intersection is about four miles. Can you take that stretch of road?"

It's probably been searched by the cops twice already but relief washes over Evyn anyway. Daire gives her a small squeeze, then lets go.

"Yes, we can do that," he says, already turning away.

"Be careful at the cliff face, don't search past the railing." Calver's hands are on his hips again and he's looking right at her, with that same look he gets when he tells her to straighten up on the nights he brings her down to the station. Evyn nods, flicks a look at Rachel, and then hurries to catch up with Daire, as if starting the search earlier than everyone else will mean they'll find her little girl first.

SEVEN

THEN

"Tape, Daire."

Evyn reached high, holding the paper in place against an old wooden telephone pole. He stretched easily over her, winding the tape round the pole and tearing the edge with his teeth. His weight pressed her against the damp wood and an odd thrill shivered down her spine. To cover it, Evyn huffed an exaggerated breathless wheeze as he lifted himself away.

"You're drinking too much of that protein shake, buddy."

Daire laughed, nudging her arm, but sobered as he looked down at her hand. She was holding the last poster.

"By the boardwalk?" he asked and Evyn nodded, squinting into the distance where the sliver of Cedar Heights Canal looked dull and grey in the cloudy evening light.

"I brought her to this town two summers ago," she said, "For the regatta. She was so excited. The rowers were dressed as mermaids and Stella screamed blue murder at the pirates chasing them downriver."

He smiled, twirling the roll of tape in his hand, "Sounds like she had fun."

"We both did, that day."

The road swerved to the left, away from the canal and Daire checked his phone to see which lane they'd need to take to get to it.

"She drove me crazy most of the time, but that day was hysterical. I'd saved up enough money to get dinner but she opted for a cheap burger on the bus home, just so she could have another go on the teacups. She was nearly sick."

He laughed again, softer, and wrapped an arm around her shoulder, squeezing her against him. They turned down a narrow lane that led to the canals' walkway.

"Maybe she could have made her way here somehow?"

Daire got quiet, nodding noncommittal, letting her imagine it: She'd hold the poster up and ask a passer-by if they'd seen her. The stranger would tilt their head and point over her shoulder. *She's just there, by the helter-skelter, do you see her?* And that would be it. All the searching would be over. She could take her sister home and never let her out of her sight again. They could go back to bickering over her terrible cartoon choices and her constant rummaging through Evyn's meager belongings.

"Alanna says you quit the athletics club," Daire hesitantly, interrupting her thoughts.

"Alanna talks too much." Her guarded tone was a warning.

Daire took his arm away with a sigh, shifting his backpack higher on his shoulder, "Fair enough."

The boardwalk was pretty, benches and wildflower planting that looked almost natural. Swans had been patrolling the water when she and Stella came here, but they were gone now. The cold was biting, the tip of her nose numb with it, and Daire's fingerless gloves showed blue-tinged skin as he took the tape from his pocket.

She tapped the ornate welcome sign, pointing at where to place the poster.

"Someone will take it down," he warned.

Evyn shrugged. "Not for a few days. Maybe someone will see it before then."

They taped the last flyer, breath fogging the air between them, and Daire led her back to his car. Evyn followed, trudging, with that same heaviness she always felt after a day searching. She always started out giddy at the possibility of finding her sister and the freedom of being outside Blackditch. No-one here knew who she was. There were no pitying looks from people in the street, no odd stares, and no veiled attempts at uncovering information about Stella's case.

Daire must have felt it too, because he was always closer to her on these trips, quicker to put an arm around her or ruffle her hair. She would have stopped him at home, waited till they were tipsy or high, before allowing him to make her laugh. But the further they got from their hometown, the easier it felt.

Daire's birthday had gained him a new car and a part-time job with his mother's firm. They met up on Saturdays now, instead of Fridays, so he wouldn't be groggy for work. It didn't matter if Evyn was tired. Working behind the till in a hardware store that never had more than two customers at a time didn't take much concentration.

By the time they reached Daire's car, they were freezing. He blasted the heating so forcefully that she could barely hear him when he told her to open the glove box.

"I got you something!" he shouted, eyes on the road as he pulled out into traffic. She must have given him an odd look because when he glanced at her, he snorted a quick laugh and reached over to open it himself. He tugged out a small turquoise paper bag, wrapped with a curled white ribbon.

"It's not a big thing," he told her, tossing it into her lap, "It's just for the woods."

She'd taken to searching the forest at night when she couldn't sleep. The month before, she'd walked all the way to Flynn's Falls and missed her first two classes when it took her too long to trek back home. Daire had been worried, fiercely telling her to keep her phone on so his app could find her if she fell or got lost. She'd teased him about it, but she never went into the woods without her phone after that.

She picked at the washi tape that held the packet closed and unfurled the delicate paper. In a small mesh pouch was a heavy necklace, a large round locket dangling from the metal chain.

"How is this for the woods?" she asked, confused and unsure. She tried to remember the last present she'd received. A handmade card from Stella maybe, or a glittery eyeliner from one of her friends before she pushed them all away. No one had ever given her jewelry before.

"Open it," Daire told her, still studiously watching the road, though she could see the white tip of his tooth against his lower lip, anxious little bites.

She pulled the necklace from the bag and held it up. A small metal circle and a catch that flipped it open with a satisfying click. Inside, finely engraved letters and numbers encircled a turquoise center with a silver dial, pointed on both ends. It moved slowly as the car turned a corner.

"A compass," she said, the corner of her mouth turning up, incredulous, "It's beautiful."

Daire grinned at her, "Blackditch Bay is west of the forest so if you lose your way in there, just point it north and, real sudden-like, turn left."

Evyn gasped and smacked his arm, "You watched it!!!" She practically screamed at him. She'd been trying to get him to watch her favorite movie for weeks and he'd kept telling her he'd rather swallow his own vomit than watch a period drama.

"You didn't tell me how sad the ending was," he said, reaching back over to close the glove box before cursing under his breath, "I think I took the wrong exit, will you open my phone and see where we are?"

She slipped the compass around her neck, tucking it into her coat, and took his phone from between the seats. He'd already set it so her face opened it, though she'd teased him mercilessly about his generic wallpaper. She scrolled through till she found the app and then studied it briefly before giving him directions to get them back to the motorway.

It was quiet while Daire merged into traffic and she was suddenly aware of his rouse. A distraction so she wouldn't think the gift was a big thing. It was like the time he'd tried to give her his old phone even though it was only two years old and more expensive than she could ever afford. But this felt different, though she couldn't explain why.

"Thank you," she said.

Daire shook his head and shrugged. There was a tell-tale pink tinge to the top of his cheeks and he stared fascinated at the car in front of them. "Yeah, no problem," he muttered, then stayed quiet the whole way back to Blackditch while she studied the twirling dial.

"Do you want to test it?" she asked him as they passed by the lavender farms, rows of darkly colored knee-high bushes that already smelled of something earthy and rich, even in winter. Though they were both tired after a day of walking, he still nodded excitedly and pulled the car over at the small car park. The headlights illuminated the murky trees beyond the verge.

Evyn checked the time and pushed the door open. Her father was working the late shift so she had an hour to spare before he came home, stinking of rotting fish and demanding enough food for two people. She met Daire in front of the headlights and held out the compass to him, flicking it open.

"The Bay is that way," she said, pointing to her left, "So North is straight ahead."

Daire peered at the compass, holding it between them, the long chain dangling from his fingers.

For a moment, it teetered to the large engraved N, but then it wavered and pointed to the south. Daire shook it, a liquidy sound, and tried again. The same small waver happened. He pivoted a half-circle and the needle turned again, pointing back at him instead of North.

"It's broken," he said, sounding more upset than she'd ever heard. He cursed for good measure and Evyn took the necklace from him quickly, inspecting it as he walked to the fence and leaned on it, pulling the hood of his coat over his head.

"Daire," Evyn said, and pointed to her right, "Walk over there."

He raised an eyebrow until she clicked her tongue at him, impatient. He jogged a few steps, turned around and raised his hands out to the sides. "I'm sorry, Evyn, I'll return it and get you a better one."

"Now, walk the other way."

In the dark, she could barely see his expression but when he jogged back through the headlight's illumination, he was biting his lip again. "I got it online, so maybe it was just a crappy knock-off."

"It's following *you*."

He stopped at the other edge of the car park, his head tilted to the side in question.

"The needle is following you," she told him, watching as it wavered toward him, this time, pointing just a little off from True North, right where he was standing. He jogged back to her, testing it by walking around her in a circle while she held it in the light. The skin on the back of her neck was just beginning to prickle when Daire chuckled and pulled off his beanie to rub at his hair.

"It's my wrist," he said, scrunching the sleeve of his coat to show her the faded scar he'd had ever since she'd known him, "It's got a metal plate in it. Jake pushed me off a trampoline when we were kids. That must be messing with it. Cheap piece of crap. I'll get you another one."

Evyn snapped the lid closed and held the locket to her chest. "You will not. I'm keeping it."

He tried to argue, even tried swiping the locket from her hand, but Evyn marched around to her side of the car. No matter what he said, she wasn't giving it back.

By the time they'd reached the cattle grid at the end of her driveway, he'd given up. "You're literally the most stubborn person I know, you know that?"

Evyn beamed at him. She only had a few minutes before her father's truck would be belching out a stream of noxious fumes around the bend in the road, so she opened the car door, stopping with one foot on the frosting mud.

"It's really beautiful, Daire. I don't know how to thank you."

"You could draw me something," he blurted so quickly that Evyn stopped with her hand on the door handle, half out of the car. Daire seemed suddenly mortified, leaning forward with a groan until his forehead thunked off the steering wheel. When he looked up, the overhead light made him squint.

"I never see you drawing anymore."

"I guess I don't have time."

He pursed his lips, trying to stop himself from talking, and Evyn sat back down and waited him out because he was never able to muzzle himself for long.

"You should... start drawing again, I mean. You were really good at it."

She grinned at him, remembering.

"Mrs. Calver told me I had potential," she laughed and he looked away, checking the road ahead.

"Maybe she was right."

"She was just being kind. I was thirteen and going through a rough time."

"That's when your mom left?"

"The year before. Stella was only two."

Daire turned his head to the side, "I can't even imagine," he said quietly.

"It wasn't that bad. Old Mads helped out, if you can believe that. She sat for her while I was in school and, when I started drawing, it was like I had this big secret. I could draw whatever I wanted, all I needed was paper and pens. I drew myself the perfect life."

Daire smiled at her. "What's the perfect life look like now?"

Her answer was instant. "Finding Stella."

Daire nodded and let out a deep sigh. She could tell he was gearing up, trying to make a point he thought she might not like. She pushed the door open a little wider, spurring him on.

"It's okay to live your life, you know," he said. His knuckles were white on the wheel.

"Excuse me?" Evyn gripped the door handle, just as hard.

"Evyn, I see you," he lifted his hand off the wheel, counting on his fingers, "You go to school, you go to work, you search for Stella, and every now and again, we get high. Is that really enough for you?"

She stared, dumbfounded, until he relaxed back into his seat.

"Look, all I'm saying is, it's okay to draw, it's okay to go to the movies or parties or just hang out with friends. It doesn't mean you've given up, just because you live a little bit. You can do both."

When she stayed silent, he continued talking, even softer than before.

"I used to see you out running all the time, for track. Now you barely leave your house—"

"Daire, stop."

Evyn pulled her foot back inside the car, closing the door and plunging them into darkness. It was easier that way, to talk honestly and try not to get defensive.

"Look, I appreciate you driving me today. And helping with the posters. I really do. But I'm not a charity case. I don't need you telling me what I should be doing with my life. Stella is out there somewhere, hoping for someone to find her. There is nothing, *nothing*, more important to me than that. I'm not gonna waste my time drawing a fucking picture when I could be searching."

Daire winced at the road ahead, his shoulders curling inward at her words.

She sat back, subdued and quiet. She'd tried to explain herself without getting angry, but the emotion had built as she spoke and now the silence was thick and uncomfortable.

Glancing at Daire, Evyn patted at her cheeks with a long sigh. He had driven three hours today, helped her hang posters, and bought her a gift, albeit a broken one. She'd repaid him by yelling at him. Sometimes, she wasn't sure why he liked hanging out with her at all. She needed to get out of the car. She didn't want to sit next to him, hurt and frustrated and wishing he'd never been kind to her. He must be so angry right now. She wished she could take back what she'd just said, find a nicer way to say it.

Slowly, Daire leaned toward her until his head was next to hers and his seat belt was pressing into the padding of his coat, still watching the road.

"Can I have a stick figure sketch?" She could hear the smile in his voice, "Just a little stick man with amazing abs so I'll know it's me."

She laughed and raised her hands into the air, gave a playful growl of frustration. "Fine! I'll draw you a fucking picture!"

The grumbling roar of her father's car sounded in the distance and she hopped out with a short wave, already thinking about where she'd left her art supplies, wondering if she'd lost her touch in the last year.

It surprised her, how much she was looking forward to finding out.

EIGHT

now

T HE GILBRIDE HOUSE SITS in the center of a small, pretty row of brightly painted cottages along the cliff face. Blackditch Bay's tourist brochures for the last few years had all featured this strip of shoreline, and almost all of the houses have B&B signs subtly displayed on their pastel picket fences.

Evyn lifts the lid of an old garbage can and stares down, riffling the papers on the top. Across the road, Daire leans over the guard wall, staring down at the beach where another group of searchers call to one another. The drop is ten feet high here, but by the time they reach the intersection at the town's welcome sign, it will be more than double that. Evyn shudders and lays down on the ground, checking beneath a row of parked cars.

When a black cat bolts out from under to car, hissing at it streaks by her, Evyn startles and rolls away. Her ribs press into the road and it takes a moment to recover, lying flat with her palm shielding her eyes from the sun. Once, she takes her hand away, Daire is there, arm extended to help her up.

"What's wrong?" he asks, frowning down at her.

Evyn bats his hand away and turns onto her undamaged side before rising to her feet without assistance.

"'I'm fine," she tells him, walking up the hill faster than is comfortable, "I'm not sure we're going to find her here, Daire."

He catches up to her, walking close so he can keep his voice low. "Why do you think that?"

"I don't know." It's true. Evyn isn't sure why, but she has an overwhelming feeling, "I just have this idea that she's in the woods. I can't shake it."

In her peripheral vision, Daire turns his head, assessing her for a brief moment before looking up at the forested area at the top of the hill. "Are you sure you're not thinking that because of where we searched before?" He's tactful enough to not say Stella's name, even in a whisper, knowing the heads of anyone within earshot would turn toward them if they heard it. "That's a long way for a four-year-old."

"She could have crossed through the fields."

"At night?" His voice is filled with doubt.

"Yeah, maybe you're right," she shrugs.

Daire comes closer, his bicep bumping off her shoulder. "You might be onto something. Earlier, before you got in the car, I thought I saw..." he trails off and she slows her walk to look at him, but he doesn't continue, shaking his head decisively. "Look, if you want to go check the woods later, I'll come with you."

He says it easily, and strides ahead to check inside a shaded playhouse at the edge of one of the gardens. Evyn is left remembering all the times they walked between stark pine trunks, flashlights wavering, looking for a different missing child.

The sun is trembling on the tip of the horizon by the time they reach the Blackditch welcome sign. The heat has lessened but Evyn's thighs are tingling from the beginnings of sunburn and her oversized shirt is sticking to her lower back. When Daire hands her the last of the water, she gulps so fast it drips from the corner of her mouth and slides in a ticklish, too-fast run down her neck.

A few of the other searchers have congregated on the grassy verge, talking in small deflated groups. Daire leans in and quietly says, "Rachel's coming."

She straightens at the approaching police car. Calver is driving and Rachel is in the passenger seat, staring out the window at the thin line of trees that block the view of the sea. Evyn is quick to look away, gathering some of the positivity and determination she had this morning. The people around her seem to do the same, standing and holding themselves with more purpose as the car slows to a stop.

Detective Calver taps at the steering wheel. It's always odd to see him outside of the station. Evyn once came across him in the supermarket, had stood staring at him while he plucked oranges from a tray, squeezed them, and popped the ones he wanted in a clear plastic bag. When he'd noticed her, she'd fled. As he climbs out of the car and opens Rachel's door, Evyn feels like running again.

Rachel seems somehow smaller than this morning, hair limp and forehead burned bright pink. But she climbs out fast, coming toward the nearest couple, reaching out to take their hands. Her voice is too low to be heard but the man's voice is louder. "Happy to be of assistance," he says in a strong midwestern accent.

"They've got search dogs coming," Daire mumbles, scrolling through his phone, one eye on the awkward exchange "This says another two units are being sent in from surrounding areas this evening to help search."

Rachel is a few feet away and moving closer to them. She's going to see them at any moment. Evyn's fingers scratch at her thighs and she catches Calver's eye, unguarded.

Immediately, his gaze flicks to Rachel and he claps his hands together, drawing attention.

"Thank you all for your help today," he calls, and Rachel turns to listen with the others, "The search is continuing and we have some more support coming in. The cliffs are dangerous to search at night so, please, let the police continue the search after nightfall. Again, thank you."

He seems uncomfortable, though he has led press conferences before, when he worked vice in the city. Their school had shown footage of him during career week, young and confident and unscarred.

Calver gives the gathered searchers an awkward wave before he motions for Rachel to get in the car. As he's closing the door, the radio hooked to his belt gives a loud static rush and Calver turns away, talking into the receiver. "Say again?" he says and another unintelligible mumble rises through the hot air. "Received, on my way," he says, moving fast to get in the driver's seat, lights flashing a moment later.

"What was that about?" Evyn turns to Daire but he's looking at her oddly, eyes roaming over her dirt-streaked shirt. He sits down in the grass as the other searchers drift back down to the road. The light is changing, coming through the tree line in yellow-tinged flares, illuminating thin clouds of swirling midges.

Daire shows no sign of moving, watching the others walk away from them, so Evyn sinks down beside him, cross-legged on the sunbaked, scratchy grass. When they're alone, Daire looks at her, some potent emotion freezing his features, but his eyes are ripe with it, flickering swift and urgent.

"Are you hurt?" he asks, his tone almost accusing as he gestures at her stomach.

Evyn stays completely still, concentrating on moving the muscles of her face into something resembling confusion. Too late, he sees the flash of her fear and he's not pulling away, not changing the subject like he usually would if she was uncomfortable. It must be the heat, or the horribly familiar searching, or the way she had slipped up last night and turned toward him when she should have pulled away. Whatever the reason, it's clear Daire has decided to cross another line in their friendship, another push against a wall she's built between them for the last two years.

When she doesn't answer he leans toward her. There's a muscle ticking in his jaw and she watches it instead of meeting his eye.

"Evyn," he says, tilting her chin up with one fingertip. "You have to tell someone."

Her body curls inward. Her face turns to stone, "I don't know what you mean, Dar."

She'd meant it to sound harsh and angry but it comes out a whisper, frightened and maddeningly weak. He doesn't respond. The heat seems to bubble around her, the sound of insects a buzzing swell. He says nothing, waiting her out until there is no choice but to give him something.

"He never hits me, OK?" It's the truth. Her father has never used his fists. But the words feel hot in her mouth, scalding. "I come home drunk or stoned and he gets mad at me. Things might get out of hand once in a while, but he never hits me."

Daire stares for what feels like minutes and she can't tell what he's thinking, what each tiny twitch of his expression means. When he looks away, scanning the empty road, Evyn's breath comes out in a relieved rush. He's not going to push it. They'll get up and go home and everything will go back to the way it was before.

"Show me how 'out of hand' it gets, Evyn."

Daire's voice is hard-edged, a tone he's never used with her before, but his fingers shake as he points toward her midsection. She draws a short, surprised breath, her upper lip tipping high, but Daire doesn't budge, holding her gaze so steadily that she feels like he's trying to pass her some of his determination.

"Daire," she says, horrified, as if he's suddenly lost his mind and she's the sane one, trying to pull him back from the edge of a bad trip. He doesn't falter, just watches her, close and quiet, until it feels like there might be no-one else in the world but the two of them on this bare stretch of dying grass.

"Show me, Evyn."

NINE

THEN

A FULL DAY. SHE hadn't heard from Daire in twenty-four hours. By lunchtime, sitting on her own in the small classroom that doubled as their homeroom, she'd sent him six texts. All unanswered. She'd even thought of approaching his friends, asking if anyone had heard from him. But talking to kids at school now seemed impossible.

It had happened quickly, so much faster than she had ever thought possible. All it had taken was a few mean words, a sullen glare, the fractured shield of her grief, and all her friends, even her teachers, had given up on her. She was a ghost, no longer taking the time to mend her clothes or bleach thrift store shirts. There was no more hiding her meagre lunch and scribbled-over secondhand textbooks. It was liberating, in a way, to have such a tenuous hold in the world.

But today, it was a nightmare.

Evyn had gotten used to near-immediate responses from Daire but, by the end of the school day, he still hadn't answered. Instead of heading to her part-time job, she cycled to Daire's house, punching the call button on his gate for an almost offensive length of time. When there was no response, she tried calling him again, left a message that was nothing more than a frustrated growl, and then scaled the oversized boundary wall into his garden.

His car was the only one parked outside.

Evyn walked the driveway as if she was a thief, slinking close to the bushes, taking note of the open ground-floor window that led to the den. At the front door, she first tried knocking and then guiltily turned the handle. The heavy bolts slid back easily and the door swung wide, cold air rushing to fill the overheated space inside.

"Hello?" she called, "Daire?"

Silence. She took a small step beyond the door frame and closed the door behind her.

"Anyone? It's Evyn, I'm just looking for Daire?"

The usually cool space was roasting hot, as if the heating had been turned up full blast. The silence was so complete that Evyn felt touched by it, forced to quieten herself, as she moved through the kitchen and reception rooms, searching.

At the bottom of the stairs, she stopped, sniffing the air. A faint, foul smell scrunched her nose. She took the stairs two at a time, following it. Daire's bedroom door was slightly ajar, the inside dim and silent. Evyn pushed the hinges, opening it slowly, to reveal his paper-strewn desk and empty chair. The heat was even higher in here, compacted in the smaller room, and Evyn's skin flushed. There was a distinct, Daire-shaped lump under the covers of his bed and she should have been relieved. But the silence was so complete that she stood stock still, her voice barely a whisper.

"Daire?"

No response. Evyn's tongue thickened, her hands coming together as she forced herself to step into his room. Turning the swiveling head of his desk lamp toward the wall, she flicked the switch, throwing dim, reflected light over the bed. Slowly, she walked toward him, watching for any sign of movement. There wasn't the slightest shudder to his thick duvet. As she crept closer, the source of the smell became apparent - a plastic bucket on the floor next to his bed. Evyn covered her mouth with one hand and pulled back his damp sheets with the other.

Daire's face was deathly pale. Even in the reflected light of the down-cast lamp, he was drawn and frowning deep. When she put her palm on his forehead, found it slick and burning to the touch, she sighed a relieved breath and leaned over him.

"Daire." She shook his shoulder a little to rouse him, "Where are your parents?"

He mumbled something that sounded vaguely like 'mom' and then retched into his pillow. Quickly, Evyn pulled him toward the edge of the mattress and moved the bucket into place. When he was done, he turned his face back into the mattress and moaned so piteously that Evyn ran her hand over his t-shirt, wet through with sweat and stuck to his back.

"Okay, big guy, let's get you cleaned up."

She took the bucket to his ensuite and rinsed it out, wetting a wash-cloth with icy-cold tap water. Back in his room, she rummaged in her bag for the painkillers she kept next to her spare tampons. Fresh bedding was carefully stacked at the top of his wardrobe and his drawers were packed with clean, neatly folded t-shirts and hoodies. With a twinge of jealousy, Evyn crossed the room and stripped the duvet away, changing it while Daire curled into himself, shivering.

"Up, up, up," she told him, hauling him upright while he groaned in confusion.

"Evyn?" he said, and then grabbed the bucket and dragged it into his lap. She patted his back while he puked. His hands were shaking so much she had to hold the pail steady for him. It would be frightening, how weak and disoriented he was, if she hadn't seen this so many times in Stella.

The worst time, when Stella was four, she had been so ill that she'd started talking gibberish. Her fever reached so high her face turned a violent shade of red and her body shook with little tremors that no amount of blankets could calm. Evyn had been terrified, begging her father to take her to the clinic. But he wasn't willing to drive that far, dismissive of her fears. And he'd been right.

Evyn had stayed up all night, cooling her sister with damp face cloths, drip-feeding her water and juice. But by the next morning, Stella had perked up as if it had never happened, begging for snacks and to be allowed out of bed to play. Exhausted, Evyn had handed over her make-up and sketchbooks and her best charcoal pencils, just for another few minutes in bed.

Now, she lifted Daire's heavy arm across her shoulders and hoisted him out of the bed, dumping him awkwardly into his desk chair so she could pull the sheet off his bed and replace it with a fresh, softener-scented one. When the bed was remade, she crouched by his knee.

"What's going on?" he mumbled into the bucket, still held in his lap.

"You'll feel better if you get cleaned up," she told him.

He nodded, sloppy, as if the weight of his head was too much for him, and tipped forward precariously. Evyn caught his shoulders and pushed him upright, then tugged the bucket from his fingers and held out a new t-shirt to him.

"Take off your shirt," she told him and noticed the heat in the room was so high that her cheeks were burning from it. She turned and opened the window, though it didn't make much difference.

Daire struggled to free one arm from his shirt, limbs twisting in the material and torso falling forward again. Evyn had no choice but to run to hold him upright. "Daire, I'm gonna help you strip, okay?"

He gave a weak laugh, leaning back in his seat to look up at the ceiling. His words were slurred but Evyn heard him clearly enough. "Not how I've always imagined it, but okay."

She froze, both her hands tightening on his shoulders and the tension seemed to sober him a little. He blinked hard and shook his head. "Are you really here?"

"Yes," her voice was thin and cautious, "You didn't answer your phone. I got worried."

A small shift of lucidity crossed his face, and some kind of emotion that she didn't recognize. He placed the bucket on the floor, struggling to free his arm and take his shirt from her hand.

This time, Evyn didn't ask. She pursed her lips and tugged the hem of his shirt until it came loose from his raised arms. The washcloth was soft as fleece, another perk of his fancy home. He hissed when she touched it to his forehead, leaning into her as if chasing the cold. Trying not to think, Evyn washed away the slick sheen of sweat on his chest and back. He'd bulked up over the season. New swathes of muscle left dips and grooves around his spine. When she held the cold cloth to the back of his neck, his head dropped forward, hitting her hip, and he mumbled something so slurred it was incomprehensible.

Once she'd pulled the fresh shirt over his head, he seemed to perk up a little. "I think I'm dying."

"You're not dying, you have the flu. Take these."

He groaned and swallowed the tablets she dropped into his palm.

"Do you want me to call your parents?"

"No. They're away for Dad's architecture award. Don't want to ruin it for him."

Despite the heat in the room, his fingers were trembling and she had to help him back into his bed. He curled up, shivering, as she tucked the duvet around him and opened the window further for some fresh air. He was asleep almost instantly, with a mumbled thank you that she didn't acknowledge. Evyn waited until the covers had stopped quivering, and Daire had settled into a comfortable sleep before leaving the house.

It was late when she got home and her father complained about the quick pasta carbonara she served for dinner. But that night, lying in bed, she couldn't sleep, unable to think of anything other than that resigned sigh, that slurred admission, and how hot his skin had felt against her cold hands, how each muscle had clenched hard, and then released beneath her.

She slept through her alarm the next morning, arriving more than an hour late for another day of overwhelming academic noise. That is what she wanted, she reminded herself. She had chosen to pull away from all distractions, for Stella. She needed to focus on widening her search, sign up to more international websites, research trafficking rings, and post more of her sister's photographs on every missing persons site that would accept it.

Still, instead of going to the library after school, to use their free computer and internet access, Evyn cycled into town and picked up Daire's favorite miso soup, some sports water and churros.

Sneaking back into his home felt like a criminal act, as if at any moment his parents would appear and call the police. She stole up the stairs and found him in exactly the same position, sleeping comfortably. Leaving the bag on his desk she wrote a short note on the side with one of his expensive gel pens.

Drink these when you wake and, next time, ask for help. E.

The next few days of school were unbearable, even worse than usual. There was no sudden glimpse of him rounding a corner, laughing with his teammates, no lightning-quick banter in the hallway to take her mind off her silent day. No one calling and waving from the pitches as she crossed to the bike racks.

On Friday, she sent him a text, asking how he was, and got a clipped message back that turned her stomach.

Thanks for the other night.

The short tone was so unlike him that Evyn turned her phone off for the rest of the day, not bothering to ask him if he wanted to meet up to share the cheap rum she'd stolen from her father. She poured what was left of his open bottle into an empty jar as he slept in his seat. She drank it on her own and let the alcohol do its work of spinning her to sleep before her father's late shift ended.

The next time she saw Daire was the following Monday. She was coming out of the art room with booted supplies in her hand and he was wandering down the corridor with his sticker-studded bag on his back. She called out and he froze, the barest glimpse of a beet-red cheek and then an awkward wave as he walked away. Evyn stood looking after him until he turned the corner and didn't move until the bell rang for lunch.

She didn't understand it. He was back in school and he hadn't texted her, not even to ask if she wanted a ride. He'd always asked before, though she had always refused so she could avoid having to talk to his friends.

Taking her lunch outside, Evyn ate on the benches, wrapped up against the chilly air, and decided she didn't need Daire Silva-Doyle. She didn't need anyone. If he didn't want to speak to her anymore that was fine with her. Better than fine. Hanging out with him was taking too much time away from her search anyway.

W HEN SHE SPOTTED HIM walking past the hardware store where she worked the next day, unusually alone, Evyn stared decidedly at the rope display, determined to ignore him.

"What's your problem?"

She hadn't meant to speak. She certainly hadn't meant to bound to her feet, burst into the street, and call after him so aggressively that he spun toward her. Daire blinked in surprise, pushing his hood back to reveal eyebrows raised so high that his forehead creased into three distinct lines.

"Nothing," he said, jamming his hands in the pockets of his coat. His cheeks pinked up and he couldn't meet her eyes. "I've been busy."

The last part was mumbled so low that Evyn could barely hear him. She raised her voice a decibel louder, an unnatural derision she'd learned directly from her father but had never used before. "Busy?"

Evyn stood and raised her arms wide, pointing out the lack of any actual activity that he was engaged in at this very moment. She pointed one finger at him, "If you don't wanna talk to me anymore, Daire, just be honest and say it."

It would have been harsh, if it wasn't for the wobble in her voice. She cursed herself and dropped her arm, turning to walk away from him.

"Wait."

His hand clamped around her elbow, holding her in place. Evyn held still, didn't pull away like she wanted to, but she refused to turn back to him either, staring at the empty store while she waited him out.

"I'm embarrassed," he told her, "About the other night."

She turned back to him.

"Why? Because you were sick?"

His sigh was so deep that his breath moved her hair across her cheek and he let go of her arm to push his own hair back. Subtle, how the sudden loss of that anchor made her feel less sure of herself, all the anger dropping away, cracking dangerously.

"I feel like I might have said some things," he gulped and when he spoke again his voice was lower, uncertain, "What *did* I say to you, Evyn?"

She thought about that huff of laughter, the half-admitted thing that had made her freeze.

"Nothing," she whispered, "You had a fever, you weren't making any sense."

Daire leaned closer, head tilted like he'd seen the crack open up and wanted to push it wider, "Did I tell you—

Evyn shoved him back, hard. "All I did was try to help and you acted like an asshole all week!" Her voice betrayed her, a bolt of pain she couldn't quite hide.

Daire rubbed his hands in his hair, dragged them over his face, and when he took them away, his shoulders dropped. "You're right," he said, wincing hard, "You're right, I'm sorry." He gave a helpless half-shrug like he didn't know what else to say.

Evyn blinked at him, unsure of what to do with this small victory. "Do you even want to be friends with me?"

Daire's whole face softened, regret clear in the twist of his mouth. He looked away from her, a soft shake of his head, and muttered *"¡Está peluo!"* at the end of a long sigh. He hardly ever spoke his mother's language but Evyn had heard those frustrated words from Mrs. Silva-Doyle before, when she'd been making tiny decorations out of icing too soft to hold its shape.

"Very much." Daire said, pulling her attention, "I want to be your friend, very much, Evyn. I'm so sorry."

Evyn didn't have much experience with forgiving. Stella had broken things by accident or cheated at checkers, but she'd never done anything Evyn needed to forgive. It was an odd thing, wondering if she could just move on, leave that little bit of hurt behind her and hope that it wouldn't happen again. She caught his eye and held it, uncomfortably long.

"Don't do that to me again, Daire."

He seemed to take that as acceptance of his apology, stepping into her with his arms wide, giving her plenty of time to pull away. When she didn't move, he wrapped his arms around her shoulders, his chin pressed to the top of her head.

"I won't," he told her, "I promise."

TEN

now

"HE DIDN'T HURT ME, Dar."

She'd meant it to sound dismissive, to match his determination with her own. But it comes out pleading, an unconvincing
whisper that she can only make worse, "I fell."

He catches her wrist, tugs to stop her twisting her hands together.
Evyn could count the tiny dots of stubble along his jawline, one small
spot slightly longer where he'd missed it shaving. His cologne is faded,
clinging to the scent of sun-warmed skin and Evyn wonders if he feels as
captured by the tension as she does, as pinned by it.

His lips move but she doesn't hear his whisper until a moment later,
like a feedback loop.

"Just show me."

And somehow she knows that, even if he were chained, Daire would
find the strength to move in this moment. She knows where that strength
is coming from, that certainty. She'd felt it when he turned toward her
on the gallery roof. Something had happened then, a seismic shift in her

perspective, and she couldn't look at him in the same way anymore, no matter how much she wanted to. The roof had been their safe place, the one spot where no-one would find them if they stayed quiet enough, where they could laugh and talk without risk of anyone hearing, of anyone putting a label on their friendship, making it something it was not.

And now here they are, as if they've stepped off that roof into the open air.

If she walks away from him now, that will be the end. He's leaving for college in three weeks, empty boxes already lining his bedroom wall, waiting to be packed with all the items he deems important enough to bring with him to the apartment in the city that he'll share with his brother. The end is so close she can taste the loneliness already, feel the lead-lining of it inside her.

She's losing him anyway. It's just a matter of time. She doesn't need to show Daire her battered ribs and she doesn't need to be saved. She's hurt now, but the pain is manageable and Evyn can count the number of times it's been this bad on both hands. Most of the time, she's fine. She puts food on the table and her father eats it and that's the sum total of her interaction with him. If she was in another family, one that cared, she wouldn't be allowed to spend all her free time looking for her sister. She'd be forced to leave Stella out there alone, with no-one in the entire world looking for her.

Daire is still watching the play of emotions on her face, still breathing shallow and quiet and waiting with that new determination she'd felt last night. She doesn't need to show him the darkest of her secrets, but she *wants* to. She just doesn't know why.

When she finally tugs her wrist away, his cheeks pale, a wavering, glassy doubt.

Her fingers move to the hem of her shirt, tucked tight into her waistband, and the doubt disappears. He blows out a sharp breath, the same way he does when he's gearing up before a game, and checks the road again to ensure they're alone.

Evyn rolls the material up and gently unhooks the bottom edge of the scarf. It takes some time to unwind, revealing half-inches of tanned skin that slowly give way to new bruising, beet-dark and mottled at the edges, viscous blue-black at the center.

It's an odd act, slowly lifting the material away so Daire can see her stomach and ribs, and she watches his reaction, cataloguing the tiny, fast-paced changes in his expression. He squints like he wants to look away but won't let himself. He rubs his hand over his jaw so hard that she hears the faint rasp. When he reaches out toward her, she takes a deep breath, expecting him to touch her, to probe the wound, but his hand hovers between them and he grasps her knee instead, squeezing hard. Without warning, he pushes away from her, standing to balance on the high curb, hands clenched at his sides.

If she could call out, she would, but her voice will shake so Evyn stays silent, re-wrapping her scarf and unrolling her shirt, suppressing a shiver. When her stomach was exposed, she'd felt the heat of the sun on her back and heard the calm wave-swept sound of the bay. But now she's chilled and uncertain as she stands to join him.

He walks away from her fast. Hands unclenching and clenching again, he turns to stride back toward her after a few quick steps.

When Evyn opens her mouth to speak, Daire spins away again, pacing up and down the verge, making fists and loosening them, silent and raging. It's everything she was afraid of. He's rearranging her in his mind, taking stock of all the times she missed a day of school, the odd bruises she laughed off, that one time she flinched when he raised his hand to show her something. He's painting all their private moments with a bruise-stained brush and he'll never see her the same again.

"How long has this been happening?"

He points at her. His voice is wavering, glassy and angry, as if she's betrayed him somehow. She shakes her head and shrugs one shoulder. That must be answer enough because he paces again, longer strides this time, and his fists don't uncurl anymore.

"Daire," she calls to him, a sudden coldness sweeping in her voice. He doesn't hear it, keeps walking a line into the dried grass, mouth twisted like there's a roar trapped right behind it. Her faltering explanations fall on deaf ears: Her father hadn't hurt her, he'd just caught her off guard and she'd fallen. He hadn't meant it, he was angry and didn't realize his own strength when he was drinking. It doesn't hurt that bad. The bruises will fade in a few days.

All her justifications and reasoning sound small and pathetic.

She's made a huge mistake, she can see it in the tensed line of Daire's shoulders as he shakes his head at her words. Eventually, he turns to her, pausing only to raise his hands, pleading with her to stop talking, to stop trying to defend this.

"Your ribs, Evyn," he sounds desperate, strained, "How the fuck could he do that you?"

She never should have shown him. She should have laughed him off as she'd always done or walked away and let him leave for college with untainted memories of her. Now the bruising will fade but this moment won't. It will be all he remembers when he thinks of her.

Striding fast down the hill, arms wrapped around herself, Evyn wishes she could take it all back. Daire curses behind her, loud and echoing, his voice cracking as he calls her name. There's no way to respond. She can't focus on anything but the road in front of her, that stretch of heat-shrouded blacktop that leads back to town. He jogs to catch up with her, breathing long and slow through his nose. She'd taught him that - how silent counting can help to slow a racing mind. Evyn walks faster.

"I'm sorry," he says as he catches up to her, then curses again, vehemently, "I'm so fucking sorry, Evyn."

"It's fine," her voice is ice cold, "Forget about it."

He touches her arm and she flinches from him. When she keeps trudging down the hill, eyes trained straight ahead, he pulls back. Evyn lets him go. She doesn't want to turn and see his face, the confusion and the anger.

It doesn't define her, this red-streaked, bruised skin. She's more than that and if he can't see it, then she needs to get away as fast as she can. Evyn isn't even sure what she'd expected his reaction to be. Empathy maybe - he'd been hurt more times than she can remember playing basketball. He'd spent the first three weeks of the summer with his fingers in a splint, complaining about how sloppily she rolled a joint and moodily asking her for help with beer bottle tops or jacket zippers. He should know a thing or two about just getting on with it.

Daire jogs in front of her, spreading his hands wide to stop her. "Are you hungry?"

The pleading is gone and his mouth is twisted into his usual semblance of a smirk. He's always gotten her with food. A flickering hope burns brighter inside her.

"I could eat," she tells him with a shrug. The laugh she's expecting doesn't come but he nods eagerly.

"Seafood Shack?"

It's her favorite spot and Daire knows she'll brave a throng of tourists for their spicy crawfish. This is an apology. The relief floods her. She still has time with him before he goes, it doesn't have to end quite yet.

She gives him a tentative smile and Daire raises his hand toward town, motioning for her to start walking again before he falls in step beside her.

There's little traffic, and the music from Pier Street reaches them even before they hit the midway point, bouncing off the sunset-streaked water in the bay. With Daire, it's always easy to be quiet. Evyn never usually feels the need to fill their silences with awkward conversation. But there's still a lingering tension between them, in the light frown that won't wear off his face. For the first time, the quiet is too much.

"What do you think that was, with Calver?" she asks him, breaking the minutes of empty breath, "He drove off pretty quick after he got that call. Do you think there's more news?"

Daire glances at her, a hint of guilt widening his eyes. He hasn't heard her. She repeats her question as if he's lost brain cells on the walk down to the harbor but he just shrugs and holds open the blue door of the Shack. He rubs at his hair, which seems unaffected by the whole day of searching in the hot sun. Evyn feels wilted, strands sticking to her skin, but Daire is barely sweating.

Inside, the tables are packed together and filled to capacity. Evyn spots a booth in the back corner, a family clearing away their leftovers into greaseproof bags.

"I'll get us a table," she says and Daire nods absently before she pokes his arm and points him toward the counter "Spicy Craw."

He laughs at her tone, but it sounds stilted and unfamiliar.

She waits until the booth is clear and looks around for anyone familiar. It's a habit she's developed since Stella went missing, scoping every room to see who's pitying or curious eye she must avoid. There's no-one here but tourists. They're not subdued, despite the missing child, as if they can pretend the world outside doesn't matter while they're on vacation. They tug at the cheesy fishing nets that decorate the walls, tapping at the crossed wooden oars that serve as art. They wipe their children's ketchup-smeared chins like nothing bad will ever happen to them.

In the queue, Daire smiles tightly at an unfamiliar girl, her hand on the back of his arm as she talks. It's not unusual. He never talks to her about other girls, though sometimes Evyn wants to ask, like pressing on a bruise.

When he comes back to the table, tray lifted high over a group of boisterous kids, Daire is still quiet and withdrawn. He sets the food in the center, pulling thin wooden forks from the bag and divvying up the trays. Evyn is starving and she downs half her drink as Daire packs away the excess packaging. She devours four fat, chilli-tinted crayfish without stopping to breathe, waiting for his sarcastic comment. It doesn't come. He's pushing at his food, a round foil tray of buttery crab claws that smells lemony even over the spice burning her nose.

"So, what do you think they told Calver? He drove away so fast, and you know he never speeds."

Daire picks up a claw, swirls it in butter, and puts it back down again. It's infuriating, this half-present, barely-there nonsense, and she slaps the table lightly. His eyes flick to her, almost angry again.

"Sorry, what?"

Evyn sits back in her seat, points her fork at him. "This is important, you know. The first 24 hours are crucial."

"I know," he says, reaching across to take a crawdad from her tray, "Sorry." He watches her as he chews it, and suddenly all the tension creeps back in between them. There's the slow dawn of understanding as she watches his facade slip. He's tricked her. He isn't trying to move past what she showed him. He isn't going to accept it.

"Evyn," his voice is low enough that no-one will hear him over the din of conversation, "We need to get you some help."

The food she'd swallowed sits square in her chest.

"Your ribs, Evyn," Daire's voice drops even lower, "I play ball, I've seen some injuries, but that is..." He trails off, rubs his fingers hard over his mouth, "You can't go home. We have to get you out of there."

She looks away. Through the netting-strewn window, the light over the bay has faded to a dull smear. People pass by, on their way to the bars and the arcade. The normality of it raises her hand to the glass, as if she could absorb it. Daire keeps talking, urgent and quiet. He reaches across the table, though stops short of touching her. "We can talk to my mom, or go to Calver. We can stop him from ever hurting you again."

Evyn reaches into her pocket to take out a bill. His face falls as she slides it across to him, topping it with a novelty salt-shaker shaped like an anchor. She pushes away from the booth, winding through rows of red-checkered tables and out the door. Daire doesn't call out and she doesn't look back, though she knows he's still sitting there as she steps out into the darkening street.

The tide is out, small dinghies stranded on the wet sand of Hangman's Beach. The warm air is seaweed-scented and sour. She can hear the muted music from three different bars, all melding together in a way that sounds off-key and clamorous. It makes her walk faster, speeding down to the harbor wall.

There's no way to undo it. No way for him to un-see what she'd shown him. And she should have known better. Evyn had never slipped with anyone else. She should never have confided in him. How could he, with his expensive car and his laughter-filled mansion, ever understand what her life is like?

It was the gallery roof. That one desperate, stomach-fluttering moment had ruined her carefully-laid defenses. His lips parted, eyes blown and out of focus, he had waited for her, held still, unbreathing. Why hadn't she run then? She'd have three more weeks with him. Three more weeks of secret texts, stolen alcohol, and drugs that softened all her hardness. Now, she'd have nothing. It burns in her mouth, the wish to turn back the clock and undo it. But she can't. And she already knows what she has to do next.

The door opens wide behind her, a burst of chatter and laughter from the people within. Daire's familiar run, the swift and steady thump of his sneakers on the sidewalk.

"Please," he says, rounding on her to stop her walking. She ducks her head, swerves, and carries on as if he's nothing. She has done this before. It's never felt this difficult.

"Evyn don't do this," he tries again.

She keeps walking, staring blankly at the ground. Daire catches up and jogs backwards, facing her.

"You have to know you can't go back there," he tells her. There's something wrong with his voice, the pitch is higher than usual, as if he's out of breath. But she's raced him across the beach for most of the summer and he's never let her win once. He can't be struggling with a slow jog.

"You can't let him hurt you like this. Evyn, you deserve better."

It's his surety, the solid certainty of someone who's never had to learn how to wash blood from a collar, or which floorboards will creak loudly enough to make someone angry. It's infuriating. She lets the anger settle over her. She already knows what she needs to do, has done it with every one of her old friends. It doesn't matter that he is the only one she could ever really talk to.

It will hurt, bad, but it will only take a moment.

She comes to a stop at the crossroads and meets his eyes, another mistake in the litany she's made today. He's never looked so desperate.

His hair is sticking out like he'd pulled at it, jaw so set that there's a hollow under his cheekbones. His body is tensed rigid, waiting for her to speak, and there's a part of him that already understands what happens next. She can see the fear of it already hovering.

"You think you know what I deserve?" she asks him, and all the coldness is there, right where she wants it.

Daire blinks and purses his mouth in determination, "I know you don't deserve broken ribs with no first aid, Evyn."

His conviction works to spur her own, like she could pull his certainty into herself and use it as armor. She doesn't even flinch, so wrapped in her defences that she can barely see him.

"You don't know a fucking thing about me, Daire!" His name hurts, just saying it, "You think you know what's best for me because I showed you a bruise? Think I'll go back to your mansion on Pen Hill and have your mom file a case against my dad? What happens to me then? What happens when my sister comes home and *I'm not there*?"

The last three words are a scream. Daire's shoulders drop and some of the tension leaks from him. He moves toward her, as if to comfort her. There's heat behind her eyes and a thickness in her throat and Evyn feels the control slipping. It's the same drop in her guard as last night. He's seeing too much and she can't pull it back. She does the only thing she can think of. Raising her hands, she shoves at him. He's not expecting it, has to take a step back to steady himself.

Daire squints at her, breathless at her fury, unsure of how to respond.

"I'm seventeen, unemployed, and failing school. I can't sign a rent contract or get a loan. Where would I live, Daire? With you?"

The smooth skin of his throat moves in a slow gulp and his sudden vulnerability almost makes her falter. She conjures an image of her sister's face like a shield and the anger floods back. Part of her wants to run, to

hide from what she has to do next. But she's made so many mistakes, she
has no choice now but to hurt him. Irrevocably.

Eleven

Then

"T HANK YOU BOTH FOR coming."

Calver closed the door softly behind them, coming around to sit at his desk. He picked up papers from a metal tray, shuffled them, and cleared his throat, looking up to where Evyn was standing.

"Would you like to sit?"

"No."

Her father leaned back in his seat, crossed his arms and raised one ankle to rest on the opposite knee.

"What's this about?" he asked, his tone rough and impatient.

Calver cleared his throat again, loosening his tie. "I've called you here, Mattie, because there have been no updates on Stella's case in the last ten months. We've reviewed every available lead, without success. We've extended every resource we have in trying to find your daughter but we've reached an impasse. There's been no new information since she went missing despite repeated calls to the public and international authorities."

He looked up at Evyn again and took a deep breath, glancing away before speaking again. "Her ICMP file is still active, her case is still open, and any new leads will be investigated as a priority, but until such time as new information appears, we are unable to take this case further." Rubbing at his chin Calver addressed her father in a less formal tone, "It's gone cold, Mattie. I'm so sorry."

Evyn stared, her fingertips pressing hard into her arms. She wanted to tell him he was giving up, to shout at him and force him to keep looking. But her throat was burning and she could feel the back of her eyes heating up. She couldn't take the risk of opening her mouth in case all that came out was a sob.

"That's it?" her father uncrossed his legs, planting his feet on the floor with a dull thud, "That's all you're gonna do? Just wait?"

Calver looked up at Evyn again, "I'm so very sorry."

Her father stood and sniffed.

"You're sorry." He put his hands on his hips and leaned forward a bit, so the detective had to sit back in his seat to maintain eye contact. "I came down here thinking you'd got something to tell me about my little girl and instead it turns out you're just tired of looking for her. Done all you can. You're sorry."

Evyn's head shot towards her father when he said the words 'little girl'. She'd never heard him phrase it that way, it sounded odd coming from him. But then he laughed, a harsh cackle that hardened the expression on Calver's ruined face. "You're a sorry piece of shit, alright."

Her father walked out the door, leaving Evyn standing frozen in her spot by the back of his chair. Calver frowned, waiting for her to speak, as if he expected her to scream or curse, maybe even kick a chair over, or swipe the files from his desk. But she was struck dumb. No-one was looking for Stella. No-one was out there searching through all the places she might be. She was alone. Evyn couldn't open her mouth because all that would have come out is the sound of her heart grinding as it cracked and splintered.

So she did the only thing she could think of. She let him see her devastation. As Calver watched, she let her practiced, stoney expression slip away. Let the feeling in her stomach, the pain in her chest and her throat, rise up into her face. She let the tears come, met Calver's gaze through them.

He winced and rubbed one hand over his eyes. The movement made the scars on his face twist.

"Ah, Christ," he muttered to himself and Evyn knew what he would say next. He'd try to explain it, as if she were the six-year-old he was supposed to save, instead of poor Stella. He'd try to make her see why this failure wasn't his fault. She couldn't bear to hear it. She turned and ran, following her father. Calver called out her name with a deep regretful tone that meant her sister was never coming back.

Her father's van was already gone when she ran into the street but Evyn didn't care. She turned up Pier Street, racing on numb legs until her breath came in massive gulps and the tears dried on her cheeks. She punched the code to open Daire's gates and tried to calm down on the walk to his front door.

"Evyn! What's wrong?" Mrs. Silva-Doyle, crouched beside a planting area, dressed in slacks and a silk blouse with flowered gardening gloves that matched her oilcloth apron. Her hair was down and curling around her face, the exact opposite of her sharp-cornered work style.

Evyn had come to see Daire but the words flew out of her mouth before she'd thought them through. "How do I file a complaint against the police? How do I make them keep looking for my sister?"

There it was. The pitying look she hated.

"Oh sweetheart," Mrs. Silva-Doyle's accent got stronger, a softening of hard sounds, "Come inside."

Evyn was already shaking her head. She couldn't listen to another adult talking to her as if she'd fallen in the yard and scraped her knee. Stella was out there alone. Frustration and anger heated her cheeks and her mind raced. She needed to calm down before she made more of a fool of herself.

"No, I'm fine." Evyn's feet were already moving, backpedaling the way she had come, "I'm just upset. I'll go cool off."

"Evyn, please, of course you're upset! Please come inside and we can talk..." Mrs. Silva-Doyle trailed off as Evyn waved her hand and turned to run back up the driveway, slipping through the gates as they closed automatically.

S HE'D REACHED THE HARBOR wall by the time Daire's caught up to her. His car veered into a parking space and he jogged to catch up, trailing beside her with his hands in his pockets in complete silence. He followed her down the pier in silence, watching her traipse circles around the packing area.

Eventually, on her third lap, Evyn swung herself onto the wall and sat with her legs dangling over the edge. The water below was good for diving, but the season wouldn't start for another month so the pier was free from whooping teenagers daring the summer kids to follow their lead.

Daire hauled himself up beside her, looking out over the bay. "Fuck Calver," he said to the horizon, a hint of amusement in his tone.

"It's not funny." Evyn rounded on him, frowning.

His mouth pushed out, considering, and then he turned away and roared at the sea. "Fuck Calver! Fuck the whole of Blackditch PD!"

It was so loud that Evyn's breath rushed in and she swiped at his arm. "Daire!"

He shrugged, "Try it, it'll help."

"I'm not doing that. They've stopped looking for her, Daire. He just stopped." The words came out a hiss, angry and bitter.

"Yeah," he replied, calm, and then leaned to brush off her lightly, "Try shouting, kid. It's gotta come out somewhere."

Evyn narrowed her eyes at him, "You're only a year older than me, Daire. I'm not a kid and I'm not shouting at nothing. It won't help"

Without missing a beat, Daire copied her narrow-eyed expression, dipping his head to bring his face closer. "Do it or I'll push you in." His face was deadpan.

The briefest moment of silence cracked when Evyn laughed unexpectedly. "Come on, Dar."

She turned to face the water. He was silent, the bulge of his bicep pushing into hers, tensing and releasing like a drum beat.

"Fuck Calver." Her voice was quiet, giving him what he wanted so he'd stop bothering her. But Daire wasn't satisfied.

"Come *on*, Evyn."

She rolled her eyes and took a deep breath, roaring the words at the top of her lungs. Her voice cracked in the center, dragging back in with a hiccupping sob. And suddenly she was crying, unwanted tears that she ducked her head to hide.

Daire didn't say anything else, just leaned so his arm rested against hers, a steady warmth the whole way to her wrist. His little finger moved, looping over hers as she caught her breath. It was easier than she thought to lean into him, to lay her head on his shoulder. They stayed on the pier until a light misty rain began to cool their arms and legs, and Daire's stomach rumbled so loudly that Evyn sniffled and stifled a laugh into his shoulder.

"Come on, let's go get lunch," he said, swinging his legs back over the pier wall, "Mom's probably worried sick about you by now."

She warmed at the thought of sitting around his beautiful kitchen table with its perfect white plates and fresh-cut flowers. But somewhere out there, Stella was alone, with no-one to sit beside her in total silence when she cried, or make her laugh when there wasn't anything else to be said.

"I have to get home, Daire," she told him and held up her hand to stop him arguing, "My Dad's probably upset so I should go be with him."

The guilt of lying to him made her look away but she was cold out here, exposed by the thin cries she'd let slip in front of him. Another crack in the wall she kept between them and lying felt like filler, like plugging it shut again so she could breathe.

"I'm sorry I got so…"

Daire shook his head, jutting his chin toward the harbor wall where the roof of his car was just visible. "I'll drive you."

"I'll walk."

He sighed but didn't push her, just walked her to the crossroads and waited till she got to the other side before turning back to drive home.

At her house, her father sat in the living room with his work boots crossed on the ancient coffee table. He held a beer loose in his lap and the sound of a football commentator was too cheery and excited and loud for her to interrupt. She took a microwave dinner from the tiny freezer and heated it for him before she went to her room to hold her breath and hope for an impossible thing.

TWELVE

now

"WHAT THE FUCK GAVE you the idea that I need *your* help?"

Evyn's voice fills with a sickeningly familiar tone she both hates and has learned weaponize, as effectively as it is used on her. Mouth pulled back into a sneer, she takes another step toward Daire, her face inches from his.

She should be focusing, concentrating on what she has to do next, but instead, Evyn finds herself thinking of her friends. She'd had so many before Stella disappeared, so many people who'd dropped away from her, or been pushed, until only Daire remained, stubbornly there every time she needed him. This would be the last time she would have to do this, the very last remnant of her old life she needed to clip away. And it would hurt the most.

"Did you like it?" Her voice drops low, mouth tilted up toward his. She's so close she can feel his breath and there's that same urge to lean into him that's always there. It's harder to ignore than it's ever been but she does it.

"What?" he whispers, but he already knows where her train of thought is going, Evyn can see it in the stiff way he holds his jaw high. She tilts closer.

"Me lifting my shirt up. What came next, in your imagination? Did you think I'd take everything off, for you?"

"Stop."

His voice is hard, a coldness she didn't know he had in him. It shocks her silent as he steps away from her, so far he ends up teetering on the curb, one hand raised to catch his balance.

She'd worked so hard, building up a mask that he wouldn't see through, creating a version of herself that Daire would hate. But it slips the moment he wavers on the curb, about to step back into the street.

"Daire!" Her fingers bunch in his t-shirt pulling him back toward her.

She'd barely seen the car, barely heard the noise of it over the rushing in her head. A horn blares as it speeds past, an inch from Daire's back. He stumbles forward, knocking against her, panicked limbs tangling. She falls with him, careening toward the rough brick wall behind them. Her ribs flare with pain, searing down her legs. Daire hisses and catches her, one hand cupping the side of her face. His knuckles scrape along the mortar, the dull tear of his skin loud against her ear. His free hand holds her steady against him.

For a moment, the only sound is the catch in their breath and the faint curl of music from the casino. His chest is moving harshly, pressing into her with a comforting rock. Slowly, the stiffness of shock releases and Evyn lets herself lean against him.

It's easy, burrowing into him. It must come naturally to Daire too because he pulls her even closer, his hand cradling her head and her cheek pressed to his chest. The material of his t-shirt is loose, pulled limp where she'd dragged him, and the scent of his warm skin feels like spinning.

Evyn has to ball her hands into fists to stop herself from choking out an apology. He'd forgive her. But he won't stop asking her to set fire to her life either. And who would search for Stella then? If she let herself be taken from her home, tossed into the foster system for the last month of her teens, moved to wherever they had the space for her. How much time would it be before she could get back?

A sob wracks her, shuddering that makes Daire wrap himself around her, the muscle of his arm firm against her back and his chin pressing unbearably soft on the crown of her head. She readies the words, turning them over in her mind until she can think them without her throat closing up.

Numb, rises on her tiptoes, jamming her cheek against his. The corner of his mouth is so close to hers that she can feel it when his breath sucks in and then stops altogether. He tenses around her, even the fingers in her hair freeze, waiting.

An image flashes in her mind, that fleeting moment on the gallery roof, so real she could reach out and be there again. His lower lip, soft between her loose-held teeth, the hardness against her inner thigh, the urgent press of his palm at the base of her spine. She sobs again, squeezing her eyes shut when he pulls away to look at her.

"Evyn," he says. It's the softest she's ever heard her name spoken.

If she keeps her eyes closed, it won't hurt him as much. He might not believe it and she needs him to *know* it. She makes her mind blank and forces her mouth into a sneer she knows too well. Her eyes snap open and she targets the one place he's soft. His brother.

"You're so fucking pathetic, Daire," her voice is hissed but steady, "Jake was right. Just leave me alone."

Shoving herself back from him takes everything she has left. He lets her go easily, leaning back against the wall as she walks away. Evyn holds her breath to stop herself crying and walks fast so he won't be tempted to follow her. Her neck is tight, stopping herself from glancing back at him. She can't see the damage. It will be written all over his face. Instead, she focuses on physical pain, pressing her elbow into her injured side till there's a roar of agony held fast in her chest.

On Main Street, a crowd of summer kids quieten as she passes, the whispered hiss of 'that's the girl' and 'never found' meets her and, if Evyn had anything left in her, she would turn on them, screaming. But her eyes are swimming and throat is burning and her rusted cot-bed is so far away. It's all she can do to keep walking, past restaurants and bars, rows of RV's on Harley's campground that look as run-down as her own house, passers-by who know her but have long ago stopped nodding to her in the street.

By the time the footpath ends and the last streetlight is a fading cone of insect-ridden light, her mind is blankly following the path. Every friend she'd had is gone. Some had drifted away on their own, unsure of what to say in the face of her grief, and some she'd had to push, refusing their help until she'd had to snap at them to stop. But nothing had hurt quite as much as this.

At the cattle grid, she pauses. From the road, the house is barely visible through the thicket that lines the broken, paint-chipped boundary wall. But there's a faint, blue-ringed light through the branches, flickering, that can only be from the television in the front room. She skirts the grate, walking along the side of the dark driveway, on the edge of the brambles.

Her father's car is parked outside the house. Early, for a Thursday night. He'd usually be at the poker game in The Ditch, drinking until his week's wages were depleted enough to make him sour. She moves lightly over the gravel, trying not to disturb him. He's had enough of her, his talk of kicking her out last night had proved that. But she's home late again and avoiding him is a priority.

Opening the front door quietly, she slips through and closes it with a soft click. She makes her way down the dark hallway, stepping only in the places she knows won't make a sound.

"Get in here," her father calls, and her stomach drops. Evyn comes to the doorway, moving into the light so he can see her more clearly.

"I went to the Ditch after work." His voice is mild, distractedly watching a talk show where politicians are feigning politeness, "Ran into old Mads."

He looks at her suddenly and all the calm disappears. "She said you were helping with the search. You and that Silva boy I chased off *just* this morning."

For a moment, she can't move. Usually, after she gets hurt, her father doesn't speak to her for days. It's like living with a ghost, or being one. This is new. Her legs tremble and she leans against the door frame for support. "Yes, Dad," she says, "But I wasn't with him. A few people were doing it."

"I told you not to see him anymore"

"I won't." Her voice betrays her just enough to pique her father's interest. He stands, coming toward her with a slow gait and the beer bottle held with his thumb plugging the neck.

"You lying to me?" He towers over her, blocking the light from the television so his face is shadowed and menacing.

"No, Dad."

Lightly, he takes her chin and tilts it so she's looking up at him. Evyn tries to meet his eye, to square her face so it shows no emotion, but she's so tired that it's too difficult to force her lips still. They tremble over his thumb.

He stares for what feels like hours, till her whole body fades to his thumb and forefinger and his unwavering, searching glare. Then he scoffs, a snorting, ugly sound and leans down to sneer at her.

"What good would you be, searching? You couldn't find a dog if it jumped up and bit you."

"No, Dad." It's a whispered agreement, pulled from the bottom of her belly like vomit. Her father clicks his tongue and pushes her chin away, turning back to his armchair.

"If I see you with him again, you can pack your bags. You hear me? I don't need half the town talking about you whoring your way into those people's money."

"Yes, Dad." She hates how sincere she sounds. Like she agrees with him. But this is the second time in two days he's mentioned her leaving. Where would she go if he kicked her out? She imagines Stella, somehow coming home, searching through empty rooms and calling out only to be met with silence. Or worse.

Evyn waits to be dismissed, unmoving though her legs feel like jelly and she's so exhausted she can't think straight.

"Get out of my sight," her father says, finally, giving the bottle a lazy swoop before he kicks up his feet and rests them on the coffee table.

She moves like he's dropped a checkered flag, staggering down the hall and into her tiny room with its yellowed net curtains and poster-covered cracks. She doesn't have the energy to change out of her clothes. Or even to ice her ribs like she should. She lies down, gingerly pulling her phone from her back pocket, checking for a text from Daire.

The screen is blank, a photo of Stella's smiling face with app-added cat-ears as wallpaper. Evyn turns her face into the pillow.

Until now, she hadn't noticed how much she'd relied on those texts. They were glimpses into another type of life. One where college was an option, where moving to the city was a possibility, where family was a source of mild embarrassment, deep love and pride. Daire never had to hide behind a wall of his own making. She'd built hers so tall but he'd still climbed over the top and asked her if she wanted to study with him, or smoke a joint, or search the woods yet again.

She turns her phone face down, curls away from it, and picks at scraps of flowery wallpaper. There would be no more glimmers of a different life now. Daire would go to college and meet new friends, new girls whose futures were bright and whose pasts weren't riddled with fear and loss and pain. He deserves that. He deserves fun and ease, a girlfriend who lets him in and doesn't immediately regret it. He deserves anyone but her.

THIRTEEN

now

SHE WAKES TO THE sound of birdsong and the blind sense of a small body beside her. Evyn pats the mattress, finds it empty as always, and lies with that familiar sinking in her stomach.

There are no texts from Daire, or anyone else. That sinking feeling dips further, and she turns onto her sore side to distract herself with the sharp pressure. Though her phone is set to silent, a quick check of her scant social media pages shows hundreds of notifications. She swipes them away without reading any of them and opens the Blackditch webpage.

Aimee Gilbride is still missing.

There's a clickbait headline blasting the canine unit's dog trainers and Evyn scans the article to get the details. The dogs had spooked in the woods, turning back the way they came, refusing to go further than Flynn's Falls. That explains Calver's quick departure from the civilian search and Evyn has that odd feeling again, the one that tells her to search the forest. The bottom of the article gives the information she needs, in bold print. Another search, this one organised by Daire's father, will be held today in Blackditch woods. It starts in the car park at 8am.

Evyn eases herself out of bed and hurriedly washes. Some reckless part of her comes to life as she turns the tap full blast, not caring about the sound. It's her father's day off from the docks and most likely he'll have drunk enough last night to keep him unconscious through a hurricane.

She moves around the bathroom as if she were alone in the house, clinking her toothbrush in the glass, gasping as she unties the scarf from her ribs and trying to ease the tension from them with small stretches. The shower runs long and gurgles the pipes and she doesn't switch it off, lets the water flow into her hands and onto her body. When she leaves the bathroom, there are flecks of water on the floor and spatters on the mirror.

Once her ribs are re-wrapped, she tugs her boots from under her bed, pulls on denim shorts and covers her bruised arms with a thin, oversized plaid shirt. She makes no effort to be quiet, to move like a phantom through her room. With every small noise she makes, there's a satisfied part of her that feels a little freer, a little less broken, and somehow closer to the people she's lost.

When she leaves the house, pulling her hair through the clasp of a baseball cap, she doesn't even try to stop the door from slamming, letting the sharp reverberating thud startle the birds along the tree line. There's a part of her that feels like she could take off with them, as if by losing Daire, there's nothing left to keep her on the ground.

The woods are a twenty-minute walk away but Evyn takes a well-worn route through the overgrown field where she'd once tried to grow vegetables. She walks through the rows of uniform evergreen forest until she reaches the small car-park where searchers are already gathering already. A small group of people hover by the turnstile gate. Daire's father is pointing at a map on the woodland information sign, talking with Old Mads, who knows these woods like the back of her hand.

Daire stands off to the side, staring into the trees.

He must feel her watching him because he turns to her and then away again sharply before he can meet her eye. He doesn't look angry, not like she expected. It would be easier if he was. But Evyn knows every muscle of his face, drunk or sober, and it's an odd, gulping guilt she sees there now. His eyes slide as if he's done something wrong and that's so much worse.

Evyn had meant him to hate her, to never want to speak with her again. She'd said the worst things she could think of, used their most intimate moment as a weapon and, somehow, *he* looks guilty.

Marching to the opposite side of the gathering, Evyn makes sure to jolt her ribs hard, focusing on the sharp stab of pain that spindles over her. She will not cry.

Old Mads spots her in the crowd and turns to jab her elbow into Mr. Doyle's arm, alerting him. Evyn sighs. After searching all day yesterday, she'd hoped that the looks would stop and she could go back to being ignored. She should have known from the vast number of unopened social media notifications on her phone this morning, she was probably more noteworthy than ever. Tourists filling the town will know Stella's face now – the other missing girl, the one who never came back. Evyn will put up with all the pitying looks and tight-mouthed scrutiny if it means more eyes on her sister's last photo.

Daire's father looks up, gives her a small nod, and then leans to whisper to Mads. He shakes his head, shoulders shrugging, and the gesture is familiar. Last summer, standing in his huge kitchen, she'd been covered in barbeque sauce, eating the leftover ribs that Daire had heated in the microwave, both of them giggling and hovering over the dish set in the center of the kitchen island. Mr. Doyle had taken a long look at them, rolled his eyes and shrugged in just the same way while he ruffled his son's hair.

"Take a shower before your mother wakes up and smells marijuana on you," he'd said, walking away, "And stay out of my office!"

With that same easy grace, he waves Mads away and takes control of the search, drawing grid patterns on the large map with an authority Evyn is certain must run in families like a blood type. Her eyes keep drawing toward Daire, where he stands by the metal gate and waits. He's a million miles away, staring into the trees, and there are dark circles under his eyes that weren't there yesterday. No matter how many times she glances at him, he never once looks back.

A subtle murmuring starts up from the crowd, heads turning in the direction of the car park's entrance at the familiar crunch of Detective Calver's truck on the gravel.

Aimee's mother is with him, her head lolling in the passenger seat, and Evyn turns away, re-tying her ponytail and watching through the crook of her elbow. Calver jogs around the help her down. He's in civilian clothes, no gun at his hip, and he lifts her with ease, both hands on her waist, and sets her on the ground. Rachel is shockingly changed from the day before. Her hair is scraped back and her face is drawn and grey. Red-rimmed eyes glance at Evyn briefly but she seems not to see her and she teeters a little when she walks.

Calver stays close to her, approaching Mr. Doyle with an outstretched hand and a grim expression. Daire strides from the gate to stand beside his father, arms crossed. He shakes Calver's hand and, for the first time since she'd arrived, his eyes slide over to Evyn's with that same guilty flash before he looks away again, focusing on the conversation. Evyn can't hear much, the talk is low and their heads are tipped toward each other.

Only Rachel is standing tall, looking at the forest as if she's trying to see through the wood.

"OK, everyone!" Daire's father calls, "We're going to split into groups and each take a section," he points at the taped map to illustrate his point, "Those of you with first aid training, please spread out amongst each group as best you can. This is a civilian search but Detective Calver is overseeing so call on him directly if you find anything."

He claps his hands together and the crowd around her disperses, forming smaller groups. Subtle maneuvers leave Evyn standing on her own. She raises her chin, refusing to scan the different groups, all distinctly not looking in her direction. She'll follow whoever leaves first, stay back from them and search on her own.

"Evyn," Detective Calver calls from the map, "You're with us."

Daire's mouth sets hard. He points to the map, drawing his father's attention to a spot near the lake. There's an old shed in the area he's circling, Evyn remembers the first time they found it. She had practically vibrated. If anyone could re-imagine an old hog-shed as a castle, it was her sister. But it had been empty, like everywhere else they had searched. Maybe this time it wouldn't be.

They set out from the turnstile, separating down three worn walking trails. It's cooler under the trees, but the heat still clings. The jolting walk along uneven ground takes far more effort than the level footpaths and roads had yesterday. The air seems denser, dried and fragrant. They've only walked a few meters before the other teams disappear from view, their voices fainter as they call out for Aimee.

Evyn falls behind the group, keeping as much space between her and Rachel as she can. Everyone in town can look at her like she doesn't belong, like she's jinxing the whole search just by trying to help it, and she will let it roll off her back. But Rachel looking at her that way will make her turn tail and run.

Evyn distinctly remembers those first few days when the whole town searched this way for Stella, everyone patting her shoulder, feeding her platitudes she didn't want. She'd felt the way Rachel looks now, bone-tired and terrified, Stella's face coming unbidden every few minutes like bolts of lightning, each one striking hard enough to make her wince. Rachel's mind will be blank now, a void that fills to capacity all at once, jam-packed with all the terrible things that could have happened to her little girl. Even now, she's trudging forward, calling her daughter's name in hoarse intervals, as if she's afraid of the sound.

Evyn pushes through thin brambles and ducks under a fallen trunk, tipped precariously against the nearest tree. There's a draping of leafy branches over it, tent-like and big enough for a small child to curl up in. She crawls into the dim space, looking for any sign of Aimee.

Close by, she hears Daire's voice, the crunch of his boots on the dried earth. She waits till she can't hear him anymore before she crawls out again. There's a bike trail, thin and nettle-lined, leading down to the fern-rimmed stream that feeds the lower waterfall and Evyn takes it, walking fast away from the group. She lifts heavy branches that look like they belong in a rainforest instead of this unkempt section of wild woodland. The heat seems to ratchet higher. By midday, it will be cloying and heavy here, but for now, a light breeze flows through the trees and birds swoop between the branches, calling warnings to each other as the team marches through their territory.

The stream is low, muddy banks drying in the heat. Evyn follows it for a short while until she spots another team in the distance, making their way toward her. She cuts through the trees and scans the thicket blocking her way back to the walking trail. It's too high to step over so she skirts around it, following a barely noticeable animal trail back to a clearer, pine-needle littered area. The air flows through the wider space and the smell of fresh-cut lavender reaches her, strong and herby. It makes her think of the clearing, the tree stump Stella had loved to pretend was a stage or a ship. Evyn has to bend forward, hands on knees, until the image of her little sister, arms wide and mouth tipped up to sing, fades away.

She's here for Aimee, for Rachel, to make sure no-one else has to feel that sinking horror when an investigation goes cold.

There's a rustle, a brittle, dry snap and Evyn jerks to a stand.

"You okay?"

It's Daire, paused mid-step, tall enough that his head and shoulders rise above the brush he's pushing back with a thick stick. She shrugs one shoulder and fills her expression with as much disinterest as she can muster. It doesn't come as easily as it had before and she can't hold his eye.

"You don't have to do this, you know," he tells her. Her throat is burning, unable to reply, which he seems to take as permission to continue, "You're hurt and, if you fall out here, you could make it worse. You should be resting, Evyn."

His voice is low, soft like they're alone, when Evyn knows there could be other searchers within earshot. She fires him a withering look, hoping that something like derision will show in her face and scare him away. But her vision blurring at the edges and his head tilts, assessing her.

"I need to tell you something," he says.

There's deathly silence for a split second and Evyn's heart begins to pull. Her breath quickens, watching Daire's arm sweep the branches back as he pushes further toward her, tramping straight through the scrubby brush.

"Stop," she says, hard-voiced and close to a shout. He must sense her panic because he freezes and the space between the trees feels almost solid, loaded. After a long moment, Daire sighs, pushing back heat-curled hair from his forehead with a whispered curse. When he meets her eye again, the softness is gone, replaced with resignation.

"Is it clear back there?" he asks, in the same tone he uses to talk to Calver, firm and deep.

Evyn can't answer, nods instead, and he turns away without another word, headed further into the woods. She rounds the thicket, careful to avoid where he had been standing, and spots Rachel in the distance, her hand touching each tree she passes for support. Calver walks close behind her, his arm held out slightly, as if she might fall.

She hurries to catch up with the detective. "There's hogweed back there," she tells him, sharp, "You might wanna warn the others. Mr Doyle and his son are both severely allergic."

Evyn doesn't give him time to respond, just pushes away again, clambering over a crumbling, fallen trunk while scanning the inside of a rivet in its side. The old cabin should be coming up, and she moves faster in its general direction. Daire must be headed there too, so she should avoid it, but there's that slippery feeling telling her to keep going and she trails toward regardless. Behind her, Calver calls out, tells her to stay close but she ignores him, pushing ahead. She should be near it now, it has to be somewhere around here. The trees are closer together, the brambles between them dense enough to scratch her bare legs as she steps through them. The canopy overhead is thicker too, dappled sunlight giving way to dim shade, a cool shiver down her spine.

The last time she'd been in that cabin was with Daire. He had swung the flashlight around the small room, ivy bursting through the broken window frame, old bait tins and fishing line tangled on the floor.

Stella could be there. No. Aimee. Aimee could be there.

The scream comes from somewhere far off, high-pitched and rasping. In this part of the woods, the sound echoes wildly, and it's hard to tell exactly where it came from. She locks eyes with Calver, her mouth dropping open, soundless, and her heart beating a rampant staccato. Rachel stops dead, completely still as Calver calls out, "Evyn, stay with Rachel. I'll go see what's happened."

He strides away through the underbrush, moving quickly enough to snap thin boughs in his wake. Then, there's nothing but the sound of their breath, fast and hitching, and the thin moans in the distance. Evyn stands apart from Rachel, out of her eye line, following Calver's back until she loses him in the greenery. The scream is still rocketing in her chest and suddenly, she wants to be home in her bed. Evyn doesn't want to know what could be found in the woods that would make someone scream. She wants to bury her head in her tattered sheets and pretend she's someone else. She wants to run from this dark section of forest, out across the lavender fields, and never come back. She wants to find her sister.

Rachel reaches out with cold, dry fingers and clasps their hands together. Evyn is pulled closer in her too-tight grip, fingers squeezing the bones of her knuckles together. She can't look away from the direction Calver had run and in her peripheral vision, Rachel is stock-still, staring too. Voices call out, and the static hiss of Calver's radio, held close to his mouth, sounds as he pushes back through the brambles toward them. "Civilian search is called off and we have an ambulance on the way, ETA seventeen minutes."

Rachel's hand squeezes hers so tightly that Evyn winces.

"They found her," she whispers but she's not moving. She's staring directly at Calver. Her face is sheet-white and the dark circles under her eyes are gaunt against her pale skin. Evyn has that feeling again, the one that told her to come to the forest, to search in the green, herby spaces for a lost little girl. She knows even before Calver opens his mouth, calling out a warning.

"Rachel!"

Aimee's mother falls, dropping to her knees so fast that Evyn sinks with her, free hand wrapping her ribs, and Calver is there seconds later, dropping in front of them and holding Rachel's shoulders, dipping his head to force eye contact.

"It's not her. It's not Aimee," he tells her, forcing slow, clear words into Rachel's vacant face, "Mads fell through an old borehole and broke her leg. We have to call off the search. Can you hear me? It's not your little girl."

Rachel falls forward, dropping Evyn's hand. Calver catches her before she hits the dirt. Evyn feels like she's witnessing something private when he gathers her up, tucking her into him like a child.

"Daire," Calver calls, leaning to see around the trunk of the tree to where Evyn can hear fast-approaching footsteps, "Help Evyn home."

He stands, taking Rachel with him, and picks her up easily, moving back the way he came. Rachel's eyes are closed, but her fingers curl in his t-shirt, pulling the material taut over his shoulder blade.

Daire's boots come to a stop a few feet from her. He says nothing, leaning down to offer her a hand up, long fingers loose-curled. Two nights ago, wobbling on the low gallery wall, she'd used that same strong hand as balance, pulling herself up into their favorite spot, already dizzy from *tizana* and rum-spiked *chicha*. There's a sob building in her chest, a cracking sound like glass under pressure. She ignores his hand and pushes to her feet.

"I'm good," she tells him, following the trail Calver had taken.

"Yeah, you seem great, Evyn," Daire says. She's never heard that hardened timbre from him before. It hurts less than she thought it would.

Fourteen

Then

"Y ou'll stay," Mrs. Silva- Doyle told her, handing both her and Daire a bright pink glass of *tizana*. She gave her son a raised eyebrow in warning, "Don't add anything to that."

Daire laughed and drew the smaller woman into a jerking hug, "Who, me?"

Tugging at the hem of her sundress, Evyn watched through the glass wall as Daire's father clinked the neck of his beer with Jake's while they hovered over the BBQ. Beyond them, several people milled around the patio, chatting easily while picking at tapas from tall round tables. Jake's college girlfriend stared out at the ocean with her hand held over her eyes and her flowery satin dress sweeping to the side in the breeze. In the distance, three white yachts rounded the headland, white sails that never failed to make Evyn wonder about the lives of the people who cruised into holiday towns.

"I only stopped by because Daire asked me to return a book I borrowed," Evyn says hesitantly, "I didn't know you had company."

The edge to her voice was only meant for Daire. He could have warned her his home would be filled with people dressed in clothes that cost vastly more than her entire wardrobe. But then, she wouldn't have turned up at his door at all, waiting till tonight to see him instead.

"You'll stay," Mrs. Silva-Doyle said again, using the same tone she had used on Daire, "I made that *chicha* you like with the salted caramel."

Evyn's mouth watered but Mrs. Silva-Doyle didn't stay long enough to hear her whispered thank you, swaying through the opened part of the wall to the soft sound of guitar music.

"Come on," Daire said, taking her free hand to pull her out onto the patio, deftly avoiding the guests. He paused at the stairs to check no-one was looking, and tugged her down the steps to the lower deck, where a long table was set with billowing white cloths and fine tableware

"Keep a look out." Daire flattened himself against the wall, comically checking for onlookers while gulping the pink drink. She snorted as he ducked into the plain wooden door behind the stairs, disappearing into the dark room beyond it.

"Daire!" she stage-whispered into the black, "What are you doing?"

The muted conversation from the patio reached her on the breeze and she was suddenly nervous that a guest would find her standing here alone and ask her to leave.

"He's got a tonne of them in there," Daire whispered when he came back out, "Must be planning a proper party this year. So much for it being *medicinal*." He snickered as he tucked three long, perfectly-rolled joints into a tin box and dropped it into the side pocket of his tan shorts, "We're all set for later, I've got a blanket and a cooler upstairs waiting to go. Let's just stay till the sun goes down and then bail out?"

"Yeah," she answered, taking a large gulp of her drink, "Sounds good."

Getting through the party was easier than she thought it would be. Daire found them a spot on one of the patio sofas, tucking her into the corner and setting the sweet milky drink she loved in front of her along with a plate of *empanadas*.

Jake's girlfriend, Annalies, sat across from her and they awkwardly tried to find a topic they had in common until they stumbled onto fantasy television shows. Annalies and seen all her favorites and more. They kept chatting all through dinner, Mrs. Silva-Doyle, swiftly swapping place names when she saw them approaching together with her two sons lagging behind on the steps.

It wasn't until Daire's father interrupted them, calling out from the head of the table with a good-natured smile, that Evyn's discomfort came back in full force.

"So, Evyn, do you plan on college after school? Or will you stay closer to home?"

Daire jerked in his seat, tipping a thin-stemmed glass of green wine onto the tablecloth that he hastily threw his napkin over.

"Dad," he said, answering for her, "Evyn hasn't decided what she's doing after school yet. She still has a year to go."

"She'll need to make her mind up soon," another voice chimed in, "My Sadie is already working on her applications."

Evyn smiled hard at the woman on the opposite side of the table, desperately trying not to roll her eyes. Daire's brother stood and excused himself, clinking four bottles of beer together conspicuously as he cleared his table space. Even that ruckuss wasn't enough to deter the guests.

"Emma will be starting with you in September, Daire," a new voice called out, a stylishly stubbled man leaned forward from their side of the table to call out, "Had to practically drag her back from her year in Australia, but she'll be studying pharmacology. You're law, right?"

"That's right," Daire nodded, absently rolling up the sleeve of his white shirt.

"You could try an Arts degree, if you're not certain about where you want to go," the first woman called out to Evyn again, "Even English, or Philosophy. Just until you figure it out."

Evyn had no idea how much money she would need for either of those courses, but she was certain she wouldn't get accepted, or be able to afford to go, even if she magically did get in.

"Evyn is an accomplished artist," Mrs. Silva-Doyle said, the summer-soft voice she'd been using all night suddenly business-hard. "Her work is strikingly mature for a young woman. I'm sure whatever path she finds herself on will be the right one for her."

"She won a young artist award a few years back," Daire chimed in as he stood and held out his hand to her, "She was just thirteen, then."

Evyn stood and took Daire's hand. "Nice to meet you all," she said to the table, but only looking at Annalies, "Have a good night."

"Be safe, you two," Mrs. Silva-Doyle called as they tramped up the steps to the upper patio, "Daire, *leve-a para casa mais cedo para que o pai dela não fique chateado.*"

"Bunker down in the living room," Daire mumbled on their way through the kitchen, letting go of her hand to bound up the stairs to his room, "I'll grab our stuff."

Instead of curling up on the couch like she normally would, Evyn ducked under the stairs into the large guest bath. She clicked the lock behind her and leaned against the door. She didn't belong here. She'd always known that. But she'd never felt quite so out of place before. Part of her that wanted to race back down the stairs and scream at them all.

The majority of the world survived for an entire year on one week of their wages. College didn't matter, her worth was more than a piece of paper. But the truth was, she wished she could just tell them what courses she was hoping for. Creative Media or Concept Art. Some fancy vernacular to throw in their faces that would make them sit back in their seats and reevaluate her skimpy cotton dress and her cheap jewelry.

"You don't know what you're talking about!"

Daire's voice, thick with anger came from the vent above her. Evyn held still, rooted to the spot at the sound of it.

"She's not coming with you, Daire. I love you, brother, but you need to let go of that idea. She looked like she'd jump off the fucking cliff if Annalies hadn't tried to talk to her."

If Evyn could have hyperventilated, she would have. But here, in this windowless room, with two brothers standing on the landing above her whispering so vehemently that their voices drifted through the air-conditioning system, she barely had enough wherewithal to hold herself back from cramming her ear against the vent.

"You don't know the first fucking thing about her, Jake." Daire's voice, snipped tight with anger she'd never heard from him before.

"I know she couldn't give a fuck about you leaving. You're the one who told me there's nothing more important to her than her sister. *Listen to her.*"

"Fuck off, Jake."

"All I'm saying is college is fun, Daire. And you don't get those years back. If you're really serious about her, she'll still be here when you come home. I don't know why you follow her around like some pathetic puppy. It's not like she's going anywhere."

There was a sickening sound. A liquid snap.

"Christ!! What the fuck, Daire?!?"

A long silence made Evyn press her ear against the vent over the sink, standing on her tiptoes to hear every tiny movement. Daire's breath was heaving, slowing down like he'd just come off the field.

"I'm sorry, Jake. Just don't talk about her like that, okay?"

"Jesus, Daire! I LIKE her! But she doesn't see you that way. I'm trying to look out for you."

Evyn didn't wait for more. She threw herself out of the bathroom and bounded across the living space. No-one called out behind her, Jake and Daire too far from the stairs to hear her quick escape.

She closed the front door as quietly as she could, racing down the driveway and through the open gates. Gathering the thin material of her sundress in her hand to keep it from snagging, she swung her leg onto her bike and pushed off down the hill.

She couldn't think. She wouldn't.

She knew she shouldn't have heard that conversation and she worked hard to snip it from her memory, pushing it down with so many other things she wouldn't allow herself to dwell on, burying it deep where it couldn't hurt her.

The brakes on her bike squeaked as she rounded the bend at the bottom of the hill, heading toward the harbor at speed. The fair would start in a few days. And then Stella would be missing for a full two years. The first anniversary had been so hard. Twelve months with no sign of her sister. An entire year of no-one to take care of, or talk to. A year of no-one truly understanding her. But she'd had Daire. They spent the anniversary on the gallery roof getting high and drinking cheap rum. He'd stayed quiet and let her talk and talk until there was nothing left inside her. When she was empty and numb and so low that she wasn't sure she'd have the energy to get back up again, he'd made her laugh at some stupid joke and they'd kept giggling till the weed wore off and their sides ached.

She brought her bike to a stop at the harbor wall, leaned against it and looked out over the water, the barest whisper of soft waves curling over the tiny lip of sand.

Jake was right. She hadn't been comfortable at the party until Annalies had spoken to her. But the knowledge that he had seen it, that he'd instructed his girlfriend to rescue her, reddened her cheeks and set her fists tight.

He was also wrong. She knew it, bone-deep and shuddering, Jake was wrong about her. Whatever Daire felt for her, she felt it back, just the same, if not more. She'd tried so hard not to but it had happened anyway. He'd slipped under her skin until being near him felt like emerging from a chrysalis, like spreading trembling wings and soaring.

But he was leaving and she couldn't. What would be the point in letting herself feel more than friendship, even if she wanted to? No matter how she felt about Daire, Stella needed her to keep looking.

Where r u?

Her phone pinged and she held it steady in her hands.

Went home to change. I'll meet you there.

She'd felt pretty in her little sundress this morning. Now, despite the heat, she just felt exposed. Evyn didn't wait for his response. Instead, she stared out over the bay and took ten deep breaths, counting them one by one until she had packed up everything she felt, and let it drop.

FIFTEEN

Now

IT TAKES ALMOST HALF an hour for the team to reach the main road with two men carrying Mads between them as carefully as they can. The searchers slip out between a small gap in the old stone wall and lay Mads on the grass, covering her belt-tied leg with a crumpled hi-vis vest.

By the side of the road, sweltering in breezeless heat, the group gathers around Mads. Her face is pale, stoic grunts of pain that brings hands to her shoulders, squeezing solidarity. Once her legs had steadied, Rachel had walked most of the way. She'd still called out Aimee's name, hoarse cries that others joined in, just in case her child was within earshot.

Evyn makes sure to stand a little apart from the others, hanging back by the old stone wall, leaning against it so it covered her from sight. No-one would notice if she left, and their unexpected detour has taken her closer to home. She could be there in less than ten minutes if she walks back up the road. But no one else is moving so it feels odd to walk away.

Rachel has been staring dead-eyed at the forest since they got here, and Evyn has the oddest feeling, like they've been pushed out of the dim, into the glare of mid-morning sunshine by the trees themselves. As if they weren't wanted.

Sirens wail in the distance and the ambulance pulls into view around the sharp bend, racing down the hill toward them.

"Wait, please," Rachel says as the paramedics complete their triage and lift Mads onto a gurney. She hurries over, reaching out to hold Mads' hand and lean over her. Evyn can't hear what is said but Mads tears up and shakes her head full of tight red curls before pulling Rachel into an awkward hug.

Once Mads is loaded aboard the ambulance, Rachel turns to the others in the group, one by one, holding out her hands and whispering thanks. In the background, Calver is watching her. There's a flicker over his face that even the low-pulled cap can't hide. It's a look Evyn recognizes, a feeling so clear it wells inside her.

Want.

She knows it well, that fear-filled, desperate desire she's come to hate. It's the same kind that makes her wish for things she cannot have and hold her hope in a painful grip. It's a feeling that had crept up quickly many times, changed her breath, slackened her mouth so she had to cover it with a palm, or a joint, or a bottle, in case it slipped out and ruined everything.

She works out how long it had been since Mrs. Calver died. There's the tinted memory of her art teacher, leaning down with one hand on the back of Evyn's chair, pointing to a detail on her canvas with a surprised smile that had filled a part of Evyn she hadn't even known was empty. That was five years ago.

With a sudden jolt, Evyn realizes that Calver has been alone much longer than she has, wearing the night he lost everything plainly on his face, with no way to hide it.

It hits so hard that Evyn turns around and heads back toward the gap in the wall, planning on slinking back through the forest rather than walking around the group to get by them. She hates Calver, has every reason to hate him for what he did. She won't allow herself to feel anything but that.

"Miss Donovan!"

The call is quiet, but the dense heat warps the sound, as if Rachel is right behind her. Evyn spins back, hands clasped together, and a tense, limp smile drawn thin over her face. "I was just leaving," she says in a too bright voice.

"Will you wait with me a minute?" Rachel asks, not waiting for Evyn to agree before hoisting herself up onto the uneven wall and patting the moss-covered stone beside her. Evyn follows her lead, but the wall is hip height and her ribs are too sore to climb it without pain showing in her face. She leans against it instead, both of them staring out across the road as the paramedics close up the ambulance and turn in the tight space.

Daire moves to Calver's side, talking low and heated. His eyes flick up once, meet hers, and then slide away. They're too far away to hear anything but Calver's hands make a subtle, calming gesture, open palms pressing toward the ground.

"Is that your boyfriend?" Rachel asks quietly, though she's still staring at the woodland on the other side of the road.

"No, we're friends," Evyn says. Any way she tries to look at it, that's a lie. But she can't bring herself to say 'were.'

"He's a nice boy," she tells her, "More mature than I remember boys being when I was younger."

Rachel can't be more than ten years older than Evyn. She's about to point that out when Rachel tilts her chin up, following a line of birds as they lift off from the trees.

"Aimee was two when Stella went missing," she says, her voice watery, "I held her for a month straight after it. Wouldn't put her down."

Evyn is unprepared for the tears that threaten hot at the backs of her eyes. She swallows, stays quiet, and Rachel fills the silence.

"It was kind of you," Rachel tips her head closer, like she's sharing a secret, "to help today, when it's still so raw for you."

Evyn nods because that's all she can do. There's no way to speak when the lump in her throat threatens to burn all her words. But when she turns to Rachel, sees her puffed, swollen eyelids and grey-tinged features, Evyn pushes through it, ignoring the shake in her voice. "This isn't the same," she tells her, hissing conviction that comes from a place that feels secret and shameful, "We'll find Aimee, Rachel. Calver will."

Rachel turns and suddenly their faces are too close. Evyn's breath catches at the desperation in her expression.

"How do you know?"

"I don't. I just feel it."

It's not a good enough answer. Rachel's face falls, suddenly withdrawing into herself, and Evyn is left wishing she hadn't spoken at all. She scans the road till she finds Calver, still talking to Daire but further away now, as if whatever they're saying can't be overheard by the group. When she catches the detective's eye, he stops mid-sentence, holding up a hand to silence a frustrated Daire. Without another word, Calver jogs toward them.

"See you later, Rachel," Evyn says and slides through the broken section of wall, winding quickly through trees to pass by a group of searchers without having to interact with anyone else.

By the road, the trees look dense, but there's less bramble here and Evyn knows from her adventures with Stella, that there is another break in the wall further up the hill. She comes out onto the road well beyond the bend, squeezing through the small gap with much less ease than she remembers, and sets off for home at a much slower pace than when she left the house this morning.

By the time she reaches home, she is tired, overheated, and dreaming of the ice-cold water Daire's mother keeps in their fridge, a bulbous jug filled with lemon and mint. She crosses the cattle grid, trudges up the center of the dirt track where the short grass is softer underfoot, and stops cold as the house comes into view through the scrubby brush.

Her father's battered truck is still outside the house. It's after 3pm, he should be out drinking already, trying to double his earnings in the small room at the back of The Ditch where the poker games run cheap buy-ins and half-price shorts. She holds still for what feels like hours but there's nowhere else to go. Too tired to keep walking, Evyn just wants to lie in her bed until she has enough energy to eat. So she takes small, quiet steps that slowly bring her to her open front door.

After the brightness of her walk, the hallway is dim enough to make her squint. It's quiet, no TV sounds and no sign of her father. She walks slowly, her breath tight in her chest, and her throat so dry and scratching that she has no choice but to aim for the kitchen.

He's leaning against the counter, the drawer beside him open wide and empty, its contents strewn over the floor. The room is trashed and he's smirking with a strange satisfaction that makes Evyn's sweat-sheened skin run cold as ice.

The fridge door is open, the food piled onto the floor. From the smell, it's been like that for some time, turning sour in the heat. There are eggs congealing on the countertop, dripping down the doors of the presses and pooling on the torn lino. A bowl of cereal is cracked on the floor, milk and crusted flakes staining a wide arc on the wall as if he'd flung it across the room. Chairs overturned, table tipped and leaning against the sink, even the net curtains over the window are smeared red, the jar of sauce cracked in the sink.

"It's not gonna clean itself." The cigarette clings to the corner of her father's lip, dripping ash careless onto his shirt front. He swipes at it and moves to the door, crossing his arms to watch.

He'd done something like this before when she'd read about a trafficking ring in the city and had tried to search the area for any signs of her sister. It was dangerous and stupid, a four hour round trip on a bus she'd taken a weeks' wages to be able to afford. She'd come home late to find her art ripped from her bedroom walls and her bed tilted, one leg stuck through the plywood door of her closet. It wasn't her safety her father had been concerned about. It was the beans on toast he'd had to eat for dinner, the only thing he could cook. The remains of it had been smeared on her sheets.

Back then, he'd been content to let her clean up the mess alone, refusing to even acknowledge it the next morning when she set his breakfast in front of him. But now, he leans back against the back door and watches her sink to her knees to pull cleaning supplies from behind the faded, paisley curtain that conceals the sink outlets. She can't look, though the white-tinged fury of his looming stance keeps drawing her eye to where he stands.

Without a word, Evyn begins to dredge the foul-smelling eggs into a paper towel, the slick slide of it making her stomach roll.

Her father finishes his cigarette, drops it to the floor and twists the toe of his shoe over it, smearing the ash in a wide circle. He's watching her reaction and the smug flicker at the corner of his mouth makes her sit back on her heels.

For the first time in her life, Evyn feels no fear. It leaves her all at once, in a rush that's both calming and dizzying. She snaps into cool blankness, as if all the consequences are far away, unreal things that won't ever come to pass. It feels momentous somehow, like she's tipped off the edge of a high place, but it's too late to protect herself from falling and the ground is so very far away. When she looks up at him, studying his darkening frown and the push of his mouth, he snarls at her.

"What the fuck are you looking at?"

If it wasn't for this calm space that's opening inside her, she would turn away, work faster to clean the mess he's made. But there is something she has always wanted to know, so she asks. If she understands the problem, maybe she can fix it. Maybe everything could be different.

"What is it about me that makes you so angry?"

Evyn has a follow-up question because she's not sure he knows how to answer something so direct. But she doesn't get to voice it.

His face pales and his lower jaw pushes out against his clenched teeth. She barely notices him raise his foot but he kicks the small kitchen table and it hits her with a blinding crack that sends her tumbling backwards into the fridge. There's a swooping darkness, like a blanket thrown over her and lifted again too soon. Evyn can hear the rattle of her own shocked breath.

She's on the floor, bright light in the tiny kitchen making her squint. There's something hard across her cheek and her legs are curled awkwardly under the table. Her mouth and nose are wet, pain just beginning to take hold and grow outward. When she swipes at her face, her fingers come away a terrifying shade of red.

She breathes in a huge gulp of blood-flecked air, coughing up the droplets of irony liquid that catch in the back of her throat. She hasn't finished hacking when the table is pulled away, dragging her legs out straight.

Her father looms monstrously tall from her position on the floor. He grabs her ponytail without a word, hauling her to her feet. Evyn holds his wrist, trying to lessen the pressure on her scalp.

The edges of her vision are dark, as if she's looking at his rage-filled face through a keyhole. His mouth is moving, but she can't hear the words over the rush of blood in her ears. There are stabbing pains in her ankle as he drags her into the hallway and bursts into the small toilet.

He hits the door so hard it ricochets off the wall and comes back to them. Roaring, he slams his fist against it and holds it open to push her into the room. If Evyn could scream, she would, but she can barely catch her breath.

He drives her toward the sink, the toothpaste-flecked mirror above it, and holds face toward it, squeezing her jaw so tight that stars bloom and burst in her vision. When he leans to talk over her shoulder, his leg pushes the point of her hip into the sink, spindling pain down her leg.

She locks onto his bloodshot eyes, barely recognizing him. The veins in his temple pulse dark blue, and his eyes are wide and glassy, rimmed with red. It looks as if he's on the verge of tears.

Without warning, Evyn isn't in the room at all anymore. She's back in the first few days after Stella went missing and she's following a choking cry to her father's bedroom. He's on the floor at the end of his bed, sobbing into his hands, and the pitiful keening holds her in the doorway like a siren.

His eyes were the same then, shining and splintered crimson. When he'd sobbed and crawled toward her, she'd dropped to meet him. The door had slammed so hard she hadn't had time to move her hands. The nail of her ring finger had turned black and fallen off weeks later.

Her father shakes her head hard and she snaps back, her breath sprays a thin red mist across the mirror.

"Who do you think you are?" he asks through clenched teeth.

There's spittle on her cheek and ear. Her mouth won't open, his hold is too tight for any response other than a guttural, high-pitched moan.

"Do you know what a twelve-hour shift feels like? *Do you*?" He shakes her head again but doesn't give her time to respond. "Because I do. To keep a roof over your ungrateful head. And while you live here, you will follow my fucking rules."

She knows this house belonged to her grandmother, her mother's mother. Mads had told her years ago. There's a part of her that has always been afraid he would lose too much at poker and sell it.

"I don't ask for much, do I?"

Through the constellation of tiny red droplets on the mirror, Evyn looks at her own face. There's a welt across her cheek, a wide line already raised and darkening. Blood from her nose covers the lower half of her face, soaking the collar of her shirt. Fear drops heavy in her stomach and she tries to settle it, praying she won't vomit.

"Have dinner ready when I get home and don't waltz around town with greasy little immigrants. Don't have half the town stopping to tell me about you helping that Gilbride whore. *Again*."

He pulls back to growl and the sound loosens her belly so she has to squeeze her legs together. He draws her backwards and Evyn clamps her eyes shut, trying to twist the undamaged side of her face toward the glass.

But instead of knocking her face into the mirror, her father lets go of her completely, leaning back against the bathroom wall to breathe heavily. He wipes his mouth, smearing a fine swipe of her blood across his stubbled chin and the room is filled with the sound of their breath echoing off thin walls.

"It should have been you," he says, eventually, "Not your sister."

Evyn grips the sink, trying to steady her shaking legs, and doesn't dare to speak, even to agree with him.

"Jesus," he says, his top lip raised in disgust, "Clean yourself up."

He pushes past her and Evyn holds entirely still, listening to the stomp of him through the house, the heavy clink of bottles from the living room and the clash of his car keys from the hook in the hallway. With the revving of his choking engine, she's alone, finally able to sink onto the floor to try to remember what it feels like to breathe without terror.

SIXTEEN

now

IT TAKES TIME FOR Evyn to come back to herself. She's not sure how long she's been on the bathroom floor before the dripping tap catches her attention, pulling her from her blank state. She watches how the water clings to the metal and forms a fat bead that holds on until its own heaviness pulls it loose.

She's heard nothing but birdsong for a while, but that doesn't mean her father's truck won't rattle over the cattle grid at any moment. Coming home to find her in the same spot is enough to make her move. She reaches for the sink, drags herself to stand, and ignores the sharp sting in her ankle as she gets to her feet. She can deal with that later.

Evyn starts by wiping the blood from her face and arms. Her nose has stopped bleeding, but she has to wash her mouth out with tepid tap water several times before the taste of it leaves her throat.

She pours bleach into a bucket and tops it with water, then strips off her clothing to soak the stains away, pushing the pan under the sink. In her underwear, she limps across the hall to her room to pull on running shorts and a cropped t-shirt. It doesn't matter about the bruising now. No-one can see her and the heat seems to have increased three-fold this afternoon, the whole house thick and ripe with it.

In the kitchen, she cleans. It's a slow thing, tricky maneuvering to avoid pain. All she wants is to crawl to her room, close her curtains and turn her face to the pillow. Maybe if she lay still for long enough, she could vanish too.

But her father cannot come back to the mess he'd made, cannot find her vulnerable in her room. So she drags the spoiled food into bags, washes down cracked countertops and ancient cupboards, runs her wet cloth over the milk-spattered walls, and leaves unbroken dishes in the sink for later.

One of the table legs is bent and she can't straighten it herself, the metal too thick to push back into place. She drags it to the back door, almost certain that there is a plastic one in the garden somewhere that she could replace it with.

The rush of air is so thick with lavender that Evyn almost coughs. The oily, herby scent is so strong. The harvest must have started. She walks out into it, taking deep lungfuls that slow her heart rate and calm her trembling fingers.

Her ankle hurts with every step but something in the scent pushes her forward, out beyond their fallow field to the broken fence at their property line. Her nose is raised to the light breeze, and though her muscles are aching and her ankle sore, she ducks through to the other side and stands, surrounded by the whisper of that lulling scent.

The wind brings her a gift, dreamy and soft.

The sound of her sister's voice, so quiet she tilts her head, listening hard with a sudden shiver of energy. She hears it again, the softest crying, the slightest whimper that tenses her muscles and then she is running, all that listless calm like a wall she has burst through.

Loping over uneven, dry ground, Evyn follows the infrequent sound, tracking through the undergrowth, pushing trailing branches and pricking brambles aside. This path used to be clear, the track through the woods she had taken with her sister so many times. It leads to the clearing, an area of woody detritus with a huge tree stump in the center, trunk cracked uneven and torn away in a storm. The stump had offered shelter and quiet whenever they needed to escape the house.

Sometimes, when she sat still beside it for long enough, the squirrels would come down from the trees and race each other for the nearest morsels of food. They got closer and closer, braver and braver. Stella had loved it, how she could reach out and touch one, on the days she'd had the patience, and see them all race off like her fingers were made of fire. It was one of the first places Evyn searched, and she'd looked here a thousand times since, but it still makes sense that this would be the place Stella would come back to.

The wind rustles the bushes nearby and with it, her sister's small cries grow louder. Evyn is so close to the clearing that the trees up ahead are dark lines in the blazing sunlight beyond them. She picks up her pace, her hand squeezing the thigh of her injured leg, willing power into it.

Everything is going to be okay. Her life had gotten so much worse after that morning when she had woken up to the cool spot where her sister should have been sleeping. But it would all be different now.

Evyn has lost every single thing she ever cared about and it has made her stronger.

She'll take Stella away. They will run. Neither of them will ever set foot in that house again. They'll see that broken-down cabin only in their memories, and even those will fade, in time. Evyn will take her battered face and her splintered ribs and build them a life far from here, where there are no woods to get lost in and hundreds of people to witness what happens if a young girl runs away in the middle of the night.

She stumbles into the clearing, catching herself against a tree to keep herself from falling. The flare of afternoon sun makes her vision fade as she squints into it.

"Stella."

She had meant to shout it, but the clearing is so still, so silent, that her voice comes out a whisper. It takes her a moment to realise that there are no birds calling, no insect hum or brush of leaves against each other in the breeze. The area is completely devoid of sound, so quiet that all she can hear is the rush of her own breath. She listens hard, hoping to hear that quiet cry again, her uninjured leg tired from taking her weight.

Nothing.

Her ankle is swelling, the skin puffed out around her tennis shoe, but she limps further into the glade, dragging her damaged leg in a line over the dried, woody ground. There's a tiny movement at the base of the stump, something small pulling away out of sight. Once removed, Evyn can see it for what it was, as if the image registered in reverse, like an old photographic negative.

What had been part of the landscape, once absent, becomes a small, dirty foot.

Evyn walks forward slowly. As she nears the stump, the foot reappears, and then a small, thin-boned leg.

Her heart drops as she realizes what she's looking at. These little toes, curling in the dirt, are too small to be Stella's. She would be eight years old now, tall and thin. This plump, dirt-streaked calf belongs to a much smaller child, round-faced and curly-haired with soiled pink pyjamas and huge, upturned eyes.

"Aimee," Evyn drops to her knees, crouching in front of the little girl.

Her back is against the bark, body huddled between two outcropping roots that delve into the dry ground on either side of her knees. Her shoulders hunch and she takes a leaf-stuck strand of her hair and chews on it, anxious eyes darting all around.

She whispers through the strands, words so soft that Evyn is sure she's misheard her. Because what she says doesn't make sense.

There's a strange noise, a broken, cracking pitch, and the little girl reaches forward to pat Evyn's thigh. Evyn brings one hand to cover her mouth, stifling the piteous sound. She pulls Aimee into her lap with her free hand, rocking her back and forth. The afternoon heat burns across her back as she shades the child from it. Her little body is warm, curling into her hold and Evyn squeezes her a little, to let her know everything will be alright now.

"I want to go home," she says in a quiet voice that sounds like a higher version of Rachel's soft cadence.

"Okay," Evyn tells her, "Let's go find your mommy."

They set off through the trees, Aimee's tiny fingers in hers, easily keeping up with her slow, limping pace. They don't speak as they duck through the woods, but the little girl starts to lag behind after a while, tugging on Evyn's arm. She could have gone back to the house to find her phone and call for help, but the thought of bringing Aimee into that ruined kitchen turns her stomach, so she keeps going, trying to reach the road.

By the time they come to the old stone wall that borders the ditch, Aimee is dragging her feet. She doesn't whine like Stella would have, doesn't cry that her legs are tired until Evyn's jaw aches with holding her tongue. But Aimee does need help pushing herself over the wall and Evyn can barely drag her own body over after boosting the child.

The road warps in the distance, heat feathering the splay of Blackditch town like a mirage. They trudge along the yellow side-line, following like ants on a stem, but eventually, Aimee's pulling on her arm is too much.

"Stand up here and I'll give you a lift," she points to a rock at the side of the road and scoops the child onto the uninjured side of her body. At first, it's easy. She weighs almost nothing and Evyn limps faster, hauling them both down the hill toward the town.

The girl's first words twist round in her mind as she walks, and Evyn focuses on them instead of the pain and exhaustion in her body. She must have misheard. A child wouldn't know what those words meant.

Cars pass, one honks its horn as she steps wide to avoid a pothole, but she doesn't flag them down. Somewhere, deep down, she knows that she should stop at a house, beg to use their phone and call for help. But she keeps going, listening to the whispered words of a frightened child replaying in her head. They don't make sense. None of it makes sense. How Aimee walked so far from home without being seen by the searchers; how she'd found the one clearing for miles around and waited there. How Evyn had heard her sister, clear as a bell, and how it had brought her straight to another missing child who said impossible things.

By the time they reach the line of terraced stores at the start of Main Street, Evyn forces herself to stop thinking. When she can't walk another step, she switches the child to her injured side. It hurts more, but not enough to stop her. Sweat beads on her face and neck, the small of her back slick and tickling. But she keeps walking. There's no choice but to get Aimee to a place she'll be safe.

There are other voices now, and Evyn absently thinks she hears her name. But it's difficult to focus on anything other than keeping her thighs pushing forward and dragging her weight so she won't fall. She can't feel much of her body anymore, just the burning heat on her forehead and shoulders. A hand on her elbow, trying to slow her, and she stumbles away, panicked.

At the crossroads in front of her, there's a blur of purple, a painted cart with a burst of sheared flowers sitting in the raised center of the junction. She can smell its dreamy lavender scent as she turns toward the station.

More voices call to her. Another hand touches her arm, startling her enough to jerk away. She wants to speak, to shout 'don't touch me' or 'get away' but it's only a hiss that comes, drawn breath through bared teeth. Someone runs ahead of her but she doesn't take her eyes from the silver sign glinting in the late afternoon light. She's almost there.

Evyn lifts the girl higher on her hip, a blast of pain weakening her arms but she holds tight and keeps walking. Her eyes sting with sweat, beads of it running between her breasts. Everything is hazy, and Evyn can only focus on the doors beneath the shining sign.

They burst open. A huge, dark shape emerging and racing toward her. She can't see his face but she knows it's him. The cap he wears to hide his scars does nothing in this light. She tries to hold the child out to him but her muscles won't move from their rigid position.

Calver is talking, she can hear the deep city accent but the words are blurring. His hand is on her shoulder, steadying her and then Evyn isn't holding anything anymore.

It's done. It's over. The lightness of Aimee's lifted weight feels like flying.

She turns, pivots on her good heel, because she needs to rest now. She needs to crawl into her bed and sleep until the heat and the pain and the blank exhaustion are just a memory.

But there are people right behind her, blocking the sidewalk and some of the road, faces that stare at her with abject horror. Evyn looks up to avoid their eyes and everything tilts, shifting her whole body. She raises her arms, as if she might lift off into the blue sky. Instead, she falls, swooping backwards in an arc, and the hard concrete rises to meet her.

There are cries, shocked gasps, but she doesn't hit the ground. There's an arm around her, something soft and solid against her back and she's lowered slowly to the hot ground.

So many voices now, Calver calls orders, and when Evyn blinks she almost laughs at the oddness of the detective's face, upside down with a halo of brightness around him. But the light is too much so Evyn closes her eyes and sinks into the darkness, where there's no pain or bone-tired ache, no odd warnings from lost little girls who sound like a voice she once loved. There's nothing but blissful silence and she lets herself float into it.

SEVENTEEN

now

S HE DOESN'T RECOGNISE THIS room. When her eyes open, it takes a minute for the green plastic chair by her bed to come into focus. Not her bedroom chair. The cream walls have signs about handwashing above a small sink with a clinical-looking soap dispenser and a red-labelled medical trash receptacle.

A hospital room, sterile bleach smell and a mattress that crackles when she moves. Evyn stretches each of her limbs, testing her body slowly. Her muscles ache, thighs recalling her long, slow walk in afternoon heat.

She pushes back the blankets and swivels her feet to the floor. A gown. She's wearing a hospital gown that opens at the back, warm air hitting the curve of her spine. The fabric feels thick and rough and there's a taped needle on the back of her hand leading to a plastic tube that runs up to a clear IV drip. Disoriented, she feels her ribs through the gown. The scarf is gone, replaced with something tighter and there's a black brace on her ankle, a long stretch of elastic from the arch of her foot to the curve of her calf.

Evyn stands, pulling herself as tall as she can. The rib brace makes it a little harder to breathe but she feels more secure, and there's barely any pain.

Drugs. She must have been given something.

Carefully, she lifts the tape from her hand and pulls the needle out, smearing the tiny bead of blood that forms in its wake. She walks to the small mirror by the sink, setting her mouth tight at her reflection, and assesses the damage. Her eye is swollen half shut, but her vision is clear and unaffected. There's deep bruising darkening over her cheek with a violent-looking red streak running through the center. Her face is sunburnt and her lips are so dry they've cracked. Wincing, she runs her fingers over her teeth, checking for looseness. There is a little give in one of her molars but nothing that won't heal.

She stretches, putting weight on her hurt ankle, and feels nothing but the support of the brace and the bandages. It's a relief to so suddenly be pain free, and her eyes gloss over with it.

The door opens and a nurse comes in, raising an eyebrow at her.

"You're supposed to be in bed, Miss Donovan," she says and firmly closes the door, pursing her lips at the abandoned drip, "And those fluids were to help with dehydration. Come sit down and let me have a look at you."

Evyn allows herself to be firmly guided toward the bed.

"You have quite a list of injuries," the nurse hums as she checks her pulse. She tilts Evyn's head up, peering at her cheek, a small appraising sound in the back of her throat. When she's satisfied, she pokes her head into the hallway.

"Detective Calver," she calls and Evyn freezes, "You asked to be told when Miss Donovan woke?"

There's the deep rumble of Calvers' voice, a quick, low 'thank you'. The nurse smiles and opens the door wider.

"I think she's well enough, considering she took out her own drip," the nurse laughs and turns to Evyn, the humor dying as soon as she meets her eye. She goes to the end of the bed to make notes on the clipboard hanging there while Evyn struggles to stay still, wondering how long Calver had been sitting in the hallway outside her room.

"How long have I been here?" she asks the nurse, but she's busy with her notes and it's Calver who answers.

"A little over four hours. How are you feeling?"

"Is Aimee alright?" Evyn has a vague memory of him telling her not answer a question with a question at the start of the summer, sitting at a bare metal table with her lips thinned and fists clenched. But here, that defensiveness seems off. Now that she had run straight to him when she found something she needed to protect, she can't quite form the tone she was used to using with him.

"I'm fine," she says, voice softer, "Is she?"

"Aimee's perfectly healthy. A couple of scratches, a little dehydration, and an appetite like I've never seen. She wolfed four sandwiches and a chocolate bar in less than ten minutes."

Evyn tilts her head. There's the hint of real affection in his voice. But then he looks up, and all the softness drops away, like he's shoring himself up for what comes next.

"You did a brave thing, bringing her to the station the way you did. Now I need you to tell me what happened."

"Nothing."

It's instant, that ingrained response, pointless when she's sitting in a hospital bed with her face looking the way it does. "I found her in the woods, brought her into town. That's all." She twists her hands together,

her knuckles popping one after the other. The nurse hisses, setting down her pen, shuffling out the door.

"Could you leave it open, please," Calver asks, nodding in thanks when she taps a rod into place on the overhead hinge. The door stays wide, an unobstructed view of the empty nurse's station.

"Evyn, can you tell me how you got those bruises?" Calver reaches forward as if to touch her shoulder but pulls away just as fast to rub at his jaw, tugging so the scars drag down his cheek.

"Aren't I supposed to have an adult present or something?" She searches for the smug anger that usually keeps her afloat around the detective, but it isn't there, just that familiar lump in her throat.

"Yes." Calver stares at her, the godawful silence that feels like arms around her, like he can see all of the things she's never told anyone.

This is Daire's fault. It's harder to lie now, as if sharing the worst parts of her life with him, just once, has opened all her insides up to everyone else too.

"Evyn, you have hairline fractures in two of your ribs, your ankle is badly sprained, and your face has deep and extensive bruising. I need you to tell me what happened. Can you say who hurt you?"

Like a whirlwind, the anger is back in her clenched hands, heating her cheeks and the backs of her eyes.

"You did," she tells him, her voice like acid.

Calver blinks, and then waits, sitting back awkwardly in his seat until Evyn continues. "You hurt me when you closed her case. You hurt me when you stopped looking for Stella."

She stands, forcing him to move his chair back. The nurse reappears at the noise, hurrying into the room.

"Miss Donovan, you need to—"

"Give us a moment please," he says, his eyes not leaving Evyn's. He stays seated, lets her loom over him, and waits.

"You never found out what happened to my sister. I had to walk the woods looking for her, night after night. I spent hours reading through every local newspaper and website in the country searching for any trace of her. You hurt me when you didn't do your fucking job."

The last few words are a stuttering yell and Calver looks away from her, down toward the grey linoleum. It's not enough to see him lost for words, the discomfort clear in the twist of his mouth. Suddenly nothing is enough anymore.

"Why did you stop? Why? She's out there somewhere, scared and alone. She could be just like Aimee. You don't know that she's not. You don't *know* that!"

When all the energy leaves her body and she sinks back onto the bed, Calver answers.

"You're right, I don't know that. I don't know where your sister is."

He shifts in his seat, still staring at the floor, and the only sound in the room is her breath calming to a quiet murmur and the bed crackling plastic beneath her weight. Once it's quiet, he asks her again, in exactly the same tone as before, "What happened to your face, Evyn?"

It's all too much suddenly, and Evyn lays on her side, sinking into the pillow and drawing her legs up onto the bed.

"You don't even care," she says. She's meant to sound angry but her voice is too small for that, too plaintive. Calver leans forward with a sigh. His hand forms a light fist, tapping off the arm of his chair.

"You're wrong. I didn't find Stella and it haunts me. I've gone over her file more times than I can count. I should have found her. But I didn't."

He sighs again and Evyn holds perfectly still, waiting for him to add something, an explanation of how it wasn't his fault. But it doesn't come.

"I didn't help her," he tells her, "But I can help you."

Evyn has to close her eyes against the directness of his stare, that determination that makes her want to run from the room and hold perfectly still at the same time. He continues even though she refuses to look at him.

"If you don't want to tell me who did this to you, that's fine. I know what you're scared of, and I promise you, I won't get social services involved. But I can still help you. I have to."

Evyn pulls her legs up closer, like a barrier between them. "I don't know what you're talking about." She sounds unconvincing, even to herself, and Calver softly clicks his tongue.

"Just let me help you, Evyn."

His voice is strained. There are lines between his eyebrows that mean something entirely different on her father's forehead and the difference makes Evyn notice all the other things that aren't the same. She's not afraid here, there's no need to be. The room is bright and filled with the scent of the familiar flowers in the vase on the windowsill and there's no-one here who wants to hurt her. It is to exact opposite to every room in her own home.

But fear follows her like a ghost. She couldn't ask for help, even if she wanted to. Hiding so much for so long makes revealing it feel like a flood that will drown her.

"I can't," she says and already, the tears are seeping. She opens her palm. Calver's eyes jump to it, then back to her and there's an unfamiliar softness there, the same one she'd seen when he talked about Aimee. He takes her hand and holds it in both of his. Evyn's fingers disappear into his pressed palms. His grip is light enough that she could pull away if she wanted, but instead, Evyn turns her face into the pillow and cries until her swollen face feels twice its normal size. She stays there, pressed into the darkness until it's all there is, until he lets her fingers go to cover her with a blanket, and she falls asleep more soundly than she has in years.

W HEN SHE WAKES, CALVER is still in the chair, pulled a little away from the bed, scrolling through his phone. He's not been there the whole time because his shirt is a different color and he's wearing glasses as he reads, something that makes him strangely less intimidating. Calver looks up suddenly, catching her watching him, and pulls his baseball cap from behind his hip, slotting it on.

"You were discharged while I was addressing the press," he tells her and she's not sure what to make of how easily he speaks to her now. The same way he talks to Daire or Officer Obasi, as if there's been a shift and she's no longer on the other side of a glass wall that makes her different to everyone else.

The room is darker, the only light coming from the fluorescent strip over her bed and the open door to her room.

"What time is it?" she asks. Had she closed the back door? Was the table still on its side and the trash bags she'd filled still haphazardly piled in the corner, waiting to be thrown out?

"It's after eight," he tells her, oblivious to her panic, "And you're quite famous, young lady."

Evyn blinks, tilting her head.

"Mrs. Garcia filmed you on her phone, put it on YouTube," he shakes his head in disapproval, "She titled the video 'Heroic young woman with tragic past saves missing child' and Officer Obasi tells me it has over a hundred thousand views already."

There's a sinking in her stomach. It's out there, on the internet, her battered face and her ungainly fall. She reaches instinctively for her phone, only to remember that she left it behind when she'd run out into the yard at the sound of her sister's voice. She fills the silence quickly, with the first thing she can think of.

"Mrs. Garcia refused to hire me at the tea-rooms because I couldn't be trusted," she said, raising an eyebrow in response to Calver's. With a hint of bitterness, she turns her voice round and hard like a news presenter, "Heroic young woman steals overpriced muffins, probably."

It's not quite a smile, but Evyn can see the want of it at the corners of his mouth. Calver dips down to drag a police-issued bag from underneath his seat.

"These were in the lost and found." He slides the bag across the floor and comes to a quick, awkward stand, "Your clothes had to be…"

He doesn't finish the sentence, just moves to the door and motions down the hallway to the nurse's station. They must have cut her clothes from her to examine her ribs. They would have been soaked with sweat anyway. Her skin feels dry and grimy with it.

"Thanks," she says quietly to his retreating back, but Calver doesn't acknowledge it. He disappears around the door frame and a nurse appears a moment later, a clipboard in her hand. It's only once she's dressed with the signed discharge papers that Evyn starts to panic. There's no way to hide this if she's all over the internet, and she doesn't even have money to get a bus back to Blackditch. She follows the nurse into the hallway, unsure of what happens next, and finds Calver sitting on a bench, leafing through a small thin file.

He closes it and holds it up for her to see.

"Aimee Gilbride's file," he tells her, "Gonna need you to come with me to fill in some of the details. Just where you found her and how you came into town. Can you do that?"

She nods warily, following him silently as he signs the final form at the nurse's desk and directs her toward the car park.

Evyn has been in the back of Calver's police car more times than she can remember but this time, he walks to the driver's side and nods at the passenger door.

"You're not in trouble, Evyn," he says with the slightest hint of sarcasm, "You're a witness."

They don't speak on the way back to Blackditch. Evyn rolls the window down and lets the warm night air rush over her. It's hard not to wonder where her father is now, if he's seen how she'd left the house, if he knows about the video. But the thought of it makes her hands shake, so she crams them between her thighs and focuses on getting her story straight until Calver pulls into the small car park at the back of the station.

In his office, Calver flips through Aimee's file while Evyn drinks the sweetened ice tea he'd put in front of her, waiting patiently until she's ready to talk.

"This interview is being recorded," he tells her, his finger hovering over a button on the overly large device on his desk, "But you are free to leave at any time. You're just giving some supporting details, as you remember them. Do you understand?"

He hits the button when she nods, dry-mouthed.

"Witness interview with Evelyn Donovan—" he holds up a hand when she opens her mouth to correct him, "Also known as Evyn Donovan, a seventeen-year-old minor, interviewed without adult supervision, for incidental details in the missing person case for Aimee Gilbride."

Calver seems to talk more than Evyn does, and it's clear he's trying to phrase his questions in a way that doesn't mention Evyn's injuries. She tells him as much as she can about how she found Aimee. When he asks her why she didn't call for help at any point, Evyn's face grows hot and her response stalls. Calver clears his throat and declares the interview finished with another long string of well-rehearsed lines.

"Is Aimee really okay?" she asks, thinking of how the girl's little body had felt like lead by the time they'd reached Blackditch.

He nods and stands, tucking the file under his arm, and answering as he walks to the door. "Thanks to you, she is. She says she woke up in the woods. Her mother confirmed she sleep-walks but she'd never gotten out of the house before. We're still looking into why the dogs didn't find her."

"Can I go now?"

It must be near midnight and Evyn knows she has to face her father sooner or later, but Calver stops in the doorway, turning back in surprise. "I can't stop you Evyn, but I told you I would help. You can wait here, or in my office, and we can talk as soon as this case is filed. Won't be too long."

She waits, staring out the window at the dark sky, trying to work out what will happen to her next.

EIGHTEEN

now

O FFICER OBASI SLIDES BOXED salad across the table.

"That was an amazing thing you did," she says lightly as she sets down another cup of sweet tea. Evyn's mouth is watering, her stomach aching with sudden recognition of hunger. She hasn't eaten since her dinner with Daire and she rips off the plastic lid, practically inhaling a piece of lightly spiced chicken.

Calver's office is a clean, tidy space. There's been nothing for Evyn to look at for the last fifteen minutes while he went to talk to someone in reception. The only piece of decoration is a small silver photo frame. It's turned slightly away from her, and Evyn can't bring herself to study the picture inside. Her old art teacher. Calver's wife. The blurred edge of her smile is all she can see.

"I'm not sure I could have carried that child so far, not in weather like this, and certainly not on a twisted ankle," The officer is still talking, a softer tone to her voice than Evyn has heard from her since the day Stella went missing. She takes the biggest bite she can manage but already, her appetite is fading at the memory.

When she swallows with a heaving gulp, Officer Obasi leans across the table, placing one hand lightly on her shoulder.

"How are you feeling, sweetheart?"

Sick. She feels sick and exhausted and frightened, and she doesn't know what she's doing here. She should want to go home but that's even more terrifying. The only person she wants to see right now will never speak to her again.

It's as familiar as breathing. Evyn lets the anger float up and cover all the hurt. She pushes the salad away and drags one leg up on the chair, moving away from the woman's touch.

"I'm peachy," she says, mouth set into a sneer.

Officer Obasi sighs. "Sometimes," she says, her voice a little harder than before, "It's okay to need help, you know. No-one survives this life alone."

There's a faraway, dark look on her face and before Evyn can think of a response, the woman has backed out of Calver's office. Through the open door, Evyn watches her nod at the detective, striding back toward the office with his cap pulled low.

Calver settles into his seat, rocking the chair backwards with a bounce. He steeples his fingers and looks at her over them. Evyn feels like she is back in the interview room again, all those times that her throat closed up and she wanted to run. She pulls her other leg up onto the seat, ignoring Calver's narrowed eyes.

"Evyn," he starts and then hesitates, straightening some papers on his desk with a gruff throat-clearing. Eventually, when his already-pristine desk is infinitesimally more so, he sits back and lightly thumps the side of his fist off the armrest, "I'm just going to say it, okay?"

He doesn't wait for her to speak, though he does seem to notice her tiny nod.

"Your father is hurting you."

She freezes in place, every muscle bound tight and her fingers clasped around her knees.

"You don't have to say anything," he tells her, "But I want you to know that I could lose my job for not reporting it. Do you understand?"

This time, when she nods, it's more than just a flicker.

"I told you that I would help you and that's what I plan to do. We're going to get you out of that house. You can stay at my place for tonight and you'll take the guest room at Rachel Gilbride's house tomorrow."

Evyn's heart races. She cannot leave the house she and Stella grew up in. But also, she cannot go back there. She shakes her head and comes up with the only thing she can think of.

"I can't afford rent, I got fired last month."

"You let us worry about that. After what you did today, I'm sure Rach won't mind working something out."

He grins a little and Evyn takes note of the nickname and his casual use of 'us'. If she wasn't so scared, she'd push for more information. But instead, she is only thinking of one thing.

"But my father—"

Calver holds up a hand, his mouth set in a straight line. "I'll deal with your father."

He lays out his plan, short and simple, and the choice is removed from her, like someone has finally lifted a weight and all she has to do is flow along with the current. Evyn doesn't speak as he walks her from the building, doesn't try to warn him of all the ways this could go wrong. It's clear he's thought of them already, and he's doing it anyway.

Outside the police station, a TV crew has set up. She turns her head away as they pass. Calver points her to the Land Rover, bright even in the warm midnight darkness of the dimly lit car lot, and drives with a slowness that makes her fingers twitch.

In the layby beside her home, a news van has pulled up, the letters scrawled across the side unreadable in the dark. The cab at the front is empty. The scent of lavender is so strong that Evyn rolls her windows down and takes full breaths, trying to calm her racing heart.

"Did they try to talk to my dad?" she asks Calver, but he's too focused on driving quietly over the cattle grid to answer. He stops inside the gate.

"Just like we planned, Evyn," he says, leaning across to open the door for her, "No alterations, okay?"

She nods once and drops down into the dirt.

Calver dives on, slow and cautious, up the dirt track that leads to her rundown home. With a deep breath, she turns into the scrubby trees and slips through them to the back of the house.

The kitchen door is closed, no light from the web-crusted window. She takes a deep breath and leans against the broken shiplap, waiting until she hears the sound of her father's voice from the front of the house. Only then does she open the door, careful, as always, not to make a sound.

The kitchen is just as she left it, the stink of spoiled food and greasy takeaway making her throat tighten. The walk to her bedroom is quick and easy but the front door is open wide, Calver's headlights throwing a stream of light across bare, dry dirt. She tiptoes around her room, crouching slowly to pull her dusty school bag from under her bed and fill it with the things she thinks she'll need.

In the background, Calver's voice is light, as if they're just having a casual conversation. Then the heavy sneer of her father's responses, as if he knows for sure that they are not. Trying to hear the words distracts her and Evyn shakes her head to focus. Calver had warned her to only take what she needed. Everything else can be replaced.

She grabs her phone and charger from the chair by her bed, some extra clothes from the broken closet, her sketchbook, a couple of photographs she had tacked to the wall, and her make-up bag. Nothing else will fit. Outside, the voices get louder by the second, and she's almost certain she hears her father say her name. In the hallway, it's impossible to resist the urge to eavesdrop.

"...probably had that little kid hidden somewhere." Evyn stops moving, "She never was the same after her sister. Probably looking for attention."

Evyn edges toward the door frame, hugging the wall, and setting her bag down quietly.

"That girl carried a lost child the whole way into town on a sprained ankle with cracked ribs and that's all you have to say for her?"

Evyn's shoulders are so tight with tension that they lift high. She peeks around the doorway, taking a quick look outside. Calver is standing at the edge of the line of light from his car, hands resting on his hips, handgun prominent on his waist. Her father sits at the plastic table, turned upright, using a rag to clean his open shotgun. She ducks back inside again, swallowing the sudden rush of saliva.

"How many times have you taken my daughter to the station, John?" There's an edge to her father's tone.

"It's Detective Calver, and your daughter looks like she went toe to toe with a tire iron. D'you know anything about that, Mattie?"

Her father laughs, a gruff, snorting sound, "She's been hanging around that Mexican kid. Probably selling drugs. Might wanna look into that family, they got a lot of money, for immigrants."

Evyn peeks again. Calver is pulling his ballcap down and still managing to shake his head at the same time. Her father clicks the shotgun closed, resting it across his thighs.

"For a man with no family, John, you got a lot of interest in mine."

Evyn can't move. Nobody talks about Calver's family. Not ever. And certainly not this way, like it's a weapon to point at him. There's a split second of total silence and Evyn is about to pull back into the dark when she hears the tiny click of a buckle unhooking. Calver's wrist moves, the flap that closes over his gun lifting wide. His hand hovers there and even in the shadows, Evyn can see the tension in his curled fingers.

"What did you just say to me?"

Mattie Donovan might be tough, but he's not a fool. Her father raises his hands lightly, smiling a little, "Hey now, Detective, I didn't mean anything about your wife. We all know that was a terrible accident—"

"Evyn, come out here."

Calver's voice is louder and deeper than she's ever heard it.

He backs away and motions for her to get in the car. The handle slips from her grasp twice before Evyn hooks it over her elbow and shuffles outside. She's run down this wobbly front step a thousand times, but now she almost falls, off-balance with the weight of both her father and Calver's stares.

"Get back in the house, Evyn." Her father says with a quiet, steely glint. She stops automatically, as always.

"I'm taking her out of here, Mattie," Calver holds out his hand for her bag but Evyn is frozen solid, her eyes trained on the shotgun in her father's lap. He was cleaning it, it's not loaded, she's almost certain.

"She's a bit young for you, John, ain't she?"

Evyn's shocked gasp is almost a shout.

Calver snaps.

In all the times she's back-answered him, sneered at him, swore and cursed him, Evyn has never once seen him lose that cool veneer. But it's gone now, stripped back to bared teeth and a handgun that loosens from its holder in a second flat, the barrel pointed directly at her father.

Everything stops.

This is all your fault.

"You sick son of a bitch." The curse doesn't sound right coming from him. It makes Evyn move, whimpering like a child, forcing herself toward the car, as if getting into it will bring back the version of Calver she knows.

"Don't come near her again." Voice like ice, Calver re-holsters his weapon and backs toward the car. "Don't contact her. If you see her in the street, you turn around and walk the other way. If I find out you've tried to talk to her, and I *will* find out, I will make your life a living hell. I always thought you had it hard, Mattie, but I promise you, I will make it worse."

Calver clips his holster and opens the passenger door before backing to the other side of the car, wary eyes on her father, "Get in the car, Evyn."

Both of them watch Evyn stow her gym bag in the back. Her father's expression is blank but somehow still smug, like he knows she'll come crawling back soon. Calver looks like he might vomit, hand pressed to the roof of his car as if holding himself up.

Beyond him, the top of the tree line wavers gently in some unfelt breeze and Evyn is certain there are more eyes on her, as if even the trees are watching. The air is too warm and the scent of flowers so strong she can taste it at the back of her throat. It's what moves her, that cloying taste. She climbs in without looking back toward the house.

Calver opens his door and slides in.

"Seatbelt," he tells her automatically.

At the gate, there's a flash so bright it makes her squint, and then another. The TV crew, standing at the entrance to the drive. Cameras on, a blonde reporter holds a microphone out toward them despite the closed car windows. Evyn can't even hear the question and Calver ignores them entirely. Pulling slowly away he drives back toward town.

"What do they want?" she whispers.

"Same as always," Calver tells her, his jaw a hard line against his wilting collar.

It takes a while to get to town, Calver takes side-road after side road, even pushing the Land Rover up Byar Hill, a potholed walking trail, to stop the reporter's awkward transit van from following them. Still it's strange, rocking from side to side in total silence while he leans over the wheel with a white-knuckled grip.

A strange feeling is rises inside her. Her chest flutters with it, like a warning.

On Pier Street, she stares at the busy bar front, open terraces packed with people newly arrived for the fair. She searches for Daire, looking for the wide outline of his shoulders or the unkempt swoop of his hair, always a fraction longer than he can manage. She scans groups of tourist girls, usually where she would see him at the weekend, but there's no sign of him. It hits her that she'll never get to speak to him again, never get that soft, uncertain wave he always gives her when he spots her watching him flirt with summer girls.

She should be feeling relieved now, finally safe, but instead, all she feels is a looming sense of dread.

Calver doesn't speak until they're approaching the station. The car slows and Evyn looks up from the dash. Outside the station are three more vans, two separate cameras set up on the opposite sidewalk, filming with the station is in the background.

Calver curses under his breath, then taps the wheel and talks to it, instead of her.

"Evyn, I can't stop you if you want to talk to them," he tells her, "But I suggest you don't because the more you give them, the deeper they'll dig. It doesn't matter to them that you're just a kid. All they want is a story."

Evyn rests her head back against the headrest.

"You know," she tells him and her voice sounds far away, even in her own ears, "When Stella's case was closed, I contacted every news station in the country, asking them to help," she draws her legs up as she would in Daire's car, resting her sneakers on the dash and wrapping her arms around her knees, "The ones that answered only offered me advertising space. I got prices with and without her photo."

Calver sits quietly for a moment, crawling slowly toward the station with his headlights dipped.

"Okay, kid," he says, "Let's get you out of here."

Nineteen

now

CALVER CUTS THE CAR engine sharply, his long sigh softening the silence.

"Look," he says, talking to the steering wheel, "I know that didn't go exactly how I planned, but I promise you Evyn, you never have to see him again."

She nods, takes another cursory look at the houses in his gated estate, checking for curtain-twitching. At midnight, most of them don't even have a porch light on. There's no-one to see a young girl getting out of Calver's car and walking into his house in the dead of night. He catches her looking, double checks the street for himself, and then rubs at his eyebrows.

"Look, if you'd prefer to stay at the station, I can take you back. You know how comfortable the interview room is." He grins a little, a teasing lightness that surprises her, but then his face changes again, "Either way, I'll be gone for the night. I have paperwork I need to catch up on before my shift starts."

He's babbling, pushing the peak of his cap up and down on his forehead, more uncomfortable than Evyn has ever seen. It's awkward to watch it but she has something to say and it pops out before she can think it through.

"I'm sorry," she tells him, "For what my dad said, about Mrs. Calver."

He stops talking, mouth snapping shut as if she'd slapped him.

"That's not your fault," he says eventually, after the car grows so silent that Evyn is worried he'll toss her out on the street. "You don't need to worry about any of that."

"I liked her." She can't seem to stop talking now that she's started. It's odd to talk without worrying it will cause anger to flare unexpectedly. "We all did, everyone at school, but especially her art students. She was so kind. She used to let me take home supplies..."

Evyn trails off when the look on Calver's face changes subtly. It's not pain, exactly, but something like it. The corners of his mouth tip down. She whispers another ineffective 'sorry' at her knees and the car grows quiet again, warming with the lack of air conditioning. "She liked you too," Calver admits, reluctant and quick, and then pulls the handle on his door to open it a crack. Evyn blinks in the sudden interior light. His down-turned mouth has flipped, the barest hint of a grin. "She said you never followed the rules. I think she might have been right."

Evyn smiles. There's an odd moment where Calver stares, as if he'd never seen her smile before, and then he pushes his door wider.

"Okay, welcome to Casa Calver. Try not to break anything."

She follows him up the steps of a large front porch. It's a big house, for one person, and Evyn stares at the overgrown garden and the half-dead ornamental trees in pots by the front door. The hallway is bright and clean with art on the walls and a light fixture made from glazed drift-wood.

"Leah made that," Calver tells her, noticing her stare, "And the art on the walls too. All her."

"It's beautiful."

"Yup. Well, you're in the guest bed," he opens a door at the end of the hall and holds her bag out to her. "There's food in the fridge if you're hungry and the ensuite should have towels or whatever. Take anything you need."

He acknowledges her whispered thank you with a short nod, and strides to the front door like he cannot get away fast enough.

"I'll be back at around 6 a.m. to check on you, but if you need anything before then, just call the station." He closes the door with a soft click and leaves Evyn standing at the doorway to his basement, unsure of what to do next.

It's odd. Right when she should feel the safest, she can still feel the looping turn of growing dread, as if something awful is about to happen. Her hands start to sweat and she grips the handle of her bag tighter, walking down the stairs for the night.

The room is as pretty as the hallway. An ornately carved mirror in one corner catches the bruising around her face. The bed is roll-topped and made up with white sheets that look brand new, lines down their center as if taken out of a packet that day. There's a large piece of monochrome artwork over the bed, smaller pieces dotted around the room and the light switch controls both the overhead lights and the lamps by the bed. It's the nicest room Evyn has ever slept in, and all she wants to do is run out of it and back into town, to find a boy who will never speak to her again.

It's Aimee's whispered words, she thinks, causing this odd crawling feeling. Just the frightened, nonsensical words of a scared child. Evyn tries to shake them loose, but they stay put, a resounding echo, no matter how she tries to think of anything else.

She pulls her phone from her bag, dead because the battery never lasts more than a few hours anymore, and plugs it into a socket by the bed. Even taking a shower in the tiled wetroom doesn't help stop the strange, growing fear. By the time she's dried off, wrapped herself in thin cotton pajamas and her silky robe, she's even more jittery and tense, on the verge of a panic attack.

Because she can't sit still, Evyn drags herself to the kitchen, looking for a distraction. There are glasses by the sink, dried on a wooden draining board that looks handmade. She fills a tumbler with water that's cooler than she expected, as if Calver's pipes have a different water source than those in her crumbling little house.

Before she can take a sip, she sniffs and notices the small bunch of purple stems in a curved jug on the windowsill.

A gunshot rings out as clear as if the muzzle was beside her ear.

Evyn's glass smashes in the sink, sharp fragments ricocheting off the porcelain to snag in the thin skin of her inner wrist. A shout catches in her chest. Her knees won't hold her weight and she drops to the tiled floor with her back against sleek cabinets. Her hand twist in her lap.

It's not real. She imagined it.

But, eyes closed and spine pressed hard into the wood behind her, Evyn can almost see the result of that imagined shot; his body is in front of her, one arm splayed out toward her and the other caught beneath him as a small pool of blood seeps across the white tiles. She can picture the sheen of sweat on his tanned cheekbone and the movement of his mouth as he gasps for air. She can even smell his aftershave, that woody expensive scent with a hint of something herby and sweet.

"Daire," she chokes out his name, scrambling to her feet. She has to move, refusing to look at the spot on the floor that is filled with her horrific imaginings. She races up the stairs, feet catching on the thick carpet, scrambling and heaving air that won't stay inside her.

At the top, there's an open bedroom door with a shirt hanging on the handle of an old refinished dresser. Calver's room.

Evyn remembers what Daire had told her. Calver must be in constant pain. Must have flashbacks about the night he lost everything. He must have something that can help her.

She races to his ensuite bathroom, big and brightly lit. Tearing open the mirrored cabinet, Evyn pushes aside bottles of shaving foam and hair gel, searching for anything that can take this panic away. She keeps hearing the gunshot, a blast of sound that ends in a coughing gasp, a voice she would know anywhere.

There are three small brown bottles of pills, their white labels faded. The first is a sleeping tablet, she's pretty certain, and the other is something to do with blood pressure. But the third is exactly what Evyn is looking for and she pops the cap off the diazepam as fast as she can, dry swallowing one pill and stuffing another two into the pocket of her sleep shorts.

The effect is instant, as if just the act of taking the tablet is enough to calm her jangled nerves. Evyn softly closes the cabinet. Her face is illuminated in a too-bright circle. Her swollen eye and her bruised cheek and the finger-shaped marks on her jaw stand out as clearly as Calver's scars. But hers will fade.

Staring at herself in disgust, she takes the two tablets from her pocket and puts them back in the bottle. She tidies the shelf and shuts off the light. Her heart is still hammering, rocking against her breastbone with uneasy lurches. But her mind is already starting to close down. The edges of her vision dull as she focuses on leaving no trace of herself in Calver's private space. She leaves his room exactly as she found it, bar one missing pill, and makes her way slowly back downstairs.

In the guest room, she sits on the bed, takes up her phone and tries to call Daire. She just wants to hear his voice. She'll block her number and just listen to his voicemail message. But her phone won't turn on. The green light flashes on the side, but no matter how long she holds the button, the screen stays dark.

She doesn't get frustrated, her first sign that the pill she took is working. Instead, she sets the phone on the bedside table and sits back against the headboard to watch the television. She can't tell what the show is about, or keep up with the conversations, but she watches it all the same, refusing to think about what she had imagined in the kitchen. She knows what trauma can do, how it can twist minds and make fantastical things seem perfectly reasonable. Evyn clasps her hands lightly in her lap and watches the flickering TV for hours.

T HOUGH HER BODY IS languid and her heart has finally stopped pounding, she can't tip over into sleep. She's vaguely aware of time passing, of the show changing, of the slow blink of her eyes. But then, somehow, the TV is blank and she's unsure of how long it's has been off, how long she's been sitting in the dark.

Tiredly, she reaches out for her phone again, tries once more to turn it on, even to check the time, but it's still dead. The front door opens quietly and soft footsteps creak the ceiling above her as Calver walks upstairs.

It must be early morning because it's already muggy and the light from the high window is pink-tinted. She drags herself upright and into the ensuite to freshen up.

The water is ice cold pressure on her skin. Evyn scrubs with fancy soaps and shampoos that come from a drugstore, instead of the dollar store where she buys hers. Once she's dry, she pulls on fresh clothes from the bottom of her gym bag and covers the worst of the bruising with makeup.

She feels almost herself again. The fuzziness of the drug remains, and her pupils are still shot with it, but she's fairly certain that Calver won't notice, considering the swelling around her eyes.

He's still upstairs when she goes to the kitchen and it's second nature to her to open the fridge and start breakfast. It's calming even, clearing away the broken glass from the sink and setting out plates and forks as she makes pancakes, bacon, and fruit salad. There's so much food in his fridge. She's making too much for two people but she can't seem to stop herself, setting out plate after plate in the center of the table.

It's only when all of the cooking is done and she's washed the pans in the sink that she spots a set of double doors leading to a crowded back garden. She stops in front of the glass to stare.

Wood chips are scattered everywhere, blown across the grass in a wide circle around a heavy table. Large pieces of driftwood sit at the side of the patio, some glazed, some half-sanded and one still damp-looking, as if it was a recent addition that had yet to fully dry out. Evyn can make out the edge of a buzz saw under black tarp.

It should remind her of her own ragged yard, but it doesn't. There's a huge piece of wood in the center of the table and sections removed from it are curved like a sculpture. There's also a section of staircase, old pine, leaning against the back fence, and Evyn thinks of the pretty carved banister in the hallway, the smooth feel of it under her clammy hands last night.

She pauses.

She'd gone upstairs, into Calver's bedroom, stolen from someone who'd only offered to help her. The guilt makes her sit at the kitchen table, listening carefully to the dull sounds from upstairs as Calver gets ready for his shift. When his door opens and his footsteps thud on the stairs, Evyn jams her fork into a pancake and wedges it into her mouth.

That's how he finds her, sitting at his kitchen island with bulging cheeks and enough food in front of her to feed four people.

"You must be hungry," he says, eyeing the feast before heading to the fridge to take out a bottle of water. When he turns around, he spots the plate she had set out for him on the opposite side of the table.

"You didn't have to do that for me," he tells her, a disapproving tone that makes Evyn sit a little taller, swallowing her food with a thick gulp.

"I could say the same," she says quietly.

He sighs, looks out at the garden, and then comes to sit in the spot she'd laid for him.

"Thank you," he says and there's an undercurrent in his tone that makes her grip the fork tighter. An echo of that pounding heartbeat that had run through her veins last night begins to rattle in her chest. She watches him take a syrup covered pancake from the plate, toss a couple of bacon slices on top of it. Something in his movement is off, jerky and reluctant.

"Evyn, I need to talk to you about something," he says.

But Evyn had known it already. That familiar sense of dread bursts through her again as if it had been lying in wait. Something terrible is coming.

Twenty

THEN

"I T'S GOTTA BE BETTER than a party at my parents' house, right?"

Evyn raised an eyebrow and took the joint from Daire's fingers, "I'm not going, Daire."

Evyn was trying, really, but things were slipping out, little emotions she tried to reign in, dripping like a tap. She handed the joint back.

"Fine," he said, "I'll go on my own." He pouted dramatically, grabbing his chest as if he was in physical pain, and raised his voice to cry out, "Oh poor loner, Daire! No-one to take to Prom! What a *loser*!"

She shushed him and smacked his arm, trying to suppress the giggles that were threatening, "Stop pretending you don't have options. Half the girls in town would go with you."

"Yeah?" Daire turns a little, jostling her shoulder, and something uncomfortable prickled under her skin.

"Oh fuck off."

He laughed, a short, rough sound as he handed her the spliff, and laid his head on the wall to hold his breath, staring up at the stars. He could always hold it for twice as long as she could. When he swallowed, the long column of his throat moved up and down and suddenly Evyn needed to move too, to put some space between their huddled forms.

She turned to look over the wall. In the street below, tourists milled from place to place. The glare of music from the bars and the warm ocean breeze made for silence that wasn't interrupted or uncomfortable.

Evyn already knew she wouldn't come here once Daire left.

"I'll miss this," she mouthed, barely enough breath for her own ears to hear it. But Daire lifted his head, staring at her.

She sat back down, knowing that she shouldn't have said anything. He was looking at her out of the corner of his eye and she could tell from his closed expression that he was thinking hard about what to say next. She had moved the line again, tipped them toward talking, and now she needed to push it back, fast.

"Did you know I puked on Calver's coat last month?"

He hummed a little, an attempt at a laugh but there was no humor behind it. She kept going, barging through the new tension.

"I got cold in the interview room. What were we drinking that night, rum?"

He nodded but stayed quiet and Evyn began to feel the prickle of fear in her stomach. He wasn't going to drop it. He was still sitting with her words, the little leak of emotion that she was trying to plug back up.

"He's such an asshole," she stammered, and Daire finally looked at her.

"He's not, actually."

Evyn lifted her chin and ran a hand over her neck, choosing not to respond. But Daire kept pushing it, a move so unlike him it caught her attention. "Don't you ever think about how much you have in common with him?"

She wrinkled her nose, wondering if she had heard him correctly or if the dope was somehow making her hear things.

"I'm serious," he said, "Both of you lost someone you loved."

"Stella's not dead." Evyn no longer cared about the street or who heard her, her voice raised high and hard.

"I never said she was!" He raised his hands, trying to placate her. "Evyn, I just don't think he's out to get you. How many times have you been taken to the station this summer and he's never actually arrested you. He *could* have, but you already know that."

She sat back against the wall and rubbed a finger over her chin to stop it wobbling. She hadn't expected Daire to side with Calver on anything, not after he dropped Stella's case. It felt like a betrayal and she worked hard to cover the feeling with anger instead.

Daire, as if sensing what she was doing, tried to distract her. As usual, he knew exactly what to say to throw her off track.

"I was there the night of the accident."

She swung toward him, wide-eyed, her attempt at rage forgotten. He pushed back against the wall, shifting his hips. It was obvious he didn't want to say more but Evyn waited, staring pointedly until he sighed and continued.

"Dad was driving me home from practice. There were some cars stopped in front of us. In their headlights, I could see a whole fender, just lying in the road, broken glass everywhere."

Evyn leaned forward, pulled in. Daire didn't seem to notice. He lit another joint and took a drag before he handed it to her.

"Dad told me to stay put. He got out of the car and started walking away from the crash, further up the road. That's when I saw Calver. He wasn't in uniform. I guess I didn't know it was him until later. He was just this big hulking shape in the darkness and my dad was walking toward this monstrous thing."

He looked up then, briefly and sheepishly.

"I was only twelve, just a kid."

Evyn nodded and handed him back the joint.

"Did you see Mrs. Calver?"

"He was carrying her. That's why the shape of them looked so strange. Her legs were gone. He was staggering, holding her against his chest. Dad told me later he was keeping her belly against him, you know, trying to save it."

Evyn winced and put her hand over her mouth, remembering how her art teacher had taken to trailing her hands along the desks as she walked around her classroom, as if the weight in her belly was pulling her off balance.

"Oh, Dar, I can't believe you saw something like that at twelve."

"That wasn't the worst thing," he bent one knee and leaned his elbow against it, rubbing his eye with the heel of his palm as if scrubbing at the memory, "My Dad helped him back to the crash site and we waited for the ambulance. He wouldn't let her go, you know, wouldn't put her down. He just held her in his lap, and I could see his leg was broken through his jeans. He'd carried her down the road and back again on a broken leg."

Daire took a drag, short and sharp, and passed it back to Evyn. She took a long, deep pull and held it until the edges of her vision softened.

"Dad told me to get back in the car but I couldn't look away. When the paramedics got there, I saw the guy in the other car. He was fine. Not a mark on him. His truck was upside down on the road but he walked to the ambulance."

He puffed out his cheeks, and let the air out slowly.

"I've never heard anything like the sounds Calver made when they took her away. They had to pull her from him. One of them came back with a blanket and took something out of his lap. They put it, all wrapped up, beside her covered-up body, right on the road, both of them. He was trying to drag himself toward them and my dad was holding him back. They had to inject him with something to make him stop screaming."

Daire grabbed her wrist, looked at her, though she didn't want to hear any more.

"He was *howling*. Like an animal in pain. I can hear it right now, just remembering it."

He squeezed her wrist and his fingers stopped shaking.

"His face, Evyn, all that blood and skin just hanging and he didn't even notice it. I had nightmares for months. Dad had to sleep in my room."

He let go of her wrist, slid light fingertips over her goosebumped skin up to her knuckles. Sliding the joint from between her fingers, he took a long drag. After three deep inhales, he handed it back. The rise of his knuckles brushed her palm and his hand moved with hers for a moment, as if chasing the comfort of touch.

The wind picked up, warmer again, and Evyn moved closer, stubbing out the smoking butt.

"Jesus, Dar," she put her hand on his arm, huddled into his side as if she was cold. But it was for him, all she could give him without tipping over the line. The length of her side pressed into his, a soothing reassurance.

He was silent for a long while. Wafts of contrasting music from the bars along Pier Street came at them every time the wind changed direction. She studied his hands, lax in his lap, knowing later she would draw them from memory. The long edge of tendon that flexed when he moved his fingers, the jutting angle at the base of his thumb. She could stare at the lines of him for hours. But she only had a few weeks before he'd leave for college. Once he was gone, every drawing would be memory.

How would she live without this soft place?

Eventually, he turned toward her, his mouth open and soft, about to speak. But when he met her eye, he stopped.

"Evyn?" It was barely more than a breath.

Her hand was still on his arm and her fingertips were burning. There was no hiding it this time, her thoughts like kindling that flickered between them. She stopped thinking altogether, trailed soft fingertips along the length of his muscled forearm, soft hairs raising at her touch. Daire sucked in a breath, tensed even tighter.

"What are you..." His mouth closed around a gulp, quieting himself as if he were afraid to break whatever spell this was. And it *felt* like magic, the teetering power of crossing this line made her suddenly indestructible. The alchemy of her whole body tingling and floating just from slipping her fingers beneath the sleeve of his t-shirt, touching ember-hot skin she couldn't see.

His eyes were half-closed, staring down at her, and his pupils were even wider than before. Evyn brought her hand to his mouth, experimentally tracing the soft line of his lip.

"Daire." The longing in her voice ran a shudder across his shoulders.

Slowly, he leaned down. With his mouth close enough to feel, Daire paused. A hesitant, firing brush against her lips, like a question. Evyn answered with a tilt of her head, pressing, and he unfurled like a spring.

His hand curled at the back of her neck, lifting her hair. Thrills raced down her spine, the kiss deepening as Daire pulled her closer. She mirrored him, the roof rough against her thigh and the silky push of his tongue. He'd done this before, was good at it, and for a trembling moment, Evyn was unsure of herself. She wavered, pulling his lower lip between hers. The raw sound he made rolled through her, settling low in her stomach. It was almost scary, how fast her body turned liquid, her knees weak and her hands pressing into his chest.

She pulled away to kiss along his jawline. Evyn had drawn it a hundred times, imagining the rasp of stubble. But it was real now, soft skin stretched as his head tilted and his hands slid down her back.

Evyn couldn't keep her thoughts from running. Couldn't focus. Couldn't feel anywhere but all the places their skin pressed together. More. She wanted no space, no part of her untouched. Shifting fast, she pushed him back against the wall. Grinning at his surprised huff, she moved over him. Her knees hit the cool slate but she barely felt it.

"Oh fuck, Evyn," Daire sounded ruined, as if this was the very worst thing that could have happened to him. His hips tilted higher, urgent hands pressing at her waist, dragging her down.

He kissed her, insistent and hard, rising to grip her tighter. Evyn's hips moved on their own, an instinct she didn't know she had. He moaned a dazed response, mouth open over hers and the power of it filled her. Evyn kissed him harder, her fingers curling in his summer-long hair, her whole body moving with his. Her breath sounded high and fast.

"Daire, I..." the words were on the tip of her tongue, she only barely held them back. He jerked beneath her, pressing against her center. Fire-soft and consuming, Evyn cut herself off with a whimper.

"Please," Daire whispered into her neck, his hands dragging over her back and thighs, tightening and releasing, "Please say it, Evyn."

"Who's up there?"

Daire heard it first and slid down, pulling Evyn with him until they were both lying flat, below the roof wall. Evyn breathed hard into his chest, the beating of his heart fast and strong against her cheek.

"I mean it, that roof is not stable, you need to come down right now."

Officer Obasi was calling from the street. Daire cursed and muttered under his breath. He might have been talking to her but Evyn couldn't tell. She couldn't open her eyes. The roof was spinning and she had no idea if she could stand, let alone climb down. Daire held her hand and crawled to the opposite edge of the roof. Below them, Officer Obasi, was beginning to sound impatient and the lock on the gate rattled as she tried to open it. Daire pushed himself over the back wall and dropped to the roof of a steel shed.

His raised hands steadied her as Evyn slid down after him.

"Over the fence, baby" he whispered. Her legs wobbled. *Baby*. She couldn't look at him. What had she done?

Daire jumped down pulled her across the overgrown grass. In the distance, Obasi cursed and huffed, climbing over the gate. Evyn was laughing before they reached the fence, loud, hysterical cackling. She'd kissed him. She'd kissed the only friend she had left. Selfish and stupid and impulsive. How could she have broken all her own rules? He was leaving. And now it would hurt even more.

A flashlight swerved around the corner of the building, throwing light over the thick, unkempt grass. Obasi's angry voice in the darkness behind it called out for them to stop. Daire ran faster, dragging her along with him, only letting go of her hand to scale the fence. At the top, tested his balance before reaching back down to her to pull Evyn up.

She looked at his palm and burst into laughter again.

"Evyn, come on!"

Her legs gave way and she dropped to her hands and knees, the laughter shaking her whole body.

"Shit! Evyn! Get up!"

She looked up, following the long line of his outstretched arm, couldn't bring her eyes any further upward in case she accidentally made eye contact with him.

"Go," she said and stopped laughing long enough to catch it before it turned to tears, "Just go, Dar."

The gravel crunched as Officer Obasi turned toward them, the light from her torch crisscrossing the ground before her.

"Fuck!" Daire hissed and swung his leg back over, preparing to jump back down and help her up.

"Daire, get the fuck out of here!" Evyn's voice wobbled.

He froze, staring at her with a look she couldn't decipher.

"Fucking go!" she roared it, angry and accusing.

He swung back over and dropped down on the other side of the fence. Gripping the bars tight, he stared hard at her, as if willing her to get up and follow him. She still couldn't meet his eye.

"Fuck," he said, but this time it wasn't rushed or panicked. When she finally returned his gaze, she knew the swirling emotions that filtered his soft curse. Fear. Hurt. Regret.

She'd lived them all and knew the only way to fix this, to undo the stupid choice she'd made, was to pretend she was too high to remember and hope Daire did the same.

TWENTY-ONE

now

S HE DOESN'T WANT TO know. She doesn't want to hear the words. Calver is looking at her as if she might crack into fragments that he'll have to clean from his spotless tile floor and Evyn doesn't want to listen to whatever terrible thing would make him look at her that way.

"That tree will die in this heat if you don't water it." Her voice is clipped and desperate. He drags his eyes to the double doors, the wood-chip covered garden beyond. The magnolia tree's lower branches are heavy with sawdust, flower heads wilting and brown-tipped, and she can see he's willing to be distracted by it. He doesn't want to say it either.

"My wife used to work out there with a chainsaw but she still managed to keep it neat," he tells her and his voice has lost all the edge that had scared Evyn, "She worked with all sorts of mediums, used to try to get me interested in calligraphy or painting, but the wood-work was the only thing that stuck."

He looks down at his plate, frowning as if he's shocked that he's spoken at all. He pushes his bacon to the side with his fork, spearing a piece that he doesn't eat. "Evyn, when was the last time you spoke to Daire Silva-Doyle?"

It's thunderous, his quiet question and his hunched shoulders, tensed and resigned at the same time. There are dark circles under his eyes and he's not looking at her, still pushing food around his plate. When he does look up, his expression is inscrutable and it's strange seeing him without his baseball cap, his dark hair cropped so the scars appear larger and more forbidding.

"I know you and he are friends. He tried to contact you at the station last night."

She jumps in her seat a little. Daire had tried to contact her. There's a desperate hope pushing its way through her. Could he forgive her? Could he take what she said and put it aside and never speak of it again?

"Oh." It's a lame response, she knows, but her face pulls into a smile and Calver finally looks up at her, then away again fast, as she continues, "My phone wouldn't turn on, I'll go check it."

She stands, trying to not sprint to the guest bedroom like a fool.

"Evyn," Calver says and his dark tone freezes her in place, "Daire's parents reported him missing this morning. He hasn't been seen since yesterday evening."

She sits back down with a thump, the tall stool tilting precariously on its two back legs.

"I know this is a shock but I could use your help working out where he might have gone. His parents say he usually spends Friday nights with you and he comes home between the hours of one and three."

There's a sound in her ears, the same violent, resonating clap that she had heard last night in the echo of broken glass. She brings her finger to the scratch on her wrist, pushing at it till it stings. She had *known* it. She had felt the rip of it through his body when she'd closed her eyes. She had known this was coming.

"Where do you two usually hang out?" Calver asks.

"Lots of places. The beach, the pier, the arcade, the Shack, sometimes we go to see the movies. Mostly we walked so we could..." She trails off, suddenly remembering exactly who she is talking to. She grabs her fork and spears another half-pancake, jamming it into her mouth.

Calver rolls his eyes.

"Neither of you are in trouble, Evyn. We're just looking for him, okay?" he takes a bite of food, hums in surprise, and then holds the back of his hand over his mouth to talk as he chews, "We'll find him sleeping it off somewhere in the next few hours, if he doesn't drag himself home first. He was pretty cut up about your fight."

Evyn slowly spits the food she'd been chewing into a paper napkin. Calver seems to recognize what he's said, how much he's given away and busies himself scraping the remains of his breakfast back onto the serving plate.

"Daire told you," she says, leaving no room for him to argue, "That's why you're helping me."

Calver puts his plate in the dishwasher, running a hand over the lower half of his face, fingers hiding the twisted scarring.

"That's not the only reason," he says and shrugs hard, as if he's trying to rid himself of some stray thought, "Don't blame him, Evyn. He was worried about you and he was right to be."

Evyn doesn't answer. Aimee's whispered words are ringing in her ears. She rests her elbows on the table and her forehead in her hands.

"I don't understand," she says, talking to the crumb-covered tabletop, "She said I would die, not him."

"Who said that?" Calver leans over the table, one hand supporting his weight and his voice hard and urgent, "Who threatened you, Evyn."

"No-one. Aimee told me," she replies, still talking to the table, "It was a warning."

There's a scrape of metal chair legs as Calver sits back down and he's quiet for a second, thinking, but then he dismisses it, like Evyn knew he would.

"Kids say strange stuff when they're frightened," he tells her, soft-voiced, "Come to the station with me, help me make a list of places for us to check for him. Things will settle once he turns up."

She nods into her palms.

"Alright then, I'll grab my things."

Evyn stands when he does, but she can't hold it back anymore. That little voice saying such awful things.

"She told me to find Daire and run. She said if I didn't run, I would die. Why would she say that?"

Calver stares. It feels like a long time before he looks away and he doesn't answer her question.

"You've been through a lot in the last few days, Evyn," he tells her softly. Does he think of her as a frightened child too? She feels like one. "I'll talk to Rachel when we get to the station, okay? Maybe Aimee mentioned something to her."

He moves fast when she agrees, striding out into the hallway and taking the stairs two at a time. Evyn goes to her room and tries to open her phone again. The screen stays stubbornly blank. It's frustrating to know there could be messages on there, voicemails or texts from Daire that she can't reach. Upstairs, there's the distinct sound of a safe unlocking and clunking closed again and when Calver comes back downstairs, he's wearing his handgun clipped to his belt.

It's already too warm for the linen shirt she's wearing over her tank top. Evyn steps out onto Calver's front porch with her face tilted toward the sun as she yanks her bruised arms out of her sleeves.

There's a dark shadow at the back of the police Landrover, a metallic black glint, and the tall outline of a man in the corner of her vision. For a split second, she thinks of her father's shotgun, all the times she'd watched him lay it out to clean the long barrel, and she spins back to Calver, grabbing his arm with a strangled, unintelligible sound.

A shutter snap follows, rapid shucking as Evyn's fingers squeeze and Calver looks down at her with a worried frown. He turns his head when he hears the noise, looking directly at the camera. And Evyn can see how the photo will turn out: her, halfway out of her shirt, staring open-mouthed up at the detective while he locks his front door and scowls at the camera.

His forearm tightens but he doesn't show any other sign of upset. He calmly locks the door and places a hand on her upper back to urge her toward the car. Once Evyn is inside, he turns to face the reporter with his hands on his hips.

"This is private property," he says but the reporter is already shoving a device in his face, a small fluffy microphone attached to a little black box.

"Detective Calver, did Miss Donovan stay the night with you, in your home?"

The response is muffled as Calver closes the door behind her, sealing her into the warm car. He walks slowly around to the driver's side, waving at a neighbor who's stopped with a stroller, staring openly. She doesn't wave back.

Calver checks his mirrors, opens a compartment, and puts on his sunglasses before slowly pulling out of the driveway. She wants to scream at him to move faster, to race away, but that won't help. That picture will look bad and there will be no stopping it by running and hiding.

He doesn't speak until they reach the station, where another news van has joined the two from last night. This time, they're filming right outside the main doors of the building, blocking the disabled driver's parking spaces.

With a jolt, Evyn spots Mrs. Silva-Doyle, in the crowd, talking to one of the reporters with a microphone levelled at her chin. She's wearing a tailored black suit, though her hair is curling at her chin the way she wears it at the weekend. Evyn's view is cut off as Calver pulls into the back car park, sectioned off with a luminous barrier.

Once he's parked in an awkward, misaligned spot beside the back door, Calver leans his head back against the headrest and sighs a long, hard breath. The tension is rolling from him, filling the inside of the cab.

"Look," he says and he sounds as tired as he looks, "I'm sorry, Evyn. I should have found you a better spot to shore up in..." he trails off, shaking his head and Evyn tries to think of something to say to take the dismayed expression from his face. It's a difficult task; she's much more adept at trying to piss Calver off than making him feel better. But he continues before she can say anything at all, a strange half-whisper as he stares unseeing out the windscreen at the pebble-dash wall.

"If Leah was there, if there were other kids running around, maybe..."

She bites her lip, hard.

It had hit her before, the night Daire told her what happened to Calver. The night that everything changed between them and she had learned that Calver was more than a warning, that what happened to him was worse than she could have imagined. But even hearing the story from Daire hadn't prepared her for all the things he had lost. Things he couldn't even voice out loud.

"I'll talk to Rach about taking you in," he tells her suddenly, snapping himself out of his reverie, "We'll make sure you're settled before the end of the day, okay?"

She nods absently, and he tries to smile at her but it falters, and instead, he reaches forward and grabs his cap from its spot on the dash.

"People might think some pretty nasty things when they see that photo, Evyn," he slides the hat on, hiding his face entirely as he adjusts it, "I'll do my best to correct any misconceptions but if anyone contacts you, says anything you don't like or that makes you uncomfortable, you can come to me, okay?"

She nods, but Calver's barely looking at her. He's gathering his phone and his keys, his free hand already on the door handle, as if he cannot wait to get away.

"Come on," he tells her, "You can wait with Officer Obasi while I speak to Daire's parents."

She follows him blindly into the station as Calver immediately starts to call out to anyone listening that the media presence is uncontrolled out front and needs to be moved back. He points at one of the open doorways in the small corridor and tells her to wait inside. "I'll send an officer in minute. Just tell them whatever you can think of about where Daire might be. Don't worry, we'll find him."

He's gone before she can reply and Evyn is left sitting at one of three small desks in the open, glass-walled room.

She tries her phone again but it remains frustratingly blank. Eyeing the landline on the desk, she listens carefully to see if anyone is approaching before she dials Daire's number from memory. It goes straight to his short, distracted voicemail. She takes a breath at his voice. It seems like the longest stretch of time since they've talked and she hangs up and dials again right away, just to hear it one more time.

In the corridor, Mrs. Silva-Doyle's voice rises. Evyn stands up, listening as the words become clear.

"... would tell us if he was staying out all night, unless something is wrong."

She's talking to Calver, and as they pass by the door, Evyn holds her breath, almost hoping they don't see her. But Mrs Silva-Doyle's head turns and her worried voice rings out.

"Oh, Evyn, your face!"

Evyn's mouth runs dry and she's barely able to lift her hand in a small, awkward wave. Mr. Doyle has a hand around his wife's waist and Calver is behind them, subtly urging them down the corridor toward his office. But Mrs. Silva-Doyle holds firm.

"Daire showed me the video," she says, stepping halfway into the room. "He watched it over and over. I know he tried to call you and I'm convinced he went out last night to find you. Have you heard from him?"

How much did she know? What would she say if she knew the things Evyn had said to Daire the last time she saw him? "I'm so sorry."

Daire's mother seems to deflate and her husband's arm tightens around her waist, though he seems less worried than she is, his expression almost apologetic.

"Do you have any idea where he might be? I know he was upset after you two joined the search for the Gilbride girl. Did he say anything to you about what was bothering him?"

Evyn closes her mouth tight. Daire's mother might look exhausted and worried but her lawyer instincts are still sharp as a tack and Evyn can feel the appraisal.

Behind them, Calver, speaks up. "Mrs. Silva-Doyle, we'll take Evyn's statement in a few moments. I'll update you as soon as we have the information, but until then, I'd like to get the missing person's report filed as quickly as possible."

When they move reluctantly away, Evyn isn't sure whether she feels relief or whether she wants to run after them and tell them everything that had happened. The guilt eats at her. Could Daire have been so upset that he went out and got drunk? Hurt himself coming home?

Before she can think it through, Calver pokes his head back around the door. "The team is busy setting up a media station outside. Can you make a head start and just list as many places you think he might be - any information you have that might help?"

She lifts a pad of paper from the desk and Calver disappears again. Quickly, she jots down as many places as she can think of.

The pier; Daire could have gone there with a case of his brother's cheap beer and cursed the day he met Evyn Donovan. Or, he could have gone to the beach, partied with the summer kids and ended up back in someone's rented RV.

She squeezes her eyes shut, moving on fast.

He could have gone to the gallery roof, got stoned in their favorite spot and tried to take back everything that had happened between them there.

Evyn sits bolt upright. There's flashing in the corner of her eye, morning sunlight peaking over the station's side wall, glinting off the metal window frame. Something about the last thought feels right.

She stands fast and peers out into the empty hallway. Before she can think it through, Evyn darts down the hall and out into the parking area, scaling the wall over into the delivery area of the neighboring store. Her ankle and ribs twinge at the climb, but Evyn ignores them.

There's only one thing she can focus on. If she found Aimee by following her gut, maybe she can find Daire too.

TWENTY-TWO

now

JOGGING AROUND THE BACK of the building, Evyn comes out onto Pier Street. The gallery is already in sight, a line of tourists milling around outside looking at the local artist's prints hanging on the iron railings. It's both easier and more difficult to get to the roof. The gate is open, so she doesn't have to jump the fence, but the moment she reaches the second-lowest branch of the tree, there are murmurs from the crowd below. A woman gasps as Evyn pulls herself higher. She's done this a hundred times, in the dark, but she's conscious now, with people watching her, and her grip is unsteady.

But Daire could be up there so Evyn stretches her arms and hoists herself higher.

"Call the cops," comes an accented voice as Evyn stands on the branch. This building is only two floors, but it's one of the oldest in town and the ornate woodwork circling high over the entrance makes it taller than the others on the street. She quickly walks the length of the branch, watching it dip down toward the roof before she hops off onto the slate.

Ignoring the gasps from the street and the call of a familiar voice telling her to come down, she scans the rooftop, searching for any sign of Daire. There's a small pile of joint butts in their usual spot but nothing that hadn't been there the other night. Evyn leans over the side, walking the perimeter of the roof in case he fell. There's no sign of him anywhere.

She's about to give up when her phone buzzes in her pocket. It's somehow turned itself on, so unexpectedly that Evyn startles, her balance thrown. She catches herself against the guard wall and drags her phone from her pocket to find a voicemail message.

It's Daire. She recognizes his voice even before he starts to speak, the soft cough he gives is enough for her to know it's him. Then there's a shuffling sound like wind through leaves and Evyn almost gags at the words that come with it.

The compass.

The line cuts off but Evyn can't move. She's frozen, knowing without doubt, whose voice she had just heard. Stella. Just like before, when she had found Aimee at the tree stump. She forces herself to move, to listen to it again. Daire's voice, his cracked sigh, as if he's breathing through a mouthful of sand. But her sister is clear as a bell, echoing strangely.

The compass.

Evyn lunges over the railing, hanging from the balustrade to the sounds of dismay below. She drops onto the porch roof and scurries down the trellis, pushing past the crowd and ignoring the flaring ache in her ankle as she jogs toward home.

People call out to her on Main Street, the same people who had avoided her when Stella went missing, now suddenly interested in her. If she wasn't so numb, Evyn would yell at them to mind their own business. But she can't focus on anything except the sound she'd heard, that echoing whisper of her sister's voice. *The compass, the compass, the compass.*

She grips her phone tight in her fist, and runs. Daire is out there. She runs faster, her thighs pumping and her arms held low, all the miles she'd run in track coming back to her muscles as they stretch and tense.

Within twenty minutes, she's only a mile from her home. One mile from the bed she had slept in, huddled against her sister.

Worse than the fear, worse than the thought what might have happened to him, was the guilt that she had known it and done nothing. She'd heard a gunshot, had *felt* it, had heard Daire's heavy breathing, over and above her own. And she'd convinced herself it was nothing but a panic attack.

Now, as she runs, she can feel Stella all around her. That familiar ache of absence is all wrong, warped with a new understanding. There's only one reason she could feel her sister when she was entirely alone, only one explanation for hearing her voice on the breeze, or being surrounded by the scent of her when she'd been gone for two years.

Stella isn't missing. She never was.

Evyn cries out, not from fear or from the lancing pain in her ankle with every step. She slows to a stop and turns her face skyward to sob at the cloudless blue because she already knew. She'd known her sister was gone, never coming home. And Evyn had piled her old life around that truth like a stone cairn, hiding it from herself.

She bends forward and tries to catch her breath. There's no time for crying now. Daire is out there and he's alive. She knows it. She *will* find him. He will come home.

But there's still has one more mile to go.

AT THE CATTLE GRID, Evyn slows, staying close to the trees, grateful that the news vans are all set up at the station and there's no-one to witness her slipping between the weedy brush that lines the path to her father's house. She shies away from the empty front yard, skirting the bushes toward the back. The kitchen door is open, swaying on creaking hinges in the light breeze. From what she can see from her crouched spot, the inside is exactly as she left it, apart from the pizza box open on the counter and the dirty plate next to the sink.

Her father's van isn't here, though the packing factory at the docks isn't open until midday on a Sunday. She doesn't push her luck, heading toward the back door as quickly as she can, bent low to the ground. Her heart is pulling, thumping with exertion and fear as she ducks through the kitchen and into her room.

Her jewelry tin is hidden under a pile of sketchbooks. The papers scatter and float as she knocks them aside, pulling the box open and picking up the chain. She doesn't waste a moment, heading back out the way she came and racing for the back fence.

In the woods, the air is syrupy and hot, burning in her lungs. Her ankle gives a sharp twang with every step and the forest is quieter than she's ever heard it. There are no morning sounds of birds, no rustling of leaves in wind. It's eerie and odd, and Evyn knows her heart would be pounding even if she hadn't just run the whole way from town.

She pulls the necklace over her head and flips open the compass, waiting impatiently until the needle settles. It points down the same path she'd taken to find Aimee, straight to the same clearing. It takes a few minutes to get there and Evyn finds it empty. The trunk is split and dry from the sun, almost powdery in the heat.

"Daire?"

Her voice is strong, desperate but there's no response. There's a flash of movement in the corner of her eye and Evyn rounds on it instinctively. There's nothing but fallen leaves. She stares at the spot until she understands what she's looking at, a scuffle in the earth, leaves pushed into a line and the ground a little darker in one spot, as if someone had turned quickly, the foot digging for purchase. She pushes past the low bush.

The needle moves again, tilting to the right.

Evyn stops calling Daire's name. The sound of her panicked voice in such a quiet place is unnerving, though Evyn's not sure why. She follows the direction the compass shows her, through thick undergrowth and scratching brambles. There's no sign of him, but then she is following a broken compass with no reason to believe he's anywhere near here at all. Has she lost her mind?

There. A dark wine-colored stain on the trunk of a birch. Hip height and hand-shaped.

She walks faster, kicking through half-torn, low-lying vines, watching the needle until it starts to spin and spin, a frightening too-fast whirl.

"Daire! Can you hear me? Where are you?"

She almost stumbles over him. Face down in the dirt, his thin tan jacket camouflages his prone body.

"No," she says, flatly, and then repeats it, as if she could change what she's looking at by begging, "No, no, no."

She drops to her knees beside him, one hand on his sun-warmed back. The thought of turning him over is terrifying and Evyn's hands shake as she presses on his shoulder, dreading what she will find if she rolls him over to see his face. Beneath his outstretched hand, the dried leaves are tainted with the rust of dried blood.

"Dar, come on," she tells him, digging her fingers under his arm and hip, jostling him gently, "Please be okay."

He groans.

Evyn's insides flip over as she digs her hands underneath his body and hauls him over onto his side. His hand, once released from its place beneath his body, falls away to reveal a fresh swell of blood from a wound just above the waistband of his jeans.

When she eases him onto his back, Daire's eyelids flutter. He makes another incoherent sound, trying to speak, but she shushes him, grabbing her phone from her back pocket.

"Don't try to talk," she tells him, "I'm calling for help."

Her fingers shake hard and her phone falls from her grip. Scrambling for it in the dirt, she keeps her eyes on his face, his paleness shocking. How much blood has he lost?

She dials as fast as she can, jamming the cool metal against her ear as a woman's tinny voice asks her to specify the emergency.

"Please help, my friend has been shot. I need an ambulance and please call Detective Calver at Blackditch Police Station. He's looking for us."

She calls out her address, trying to give directions. Her voice is too high-pitched, stuttering. She closes her eyes as she repeats herself for the operator. When she opens them again, Daire is looking at her through half-closed lids. His hand moves over hers where she's pressing his wound and he taps her knuckles twice, light and weak.

Another voice comes through the phone, though she hadn't heard the call being transferred, asking for details of the injury.

"Yes," she responds, trying to be as clear as she can, "In his side... like, the side of his stomach, or maybe his hip, I can't tell, there's so much blood..."

Daire's mouth moves, a wheeze that she can't understand, and his eyes roll back a moment later, exhausted by the effort of trying to talk. She panics, begging the operator to hurry.

"How long will the ambulance be?" she asks, trying not to gulp air and hold it, like she had when she was a child, hiding. The voice on the other end of the line gives out directions, hard and clear, and Evyn finds herself clinging to each word.

She presses her hand to Daire's neck, calls out the faint, thready beats she feels there. Daire barely responds to her touch or voice. His pale face falls to the side, sweat-dampened skin streaked with dirt. When Evyn follows the operator's instructions, pressing the wound as hard as she can, Daire's eyes open wide, lock onto her in agony, and then close again as he drifts out of consciousness.

She leans down and touches her forehead off his.

"It's going to be okay, the ambulance is coming."

The next time he opens his eyes, she's so close to him she can see where he's looking, somewhere off to the side, and she can hear the word he's been trying to say.

"Run."

The phone lies a few inches from her knee, the speaker calling out commands and requests for more information. Evyn looks around wildly but the area is empty, nothing but trees and brambles. The operator's calls out again and Evyn raises her knee, using it to press harder on Daire's waist. He groans and tries to move away but she holds fast.

"I know it hurts, but you're going to be fine," she tells him, settling into determination now, the panic ebbing enough that she can think around it.

In the silence that follows, there's the distinct snap of a twig close behind her and Daire's eyes shoot wide open, his pupils nothing but pinpricks, flicking between her and the spot where the sound had come from.

"Hang up that phone."

Evyn's mouth drops open and all the power fades from her hands, easing up on the wound so fresh blood seeps through her fingers. Daire reaches out, a blind sweep that pushes the phone toward her. She picks it up with blood-covered fingers and cuts off the call.

The crunch of dried leaves sounds heavy and close and her father's voice is slurred.

"Get up."

Her hands press harder, stemming the flow of Daire's blood. In her peripheral vision, her father's boots shuffle into view, the long barrel of his shotgun trailing on the ground.

"I can't," she tells him.

"Get up!"

His roar startles the birds overhead. Their raucous screaming shrouds her own whimper. Daire's eyes are closed, mouth slack and, when she takes his hand and presses it to the wound in lieu of her own, it slips away a moment later. Evyn tries to haul him back over onto his side, trying to keep some of the pressure there, but her father comes closer, raising the gun to push the stock into her shoulder.

"You've shot someone, Dad," she says, surprised at the softness in her voice that she doesn't feel at all, "We have to wait for the ambulance now. If we leave him here, he'll die."

Her father is unmoved. He sways a little, stepping back to catch his balance. His eyes are bloodshot and red-rimmed, his shirt unbuttoned, and his bootlaces are open and dragging in the dirt.

"Start walking or he'll die a lot faster than that," he tells her, gesturing with the gun to show her the direction he wants her to go.

Evyn raises her hands, though the weapon is not pointed at her.

"Please," she whispers. She doesn't even know what she's asking for but he won't give it, no matter what it is.

"Walk!" he roars again but the birds don't cry this time. Evyn does. She hauls in a breath so large it stretches at the band around her ribs and swirls to a stand, rounding on him with a wordless, desperate scream.

His slap is strong enough to turn her head, and immediately, Evyn bursts into tears. Daire groans behind her, his fingers moving in the dirt as if to reach for her and her father's eyes dart to the movement like a hawk on prey.

"Alright!" she screams, drawing his attention, "I'm walking!"

She leaves Daire as he lies, face-up in dappled light, the gunshot wound in his side seeping a slowly widening circle over the dry forest floor. She tries not to cry as she walks, her father directing her away from the house, through the woods that lead to the car park and Flynn's Falls. He holds the gun by his hip, not pointing it, but Evyn still feels his eyes trained on her back, watching her every move.

"Why would you shoot him?" she asks, her voice almost emotionless.

For the first time she can remember, her father answers a question.

"He was in the woods. Sneaking around at the back fence. How was I supposed to know it was just a kid?"

"Where are we going?"

"Just walk."

As they reach the walking trail, she wonders if he would shoot her if she ran. Was he sober enough to aim straight? She trudges on her swollen ankle and lets the pain keep her focused until they get to the dirt track that leads to the car park. There, pulled into the trees and half-covered with spruce fronds, is her father's truck.

She stops in the grassy center of the path and watches him pull branches from the hood, toss them aside to uncover the vehicle. The forest is quiet, mid-morning sunshine and peaceful breeze, and behind her, lying on the forest floor, is a boy who is dying because of her.

The jolt of it hits her fast. The fair was yesterday. Today, two years ago, Stella went missing. She'd missed it, hadn't thought of it once. The day that had changed her life, morphed her from a popular girl with a lot to hide, to a someone with nothing left to lose. Except Daire.

All those months of keeping him at a distance, knowing, one day, he would leave. She had thought she was protecting herself, but now, as her father yanks open the truck's door and leans on the frame, staring at her pointedly, she wonders if some part of her might have been protecting him just as much.

"Get in."

She thought he would slide into his own seat, not waiting for her to follow his orders, knowing she always would. But he stops this time and glares at her until she moves. As Evyn comes around the side of the truck, she spots another mound of spruce fronds covering a smaller, sleeker car, a little further back from the road, rammed into the bushes. Daire's car. Her father must have driven it here in the night. He must have left Daire to lie there and bleed while he hid the evidence.

"Where are you taking me?" she asks as she closes the door and clips her seat belt in place.

"Shut up."

Does he have a plan at all? The stench of cheap booze in the car is overpowering. The shotgun is wedged between his knee and the door and he guns the engine, revving as if he's about to take off the ground entirely. He pulls a bottle of whiskey from a bag and unscrews the cap with his teeth.

The truck pulls out of the ditch with a set of heavy jolts that toss Evyn around the seat. She holds onto the overhead handle, tensing hard enough her ribs give protest.

They trundle down the potholed trail until the car park comes into view, empty except for one silver car she doesn't recognize. Her father spins the wheel with the heel of his hand and reaches into his shirt pocket for a pack of smokes. He pulls out on the main road without checking traffic, speeding away from town so fast the engine seems to rattle and screech.

When he rolls the window down, the smell of lavender takes the edge off the tang of stale sweat and alcohol in the cab and Evyn takes subtle breaths, filling her lungs with it. In the distance, she hears the sound she had been waiting for, the long, extended wail of an ambulance.

Closing her eyes and twisting her fingers in her lap, Evyn wishes with everything she has.

Please find him in time. Please get to him before it's too late.

TWENTY-THREE

now

H ER FATHER DOESN'T SLOW as the ambulance speeds by. Evyn stares at the small piles of green and purple dotting along the roadside, fallen flowers from the harvest loads as they make their way into town. The truck crushes them under its thick tires.

When she thinks he's not looking, Evyn takes small glances at her father. He's hunched over the wheel, an unlit cigarette dangling precariously from his mouth and there are swollen bags under his eyes that tell her he's been awake all night, the smell tells her he's been drinking for most of that time too. How long it will be before he passes out?

The thought of opening the door and jumping comes to her, along with the ridiculous image of her rolling away and getting up to run like a hero in a movie.

Without warning, Evyn laughs.

The small giggle bursts into full-throated spluttering when her father turns to gape at her, drooping eyes suddenly wide and incredulous, with the cigarette barely hanging on to his dry top lip. Hysteria, Evyn thinks, somewhere beyond the haze of shaking laughter. Her body is reacting in any way it can, trying to release the tension and pressure that has been building inside her since the gallery roof.

"Shut your fucking mouth."

She snaps her lips closed, sobering fast at the edge of terror his tone brings out. But, this time, she doesn't let herself cower. She sits unflinching in her seat, staring back with as much defiance as she can muster. It feels reckless to glare at him like this and she thinks of the way Daire had tried to reason instead of backing away when there was a gun pointed at his feet. Is this what it takes to be brave?

Her father looks away first, blinking slow. In the distance, the purple haze of half-shorn flower fields waver in the heat and Evyn breathes perfumed air. She can't remember the last time her father had looked at her without the barely contained edge of fury in his eyes. He must have, at some point. He must have picked her up as a child, or maybe patted her head the way Daire's parents do to both their boys so regularly.

But Evyn doesn't remember it.

After her mother left, the only softness she ever had was Stella, cuddling her when she was scared and magic-kissing skinned knees. Those moments of human touch had sustained her, more than she had realized, until they were gone. Evyn had been the one teaching herself, and then her sister, how to pour cereal and milk, how to get from one end of the house to another without creaking any of the floorboards that might draw their father's ire, how to wash when the shower stopped working. She'd had purpose, back then.

When her father had been anything but angry? Evyn has never been around him without tension biting into her shoulders, but the volume of his anger, the frequency of it, had been turned up since Stella disappeared.

"Why did you kill Stella, Dad?"

She must have always suspected it because the idea doesn't ping in her head like a lightbulb in a comic book. It floats from the deepest part of her to the surface, held down in the dark until she finally let it rise.

Her father jerks the wheel and the car slows slightly. She's almost certain he won't answer but he glances over at her, heavy-eyed and slack-mouthed. There's a downturn at the corner of his mouth. For the first time, Evyn doesn't see anger there, just exhaustion and sadness. He takes the cigarette from his mouth and plucks the bottle from where he's stashed it between his thighs.

"It was an accident," he whispers, slurred, before he lifts the whiskey to his lips.

Evyn holds her breath as he takes his eyes off the road and gulps several mouthfuls in a row, like it's water. The last two years rearrange themselves as she waits for him to speak again, unsure if he even will. All those times he'd been angry about her searching for her sister, his insistence that she be home to make breakfast and dinner, take on a deeper, more sinister reason. He hadn't been worried about how her actions would reflect on him; he'd been worried she would find the truth.

"It was your fault," he says suddenly, breaking the silence, "Skulking around that house at all hours. Couldn't get a moment's peace with you. It was just an empty bottle. It should have hit you in the chest."

She turned to look at him, the unlit cigarette is back between his lips, bobbing with his words.

"You're like me," he says, with a downturn to his mouth that tilts the cigarette upwards in a quick jerk, "You can take a hit."

Evyn closes her eyes. She feels nauseous, her throat burning with bile, but her father isn't finished.

"But it wasn't you. It was her... There wasn't one drop of blood. Not one. But she was cold as ice... I mean, what was I supposed to do?"

He turned to look at her, eyebrows raised in a pleading way Evyn doesn't recognise. She's frozen in place, cracked edges vibrating like she'll tear right open at the next bump in the road.

"I did what I had to do, the only thing I could do."

The stink of crushed lavender is thick inside the cab, the cracked windows filling the car with heated blasts of oily scent, and her father seems under its spell. His eyes are hazy, chin dipped. There's so much Evyn wants to know and, if she asks now, he'll answer her. But there's only one answer that matters.

"Where is she?"

She asks as quietly as she can, not wanting to startle him out of his reverie, but he turns to stare at her for so long that the car veers off the road, wing mirror clipping the bushes that burst from the low stone wall. For a moment, it looks like he will tell her everything. There's a waver of his lower lip and his eyes turn glassy. But then he straightens up in his seat and sets both hands on the wheel.

"In the bay," he tells her, with a hard click of his teeth like he can't stand to think of it.

She doesn't need to ask him to explain. He works on the dock, knows where all the security cameras are and which boats are left with keys hanging from hooks in their wheelhouses. Stella had never made it to Evyn's bed that night, hadn't been taken from there at all. Her father had carried her down to the bay and dropped her in.

She pictures her sister's little body hitting the water with a horrifically small splash. Had her hair been loose? Had it wrapped like seaweed around her thin arms, her little pink nightdress pulled by tidewater?

Eyes squeezed shut, she imagines the weightless drift of her sister
in the pitch dark bay until it feels so real that she could reach out
and pluck Stella from the waves. Evyn doesn't move an inch. Sitting
still, staying silent, making herself invisible, all the survival tactics
that worked to keep her safe hadn't protected Daire or Stella. All the
hiding, all the pulling away from people who would have helped her,
everything she had ever done to keep out of the foster system, had
led to this moment, sitting in a car driving to god knows where with
a drunken father, a murdered sister, and the boy who tried to help
her dying in the dirt outside their broken home.

The road opens out ahead of them, lined on both sides by the
harvested lavender fields, purple signs directing them to the garden
center or the town fair, and Evyn's breath comes in gasps.

Her father ignores the sound, clicking his tongue again as he
plucks the cigarette from his mouth. Evyn knows what comes next.
He'll unhook his seatbelt, lean forward, and reach into his back
pocket for his lighter, steering with his wrist. She had watched
this balancing game he played with some reverence when Daire was
teaching her to drive, wondering if her confidence behind the wheel
would ever improve enough to control a car that way. But now it's an
opportunity and her body reacts before she's made the decision, as
if some part of her had been waiting, coiled tight. She already knows
exactly what to do.

Evyn reaches out with both hands and pulls the wheel so hard that
her upper body rolls forward with it, ribs striking the handbrake and
head ducked below the dashboard. Her father pushes at her ineffectually,
a weak swipe of her shoulder that she barely feels because the car is
swooping, a wild lurch. The sudden change in gravity lifts her from her
seat, hips biting into the seatbelt. There's the scream of metal tearing

and her father cries out a thin, shocked yell as the car hits the ditch at an angle.

The cab dims, crunching metal sounds and clumps of dirt battering the windshield until it shatters and rains earth, stems, and glass across them both. Evyn is thrown forward into the dash, the seatbelt pulling tight as her father's airbag erupts beside her. Her head cracks against the passenger window and there's more shattering glass as the car lifts high and rolls again. Clear blue sky dawns across the broken windscreen and the driver's seat is empty. Evyn's careening arms hitting the empty spot where her father had been. And then dirt and sky in such a jumble that Evyn can't tell how many times the car rolls before her seatbelt snaps and tears under the onslaught of her thrown weight.

She's flying, out through the shattered windscreen into a torn purple haze with burnt orange fire behind her and cool, lilac-tinged darkness before her. It's almost a choice, to face toward the dark. It comes with a voice, one she'd longed to hear for two years. Evyn breathes in the dense smell of lavender and smoke and listens as a little lost girl welcomes her home.

TWENTY-FOUR

now

H ELL SMELLS LIKE DESICCATED soil and hot, acrid air. It feels like burning and choking and drowning all at once. In hell, time is a strange concept. A minute seems like hours and like no time at all. A nanosecond of pain, so intense that Evyn isn't sure it's real, is also hours of drifting mindless, until a noise or a smell pulls her back like a tide. She's pushed into waves of half-life, doesn't want to come back from the darkness at all, floating and cast about with her conjured images of Stella, sinking beneath still waters and rising from them again, wafting in and out of her own mind.

Without warning, there's a huge pull, lilac stars exploding all around her with the strength of it, blinding light, and something moves in her mouth, pushing over her tongue. There's pressure on her chest and so much movement around her and inside her body that she wants to scream with it. But to do that, she has to pull clean, cool air into her lungs. What she had been breathing before was thick, dirt-filled and clammy, made of her own frail exhalations.

After days, or maybe weeks, Calver is there, right beside her, so fast she wonders if he had been following their car. He's talking in calm murmurs but the words are lost and inconsequential, like whispering in a crowd.

The thought of the car flipping, of what she had done, pulls her back into her body and the sandy crust of her eyelids move. That one tiny motion brings pain. Like a valve releasing, it's everywhere. Evyn tries to cry out with it but the air wisps in her throat like screaming in a dream.

"Thank Christ," Calver, his voice strong but cracked at the edges, "Evyn, can you hear me?"

She can't even begin to answer. The words won't form in her mind, even if she could make her lips move.

"How long for the ambulance?" He calls to someone else and a thought begins to form about who might be with him, but it evaporates before she can catch hold of it.

A beat of time seems to waver into months.

"Get the first one to circle back. She can't wait."

The urgency of his voice is enough; Evyn doesn't want to hear or feel anymore. This time, she pushes herself under, shallower now, the waves lulling, and the pain is above her, across the water-line, where she'd have to reach out and grab it if she wants to hear more. A moment later, there are arms beneath her. Her body lurches, limbs limp, swinging at strange angles as she is lifted high and cradled against something broad and warm.

"Not this time," Calver's voice comes near her ear but he's not talking to her. "Not again."

She wishes she could open her mouth and scream at him to put her down. Every jolting step he takes brings her back into her broken body. He keeps going, carrying her, talking to her, urging her to stay conscious, and the faint sound of sirens mixes with Calver's low muttering.

Evyn opens her eyes. Her head is on his shoulder, the familiar blue of his collar streaked with bright red blood and dirt. Through tangled lashes and across the torn field behind them, there is a light so bright Evyn can't look directly at it.

She closes her eyes again, praying for the jostling of her body to stop.

"**Y**OU LIFTED HER?"

The voice is alarmed and severe. Time must have passed because she's lying flat now, shaded from the afternoon sun, though the heat still burns through her.

"She was buried in the harvest piles, I had to pull her out for CPR."

"How far from the car was she?"

"About 30 feet, past those mounds back there"

"Behind there? How'd you see her?"

IT'S DIM WHEN SHE surfaces once more, fully in her body, alive and crackling with pain. The waves of her half-conscious state are a solid wall behind her, she can no longer escape. Evyn tries to turn her head, to open her eyes. The movement produces a sound that is half cough, half cry. There's a flurry of activity, clipped voices talking around her in snapped half-sentences.

"Blood pressure rising."

"Fluid sounds from the left lower quadrant."

"Right side's hollow, her lung's collapsed."

Evyn squeezes her eyes tight against the panic. She's going to die. Her chest burns with her breath, tight in her throat, and her fingers open and close on nothing. A rough, gentle hand covers her forehead and eyes and Calver's voice is in her ear again, cutting through the buzzing anxiety and confusion, the rapid beeping, and the efficient, clipped chatter of the paramedics.

"Easy now, Evyn," he tells her, "You're safe, you're alright. You're in an ambulance on the way to the hospital."

She can suddenly feel the vibration of the engine beneath her body.

Calver had come with her. Not left her to the paramedics. Was he supposed to do that? What about his car? Shouldn't he go back to work?

All the thoughts that had crowded at the edges of her mind begin to push to the center all at once. Is her father alive? How badly is she hurt? Why can't she move?

Daire.

She forces her eyes open and crumbles of earth loosen from her lashes. Calver takes his hand away, revealing bright lights in lines on either side of a metal roof above her. Wires run down her body and Calver's dark blue cap is moving gently as he nods. For a horrifying moment, looking into Calver's face, she wonders how badly her own has been damaged, whether his scars might somehow have become hers.

When she tries to speak her throat constricts around something foreign. Her mouth can't form Daire's name and she understands why with a wave of nausea. There is something in her mouth, a tube, lying on her tongue and disappearing down her throat. She gags more at the thought than the sensation, her body convulsing with it.

Immediately, Calver's face disappears and a stranger replaces it. Calm and stoic the woman places a hand on Evyn's arm and raises her voice to be heard over the rumble of the engine.

"Evelyn, you are intubated because one of your lungs has collapsed. I know it's uncomfortable. Just breathe long and slow."

What if Daire wasn't found? What if he's still out there, bleeding, with no-one helping him? She jerks both hands, wrenching against the restraints.

"50 CC Benzodiazepine." The paramedic frowns in concentration. "Evelyn, I'm going to give you something to help you relax, you'll feel a small pinch," Evyn doesn't feel anything but terror.

Is he alive?

The drugs are too strong. As she goes under, hauled into the darkness in spite of herself, she hears Calver's voice, clear and low, and with an edge she has only heard from him once before.

"Please don't call her Evelyn. Her name is Evyn."

Twenty-Five

Then & Now

S HE DOESN'T HAVE A body anymore. It's a familiar feeling.

This place is familiar too, staring up at an icy-cold, night sky that seems to swirl faster the more they smoke.

"I think this is laced," Daire says.

Evyn takes his hand to quieten the tremor of a turning trip she can hear in his voice.

"Shh," she tells him, "We're floating in starlight."

S HE WHIRLS GENTLY IN a white room with crisp white sheets and the sound of faraway beeping, the odd squeak of a plastic chair.

"John, you should go home. Think of how it looks."

It's a voice she recognizes but Evyn can't open her eyes to check who is speaking, so she floats and listens.

"You and I both know I'm not getting my job back, Rach. That picture is everywhere. I've got people looking at me like I'm some kind of sick... like maybe I had something to do with the crash. People need to trust their police, especially in a small town like Blackditch. The investigation's just a formality."

"You don't know that. People here have known you for years. This is a juicy bit of gossip to roll around. But you're making it worse, coming here, day in, day out. You are handing them a story on a silver platter."

"The kid is hurt and she's alone."

"That's not your fault."

"Whose, then?"

Mine.

"D RAW SOMETHING FOR ME," Daire says. He taps his pen lightly, leaning closer, "Do you remember?"

She does. Taking his pen, she draws her mouth, tipped up, a joint curling smoke over her full top lip. In real life, this is where she had stopped. But here, in this swirling place, she makes her lips extra plump, a glossy spot in the center, and adds the wide angle of his mouth next to hers. Evyn slides the paper to him.

"You didn't draw this," he says with a soft smirk, one shoulder raised in an oddly shy gesture. She can be more honest here.

"I wanted to."

His eyes turn dark, warm. "I know you did."

WHEN SHE WAKES AGAIN, the red tinge to the backs of her eyelids is gone. It must be dark. There are more voices. Evyn doesn't even try to open her eyes.

"How did you find her, John? She was so far from the crash site. I was headed for the car. How did you know where to look for her?"

It's Sergeant Obasi's voice, that same probing edge to her questions.

"I don't know, Ebele. I saw something... I don't know what I saw."

Calver's response is quiet, but not sad. It has a flair of something tremulous, like incredulity. Evyn recognizes it, that burning desire to explain what can't be explained, to be believed even while saying impossible things out loud.

Once, she had lain in her small bed, still and silent with her breath held close. She had felt a pressure against her stomach, as if a small body had curled up there, in the place where Stella had always slept. Evyn had held her breath and focused on the feeling until it solidified against her. And when she finally opened her eyes, with lungs that burned and convulsed inside her, there before her, beyond the disappointment of her empty mattress, was a gossamer strand of Stella's hair.

If she'd had someone to talk to back then, her voice would have sounded just like Calver's did now.

"I think she's coming round," Obasi says and Evyn shies away from consciousness, pushing herself back into a darkness filled with dreams that seem safer and more real than anything else, especially now that she knows they're just memories.

"SHE HAD A CRUSH on you, I think."

Evyn had told him this while they watched a movie after a day of searching. She never wanted to go home after they looked in far-off places and found nothing. He'd always asked her to stay for dinner. She'd eaten in his home so much she couldn't eat scrambled eggs without peppers and onions and chilli anymore. She could crimp perfect empanada dough all by herself.

"Yeah?" Daire answers, throwing a piece of popcorn at her, "Most girls do."

Evyn rolls her eyes and pulls the popcorn bowl from his lap, setting her foot on the couch so he can't reach around her.

"Idiot," she tells him, though she thinks she might have said something more vulgar back then. He had laughed, then, threatened to change the movie to the sports documentary she hated if she didn't share the bowl.

But it's different now, he leans toward her instead, rests his whole palm on her raised knees, his fingers in the crease of her jeans.

"Are you ever jealous?" he asks, and she can't tell where he's looking but his voice has dropped low.

"You didn't say that," she tells him.

"I wanted to."

Evyn reaches for his jaw, leans until their foreheads are touching.

"Are you alive?" She asks him but there's another voice calling her name and he fades before he can tell her.

S HE WAKES CRYING, SOUNDLESS and unmoving, with tears slipping over her temples. Evyn wishes she couldn't feel as much as
she does, that she could go back to that hazy, drugged state. Her body
is heavy, even trying to bunch her hands into a fist produces nothing but
a soft curl of her fingers on the cool waffled blanket.

"Evyn," a woman's voice says, authoritative and calm, "We're going to
extubate you now that you can breathe on your own. It'll be uncomfortable for a moment."

The doctor leans over her, shining a light directly into her left eye, then
her right, waving it back and forth.

"Better, much better," she says, with a blurred curve that Evyn thinks
might be a smile. "You are a very lucky girl," the doctor waves the chart,
back and forth, as if admonishing Evyn for the information it contains.
"In the accident, three of your ribs broke and perforated your right
lung," she reads out, "There was a significant amount of debris that
needed to be cleared in surgery so that you could breathe on your own
again. You sustained a broken collar bone, a fractured tibia, your right
wrist is broken in two places, and you also have some deep bruising
on the right side of your body. I'm sure you're feeling pretty grim but,
considering your heartbeat was almost non-existent in the ambulance,
by all accounts, you are very lucky to have survived."

Evyn blinks and stares over the doctor's shoulder to where Calver is
leaning forward in his seat, one hand resting on his knee as if he's about to
leave. When Evyn moves her head, the warm plastic of the tube brushes
against her cheek.

"We're going to take the tube out now, OK?"

Calver gets to his feet, "You want me to stay?"

Evyn nods and he steps awkwardly closer to the end of the bed as the
doctor pulls a curtain around the area. She has been awake for almost

twenty minutes and in that time her mind had crystalized all kinds of information she'd had no idea she possessed at all. Over the back of Calver's seat, there's a thin silk scarf that Evyn knows belongs to Rachel. There are two overnight bags pushed against the far wall and the chairs are pushed close together, as if someone had slept there.

How much time has she spent drifting, listening to hushed conversations, on the edge of dreaming?

The doctor presses a call button over her head and a nurse comes in a few moments later. Calver stands with one hand on the curtain, twitching it as he watches the medical staff prepping. They help her upright and Evyn waits for the moment she's freed from the tube so she can ask about Daire.

The doctor tilts her chin upward, and pulls smooth and fast. Immediately, Evyn gags as the tube moves in her throat. Thin, watery bile streams over her chin and chest until the nurse crams a cardboard bowl close to her mouth. Her head swims and the nurse presses a hand to her back while she catches her breath. When she's steady, breathing raw, sore breaths into her tightened chest, the nurse moves away and uses a syringe to push a sedative into the catheter in her arm.

"Wait!" Evyn cries, but the dry rasp that pushes from her lips only results in a fit of coughing that sends her sprawling forward. The drugs spiral through her weakened body and the cough turns to a choked sob.

"Dar," she tries again but her eyelids are closing so fast she can't focus.

Calver's hand, huge and heavy, grips her left shoulder. He leans forward so their faces are at the same level and suddenly, Evyn is aware that her chin must still be covered in vomit.

"It's over now, Evyn, you're alright," he tells her and she sobs, frustrated.

He doesn't understand, thinking her tears are for herself, for her own pain. The idea that she might be wondering if Daire is alive hasn't occurred to him and suddenly Evyn knows it, the same way she had known about her sister.

If Daire was alright, he would have found a way to be here now.

WHEN SHE WAKES AGAIN the room is dim. Thin light from the open doorway illuminates Calver's outstretched legs. He's asleep in the chairs on the other side of the room, arms crossed over his chest and chin dropped low. His phone balances precariously in his lap, sliding toward his knees with every breath. She watches as it falls from his thigh toward the floor.

A hand catches it before it hits the ground. Rachel, standing just inside the door. She places the phone on the table and sighs, crouching next to his chair.

When she reaches out, it's such a hesitant, trembling motion that Evyn wants to close her eyes. It's too private, watching Rachel's fingers move over the scars on Calver's face, waking him gently.

"Hi," she says when he opens his eyes and slowly turns his head.

He pulls his feet off the seat, leaning forward and motioning her to sit down. Rachel sits close, and Evyn wonders when this comfortable glow had grown between them.

"They're going to arrest her tomorrow," Calver says, scrubbing his face with both hands, "How the hell am I going to tell her, Rach?"

"She's a tough girl," Rachel replies. There's an admiring tone in her voice that makes Evyn want to bury her face in her pillow. But her body won't respond, the crash of drugs through her system has left her wiped. Rachel's voice is low, soothing, "She'll know you're doing your best for her. I don't think she's one to forget that."

"It isn't enough," Calver says.

"Yes, it is," Rachel slides her hand over his, curving her fingers into his palm. "It's enough, John."

"I should have..." he trails off, looking down at their intertwined hands, and shakes his head. Rachel inches forward and Calver's whole body holds stock-still as she places a soft kiss on the corner of his mouth. For a moment, there is no sound in the room at all, not even breath, and then Rachel stands, apologizing quietly, and pulling a small box from her oversized carry-all.

"I brought you some real food," she tells him, setting it on the chair and hurrying to close her bag, "That's all I meant to do."

"Rachel," Calver calls, but it's too late, she's already through the doorway, her soft footfalls echoing as she walks away.

"Shit," Calver says to himself, dropping his head into his hands and staring at the ground between his feet.

Twenty-Six

now

"D AIRE," SHE SAYS WHEN she wakes, trying to sit up in bed. The room is empty, silent, the chairs lined neatly against the wall and all trace of Calver's presence gone.

She searches frantically for a buzzer, something to call someone to come help her. She needs to know what happened to Daire. Her brain is suddenly alight with information that seemed meaningless before now.

Calver had been here for what felt like days, he'd talked about losing his job, about the photograph in the papers. Had he lost his job because of her?

And Daire. There's pain in her chest when she thinks of him, lying face down in the dirt, telling her to run. Where is he?

The door opens and an unfamiliar nurse comes in, deftly pulling a chart from its spot at the bottom of Evyn's bed.

"Please," Evyn says, interrupting the nurse's clipped 'good morning' with a desperate edge to her voice, "Where's Detective Calver? He was right here, can you call him for me?"

The nurse makes a calming gesture, eyeing the readouts on the machines she's hooked up to. "It's okay, Evelyn, there's a social worker here to see you as soon as your check-up is done. She's going to go through everything with you."

Evyn's chest pulls inward. A social worker. Foster care. State-run homes. Surely, they can't do that to her when her eighteenth birthday is so close?

"No, please," her voice is too loud, too stricken, "Please can you call the detective, the one who was here before. I need to ask him something. It's really important, please."

She's babbling and the nurse frowns at the heart monitor.

"Miss Donovan, please take some deep breaths and try not to panic. You're on a lot of medication right now but you're still very sick and you could damage your lungs if you don't calm down."

They'll sedate her again, Evyn can see the hint of it on the woman's face but she can't seem to stop, breathing high and fast.

"Please, my friend, Daire Silva-Doyle, do you know what happened to him?"

"Evyn," Calver's voice, coming from the doorway, deep and strong, sounding the way he always did when he picked her up drunk or stoned. Somehow, it's a relief to hear it now, instead of the rage-inducing thing it used to be, "It's alright, try to relax. I'll tell you what you want to know, okay?"

She nods so hard that the nurse raises an eyebrow but she calms her breath without assistance, forcing her fingers to be still in her lap, to not fiddle with the wires that are attached to her chest and hands.

The nurse continues her assessment as Calver lifts a chair and moves it to the side of her bed. It seems to take forever for the nurse to leave.

"Where's Daire?" she demands, the moment the door closes.

"Evyn," Calver says and she can tell by the way he says her name that he doesn't want to tell her, "He had lost a lot of blood when the paramedics found him—"

"Is he alive?" She interrupts and her question is little more than a shriek. Calver's hands come up to placate her, a subtle look at the heart-rate monitor to remind her that she is supposed to be calm right now.

"He's in a coma. They induced it when he arrived at the hospital to help his brain recover from the blood loss. But when they stopped the drugs, he didn't wake up. They're monitoring him but they can't tell us when, or if, he'll come out of it."

Even though the drugs, she can feel the shimmer of pain deep in her chest, sparking dim shards in her midsection.

"Evyn, there's more. The doctors have deemed you fit for interview today which means, in a few minutes, Officer Obasi is going to ask you some questions about what happened the day of the accident."

He stops talking suddenly, pulling at the peak of his baseball cap and Evyn notices that it's not the standard police-issued one he usually wears. Her breathing slows because she's focusing on him, taking in his appearance from his tan work boots to his jeans and t-shirt, the thin plaid shirt, and the belt without a gun attached to it.

"Why aren't *you* interviewing me?" she asks.

"I'm on leave," Calver tells her, distracted, "You don't need to worry about that. Listen to me, Evyn. If there is anything you need to say, anything I should know about what happened on the day of the crash, you should tell me. Right now."

He's rushing, a quick flick of his wrist to check his watch and head turning to check the hallway, as if he's being followed. "The social worker is on her way. She's going to stand in as your adult guardian until we get this mess sorted. But I'll try to stay in the room with you, if you want."

"What mess?" Evyn's mind is reeling, "Is Daire here, in this hospital? Can I see him?"

Calver rubs his hands over his face, a gesture that's familiar now, one that means he's out of his comfort zone, and doesn't know where to start. "He's in intensive care. Only family is allowed in right now."

Evyn shakes her head, her mouth tightening. She tests her muscles, stretching her arms and legs, ignoring the raft of tubing and wires that move over her skin.

"Please," she says, her voice far higher-pitched than she meant it to be, "I need to see him."

Calver pulls his chair closer with a click of his tongue and ignores her request entirely. "Evyn, Officer Obasi is going to want to know exactly where you were and what you did in the twenty-four hours before the accident, do you understand?"

There's something in his voice, a tension that makes Evyn stop squirming and stare at him. She wants to ask him what he's hiding, what he's not telling her, but he continues before she has the chance.

"You are a person of interest in the death of your father, and the attempted murder of Daire Silva-Doyle. If you have anything that you want to tell me, Evyn, say it now."

Her mouth is open but she can't seem to close it.

"I..." she trails off, unsure of what she wants to say. She'd been scrambling, trying to think of a way she could get out of bed and get to Daire's room. Now her mind is entirely blank. "I *did* kill him."

Calver winces, holding up a hand to stop her.

"Who?"

"My dad." There's the memory of his face, that shocked look that she must be echoing now, the bottom of his boots disappearing through the windshield, and the empty seat as the car rolled and rolled. "I did it on purpose."

She can't breathe and the monitor flares in response, a beeping heartbeat that flutters too fast to follow.

Calver puts his hand on hers, squeezing gently.

"And Daire?"

"What?"

"Did you shoot him?"

Her breath comes rocking back to fill her chest and she almost shouts her response, "No! Of course not!"

His shoulders drop and he pats her wrist. Before he can tell her anything else, there's a shuffling in the corridor that makes them both look up. Calver takes his hand away, stands, as Officer Obasi and a woman Evyn has never seen before, make their way into the room.

"Miss Donovan," The woman holds out her hand, a grey cardigan slipping down her arm. She has a small black bag she places in Calver's seat, and her grip is warm around Evyn's lank fingers, "I'm Irena, I'm your social worker."

They talk over her, Obasi and Calver and this woman who acts as if she's standing guard. Evyn hears words like 'caution' and 'responsible adult' and 'fitness to interview' but she can't take in what's being said. She's still struggling to understand why Calver would ask her if she shot Daire but there's no time to ask because Obasi is dragging the other chair to the opposite side of the bed, setting a recording device on the table, and taking a notepad from her pocket.

"Evyn, I'd like to ask you a few questions. Can you tell me everything you remember happening from the day Mr. Calver took you from your home until the accident at Blackditch Lavender Farms?"

Evyn baulks at the wording, "Detective Calver didn't *take* me anywhere, he was helping me."

She looks over at him, standing with his back against the wall and the peak of his cap pointing straight at the floor.

"That's good, tell us about that," Obasi urges, refusing to look anywhere but Evyn's face.

She tells them everything. She doesn't start with leaving her home, she starts with Rachel, with the desperate plea of a terrified woman searching for someone she loved. She doesn't leave anything out, the bruises, the hiding, the awful things she's said to Daire on the last night they spoke. She talks for so long that her voice is hoarse when she tells them how she had pulled the wheel of her father's van.

"Miss Donovan," Obasi finally interrupts her, "I'm going to stop you there, and before we proceed again, I'm going to read you your rights."

Evyn listens to words she has heard on cop shows a hundred times before. It feel surreal. She holds out her hands, expecting them to finally cuff her, like she'd wanted every time she sat in a cell at the station and twisted her hands in her lap.

"This is ridiculous." Calver's voice comes from the corner of the room.

Obasi ignores him entirely, though she does smile a little and pats Evyn's outstretched hands back down onto the bed. "We're not going to take you anywhere, Evyn. You haven't been released from the hospital."

"I understand, I want to keep going," she says, and Obasi asks her question after question, until Evyn's eyes lose focus and her voice turns raw. They ask her the same question in multiple ways, over and over, until she can't think straight anymore.

It's Calver who stops it, pushing off the wall to quietly request a break.

"I think we've gotten all we need," Obasi says, and she sounds tired too. She presses at her temple after she stows her notepad and turns back to Evyn with a sigh. "I'll do my best for you," she says but Evyn isn't sure what that means and she doesn't ask until they're gone. Calver slides down the wall until he's sitting in a crouch, face in hands.

"What does that mean?" Evyn says to herself as the social worker follows the police out the door and down the long hallway.

"It means she's going to have to charge you with manslaughter. You've admitted to it."

"But he killed Stella! I didn't even know where he was going to take me!"

"She knows that, but you still have to be processed," He scrubs his face harder, "And there's some discrepancy over how you found Daire."

Evyn looks up. It was the one thing she'd glossed over, and they asked her so many times she was certain she'd given them a different story at least once.

"What discrepancy?" she asks, almost afraid of the answer.

Calver stands and goes to the window. He places his hands wide on the sill and leans until his forehead is touching the glass. Eventually, he turns and stares at her.

"The voicemail."

Strange. She'd told them everything about that, except the parts she couldn't explain. "Can't they just listen to it themselves? Look at the records or something?" she asks, settling back into the pillows, suddenly exhausted despite having not moved anything but her mouth in the last hour.

"They have, Evyn," he tells her and his eyes slide to half-mast, "There was no phone call, not in your phone records, and not in Daire's. He called you, repeatedly, the day before but the last call he made was at 9pm that night, and the doctors estimate he was shot between midnight and 3am."

Evyn remembers the shot, how black the sky had looked outside Calver's kitchen window. She rubs at her wrist.

"But I heard it," she says, "On the rooftop. It was his voice."

Calver looks as if he wants to run from the room, "I believe you, Evyn. I know that you believe he called you."

"That's not the same as believing me at all!"

"We know he saw the video, the station and hospital have records of him calling looking for you. But there are no voicemails in his phone records, or yours."

"Maybe he used an app, can't you check that?"

"No. His phone is..." he trails off again, and Evyn gets the distinct impression there is something he wants to tell her, but he's hiding it, trying to find a way to work it into the conversation, "Daire's phone was found in the wreckage of your fathers' car. Your phone was with him, underneath him actually. It wasn't charged. The battery was dead. Tech says it hadn't been used in 48 hours."

Evyn's mind is spinning again, trying to find the thread of a reasonable explanation.

"I called the ambulance!" she raises her hands off the bed, her voice ringing high, "How could my phone be dead if I called the ambulance?"

Calver presses his lips together as if he's biting them from the inside.

"That call was made from Daire's phone," he tells her. She had dropped her phone beside him in the dirt, picked it up again and it was cold. *His* phone, she understands suddenly, and Calver continues, "He didn't call you, Evyn. Whatever you heard on that rooftop, whatever gave you that message, it wasn't Daire." There's a new rawness to his voice that she remembers hearing before, from far away.

Until Calver goes to the side table and pours her a cup of water, Evyn doesn't realise she's crying. She doesn't turn her face away, doesn't even try to hide the tears. She takes the cup and holds it in her lap. Her body aches everywhere. She wants more of the sedative, anything to stop the blooming sense of wrongness in her stomach.

"When Daire wakes up," Calver says, "if he can remember what happened and corroborate your story, then all this will go away. But until then, we're going to need to set you up with a lawyer and get you an adult representative."

"Why can't you do that?" She already knows the answer, had seen it in the way the social worker's eyes had traveled over Calver before she left the room, how pointedly she'd left the door wide open.

"They won't let me. That picture, the one of you leaving my house, it set off a lot of alarms around town. People think," he pauses to scrub his mouth with the back of his hand, as if he's physically sick at the thought, "People are saying some unsavory things right now. I'm sorry, Evyn."

"That's why you lost your job."

"I'm not fired yet. But yes, that's part of it. The truth is, I probably *should* be fired."

She stares up at him, confused, with tears still running in a slow slide over her cheek, "Why?"

"Because I had my concerns about your father. About how he behaved with you. I should have looked deeper. But after your sister, I turned a blind eye. I only saw what I wanted to see. I'm ashamed of that."

Evyn doesn't know what to say. She wants to reach out and comfort him but he doesn't give her time. He turns away instead, pushes his cap lower over his face and squares his shoulders, pressing the back of his hand to his nose for so long that Evyn can see the nurse look up from her station.

"I'm going to get you some help, Evyn. Try to focus on getting healthy again, okay? I'll see you in the morning."

He leaves without another word and Evyn curls on her side, tugging the IV line with her. There are so many thoughts flowing through her that she can't focus on any one of them but the overwhelming guilt sits square in her chest, like she's breathing it in with every inhale.

"The detective says you've had a tough day, honey," a nurse calls. There's a soft hand on her back, a gentle pressure, "Do you need something for the pain?"

Evyn shakes her head and turns her face to the pillow. Her sister is dead, killed with a bottle that was meant for her. The man who'd tried to help her is out of a job because of her. And the boy she loves is somewhere in this building, shot through with a bullet that was probably meant for her too.

There is no medicine for what she feels.

Twenty-Seven

now

W HEN EVYN WAKES, RACHEL is sitting in the chair by the bed, reading a book with a suspiciously familiar-looking, bare-chested man on the cover. She snaps it closed and tucks it into her bag the moment she notices Evyn looking at her.

"You're awake," she says, in a too-breezy way that tells Evyn she's a terrible liar.

"Where's Calver?" Evyn asks, and then, before Rachel can answer, "Is there any news on Daire?"

Rachel smiles, "John should be here later today," Her smile fades, "And no, there's no word on Daire but, in his situation, no news is good news."

Evyn is unconvinced and her expression must show it because Rachel looks away fast, digging deeper into her huge carryall to pull out a paper bag. The smell of fresh-baked croissant seeps from it. Evyn is suddenly hungrier than she's ever been and she has to force herself to take it gently, not rip it from Rachel's hand and tear it open.

Once her mouth is full of food, she realizes she hasn't asked about Rachel's little girl.

"How's Aimee?" she says, with half a croissant tucked into the corner of her cheek slurring her words. Rachel laughs, a too-high sound that instantly makes Evyn smile back.

"She's back to her old self. She won't sleep anywhere but my bed but that's more for me than her, to be honest." She is still smiling when she reaches out to grasp Evyn's wrist, "I need to thank you for what you did for her. I saw the video, how hurt you were, and you never once put her down till you got her to safety."

Without warning, Rachel is crying, both hands pulling back to cover her trembling mouth. "I don't know how to thank you for that."

Evyn shakes her head, unsure of what to say. She raises the remains of her pastry higher, "This is a pretty good way to do it."

Rachel snorts a teary laugh and then reaches out to gently brush Evyn's face.

"I want to ask you something," she says, "John tells me that you need an adult representative. Someone to be present with you during interviews and maybe to help you settle, once you're released from the hospital."

Evyn gulps. She has no idea how long more they'll keep her here, or what will happen top her once she's discharged.

"Would you like to come and stay with me for a while? I know you turn eighteen next week and you'll be legally allowed to go wherever you want but it might be nice to have some company while you work things out, right?" Her voice is too high and cheery. It sounds like she's trying to convince herself as much as Evyn.

"That's okay," Evyn tells her, "I'll be fine on my own." Even as she says it, she knows it's not true but she tries her best to sit up taller, tipping the blanket over the cast on her wrist as if hiding it means it's not there at all. There's another on her left foot, she can feel it itching under the covers.

Rachel pulls her bag into her lap with a sigh. She takes a folded, colorful piece of paper from it, glancing at the inside before holding it out to Evyn.

"Aimee made this for you," she says but her tone is off, as if she doesn't want to hand it over at all. It's a card, Rachel's writing on the front saying "Get Well Soon."

A quick glance around the room tells it it's her only card.

On the inside, there are trees, black crayon trunks and cloudy green puffs. In between the trunks are three people. Aimee, with her blonde hair a yellow scribble, is the smallest. Evyn, with her long, dark hair scratched with the same black as the tree trunks, is the tallest. They're holding hands with a third girl, shoulder height to Evyn with the same dark hair.

There's a chill in the room, running down her spine and raising the fine hairs on her forearms. "Who's that in the middle?" Evyn asks, but her voice is stilted and shivery and she isn't sure she wants to know the answer.

Rachel stands, smoothing down her sundress, and slips the strap of her bag over her shoulder. She's plastered on a terribly fake smile and Evyn isn't sure for whose benefit. "I don't know," she says, cheerily dismissive, "Kids are funny. If you change your mind and you want to come stay with us, the offer is open. I've taken the room offline for the rest of the year so it's there for you if you want it. But Evyn," her voice sharpens and she raises her chin slightly "My little girl is in that house. I can't have drugs in there. You understand that, don't you?"

Evyn's mouth falls open but she nods anyway.

It hadn't happened in a while, someone reminding her of how bad her reputation is in Blackditch. The last was her English teacher, Mrs. Ross, stopping her outside the lunchroom after she'd spent a half-hour with Daire reading a godawful spy book he'd recommended.

"He's a good boy, Daire," her teacher had said in a short hiss, "If you were a good friend, you'd keep your drugs away from him."

She'd walked away fast, leaving Evyn gaping after her and there had been the urge to shout that they weren't her drugs at all. The unwitting supplier was the world-renowned architect who chaired their board meetings every month. But she swallowed it, looking back at Daire to make sure he hadn't heard before heading to her next class.

She feels it again now, the urge to protect herself, to let a little truth show. But she can't. She nods instead and Rachel writes down her phone number and leaves it on the side table.

"You need a guardian for this next part, Evyn. Are you happy for it to be me?"

"Yes. Thank you."

"Least I can do," Rachel says as she tucks her bag higher on her shoulder and heads for the door, "I'll see you soon."

E VYN ISN'T ALONE FOR more than three minutes before the nurse comes to remove the drip and take the heart monitor away. She leans a pair of crutches against the wall.

"You're looking better," she tells Evyn, "Do you want to take a shower?"

Evyn can't remember ever feeling grimier than she does now. Her hair is greasy and her skin is dry. She doesn't know how long it's been since she last brushed her teeth. She nods furiously until the nurse laughs and helps her pull back the covers.

It's brutal, learning how to lean her weight so she can walk with the cast and crutches without putting pressure on her ribs or wrist. She manages the walk to the bathroom only with constant support from the nurse whose name she still doesn't know. But after the shower, Evyn feels brand new, like she's been scrubbed clean of more than just dirt from the lavender field.

The bedsheets are clean when she returns to her room but no-one is waiting for her. The nurse tucks her in and shows her the call button and, when she leaves, Evyn sits in an empty room and stares at the blank walls for less than a minute before pushing the sheets back again.

Daire is in intensive care.

She drags her gym bag from the bedside locker and pulls out her robe. It's too short to cover the hospital gown entirely, but it does hide the opening at the back. Slowly, she makes her way out into the hallway, checking to ensure the nurse's station is empty. By the time she gets to the elevator, she's already exhausted, but she keeps going, leaning against the walls until she's standing in front of the double doors to intensive care.

They're locked. A keypad on the wall blinks with a small red light and the sign next to it reads 'No Unauthorised Entry.'

She leans in to read the small print at the bottom, instructions for family members to follow, and almost can't get out of the way fast enough when the door opens unexpectedly. A tall man in a white lab coat reaches out a hand to steady her.

"Can I help you?" he asks and Evyn shakes her head.

"I just came to see my friend," she says, trying to make her voice sound as confident as the doctors.

"This area is restricted," the man says, a small frown at the crutches and cast, "Where have you come from?"

Evyn starts to panic. Daire is behind those closing doors, just a few moments away, and the urge to dart past the doctor hits hard, as if she could fix everything broken inside her just by seeing his face.

"I'm a patient," she tells him, straining her neck to see through the glass.

There, at the end of the hallway, striding past the reception counter, is Mrs. Silva-Doyle. She stops, though Evyn hasn't made a sound and the doors are so thick that even if she'd called, Evyn's not sure she could have been heard. But Mrs. Silva-Doyle turns her head and stares.

Evyn feels rooted to the ground under the weight of it. The doctor is talking to her, asking something she can't hear and couldn't respond to even if she wanted.

Daire's mother turns away, as if to walk back the way she came, but then stops and strides toward the doors with a blank look that makes Evyn's stomach drop. The truth is, Evyn had dismissed the attempted murder charge the moment that she'd told Calver she hadn't done it. As soon as he'd breathed a sigh of relief, Evyn had felt like that threat had lifted. But somewhere out there was a file with her name as a suspect and suddenly she is terrified of how showing up at Daire's ward would look to his mother.

Mrs. Silva-Doyle disappears from view, pushing the release button on the inside wall and then the door is opening and Evyn's fingers grip tight around the crutch.

"What are you doing here, Evelyn?" Mrs. Silva-Doyle's voice is deep and short, her chin tilted high and her soft accent clipped to almost non-existent.

"I wanted..." Evyn can't find the words, "I just wanted to see him."

"He's not well," she said, as if Daire had the flu instead of a gunshot wound inflicted by Evyn's father, "It's not good that you're here. I told Calver 'no' and you should respect that."

Evyn swallows. In all the time she's known Daire, his parents had never spoken to her with anything other than kindness.

"Please," she says, "I'm sorry. I won't stay. I just need to know he's okay."

"He is not okay. He's lying in a hospital bed and he can't wake up." She snaps her mouth closed and Evyn can hear the words she wants to say. Her body is trembling with the effort of holding them back. Evyn's fault. All Evyn's fault. "Go back to your room, Evelyn."

The doctor takes her elbow.

"I'm sorry," Evyn tries one more time. She doesn't even know why. She just wants to see him, to stand at the door of his room and look. But she won't get even that small glimpse and maybe it's right that she shouldn't.

"Evyn!"

Calver calls out from the other end of the corridor. She sags a little in relief and turns to look at him jogging lightly toward them.

"What's happening here?"

The relief vanishes. Calver is frowning at her and her vision swims, from tears or faintness, she's not sure which.

"I'm sorry," she says again, and Calver knocks the doctors hand away, wrapping one arm around her shoulder, turning her away from the intensive care unit.

"Let's get you back," he says quietly.

The doctor comes to a stop in front of them, a clipboard held in front of his chest. "These patients are very sick, young lady" he says but he doesn't get to continue because Calver stops, half-turned as if speaking to both Mrs. Silva-Doyle and to the doctor.

"So is *this* patient," he turns a little more, talking directly to Daire's mother, "She's seventeen years old and she's been through more than we'll ever know. She didn't shoot your son, Gabriella, she saved him."

Daire's mother stands still for a moment, her eyes flicking between Evyn and Calver. She gives a short nod and turns away, letting the door close behind her. Calver ignores the doctor, helping Evyn back to the lifts, saying nothing until he reaches her room and sets her on her bed.

Evyn's hands are hurting from the crutches and her ribs are aching and sore, despite the medicine she'd taken only a few hours earlier. She's still on the verge of tears, the muscles of her mouth tight, determined to hold them back.

"I'm sorry," she says, her voice thick, "I won't do that again."

Calver sighs and hands her a cup of water. "Gabriella is worried for her son," he tells her, "Try not to take it to heart."

Evyn is worried for him too, but she closes her mouth and lets herself rest back onto her pillows. She hurts everywhere but pain is something she can handle, it's the fear that makes her want to close her eyes and pretend to be asleep.

"Did Aimee make this?" Calver says, and Evyn opens her eyes to see him smiling at the card. She watches him open it, sees the small frown of confusion, his eyes flicking to hers almost reluctantly.

"Rachel brought it this morning," Evyn answers and even she can hear the trepidation in her voice, like she's asking him not to ask the question that he obviously wants to.

"Who's the third girl?"

Evyn closes her eyes again, unsure of how to respond, but there's a flickering light on the back of her eyelids and, when she opens them, she's not afraid anymore.

"How did you know where I was, at the crash site?" she asks. Calver snaps the card shut and puts it on the table, taps it with two fingers like he's gearing himself up.

"I saw something," he tells her and she recognizes the reluctant shift in his voice, "I don't know, I guess I got lucky."

She waits, twisting her fingers in her lap because she thinks she knows exactly what he saw. She thinks she saw it too, half-conscious with her chin resting on his shoulder as he carried her out of the field. All those times she felt like her sister was close to her, right there in front of her if she squeezed her eyes shut and held her breath - Evyn knows exactly how she was found.

"Look," Calver says, sitting at the edge of the hospital chair, elbows on his knees like he's ready to leap up again, "When I found you, it was... strange. We should have had to search that field. You were buried so deep in the harvest piles you weren't visible and you weren't making noise because you weren't breathing. I found you because I saw something. Something bright caught my eye, over and over, like a flash or a flicker, and I never really saw what it was. But I think I *know* what it was. And I think you know, too."

"I do," Evyn says. It takes every last bit of strength she has not to cry, but she does it. She curls her hands into fists and hugs her arms into her body, "I think Aimee does too."

Calver puts his hand on top of hers and takes a slow breath. "She says someone helped her, turned her away from the cliff face and toward the woods. Showed her where to go. So yes, I think Aimee knows too." Evyn can already tell it's the last time he'll ever speak of it, can see him shutting it away as if it never happened. Almost immediately, he takes his hand away and rubs it over his jaw. The white scars stretch pink. "There's a hearing tomorrow. I've found you a good lawyer and Rachel has agreed to be present as your advocate. It's where they'll decide on how to proceed with the charges and where you'll go once they release you from hospital."

Evyn can feel the blood draining, her head light and heavy all at once.

"I don't want you to worry," he tells her, "The attempted murder charge will be dismissed once Daire wakes up. I'm working on how to handle the manslaughter charge."

She almost smiles, "Oh, so I shouldn't worry?"

Calver blinks and then lets loose a small laugh at her sarcastic tone. He leans forward and chucks her chin.

"There she is," he says. He has that same look as when he'd picked up Aimee's card. Evyn isn't familiar with his expression, but she's pretty sure she knows what it is. The tears come unbidden, her mouth twisting.

"I'm so sorry," she says and Calver is shushing her before she can tell him why but she says it anyway, because it hurts worse than any broken bone, "I'm so sorry I caused all this."

Calver stops cold and stares down at her. For the first time since her father provoked him, Evyn sees anger flash in Calver's face.

"I couldn't' protect them." She's hiccupping now, almost hyper-ventilating, "I tried, but it only made things worse. I should have told someone. I shouldn't have hidden it. It's all my fault and I can't take any of it back! I can't fix it!"

She's howling. Her voice is turning over and rolling loud in the small room. Her eyes are burning and she can't control any part of her shaking body.

"If I had taken Stella, run away, she'd be alive now!" she clutches the blankets, balls them in her fists, and pulls them into her chest, "And I tried to keep away from Daire, I really did, but he wouldn't let me! I was so lonely and so afraid all the time and he made it feel like I wasn't so broken anymore. But now he's up there and I can't see him and he might never wake up and it's all my fault!"

She tries to say more, but her words choke her.

Calver sits at the edge of her bed, hauls her into an awkward hug, as if he hasn't held anyone in years and has forgotten how. She's getting tears and snot and saliva all over the front of his t-shirt but he doesn't move away or seem to care and Evyn can't stop now that she's started. Heaving breath and choking sobs and her body hurts every time it shakes but that only makes her cry more.

Through blurry eyes, she sees someone standing in the doorway, curling dark hair and the curve of a feminine hip. A moment later, a blonde nurse is coming through.

"Sweetheart," she says, soft and sure, "I'm going to give you something to help you sleep now, okay?"

Evyn doesn't have the strength to shake her head. She says nothing, hides her face in Calver's shirt as the needle pricks her arm. The sedative works through her in seconds, calming her and slowing the pounding pulse in her ears.

"It's not your fault, Evyn," Calver tells her, settling her back onto the pillows. He pulls the blanket up to her shoulders, the wet patch on his shirt extending almost to his shoulder, "You didn't do any of this. You're a kid. You should have been protected."

Her eyes are too heavy. It's impossible to respond.

There's a shadowy shape in the corner of the doorway again but Evyn's asleep before she can see who it is.

TWENTY-EIGHT

now

RACHEL SIGNS THE DISCHARGE papers while Evyn rigidly ignores the social worker. She has nothing against her, but her eighteenth birthday is in less than a week and then the social worker will be removed, like a magic switch has been flicked.

The drive to the district courthouse is short and quiet. Evyn stares out at the streets and wonders if, somewhere near here, there might still be a picture of her sister pasted to a lamppost or a traffic light, a poster that she and Daire had put up together.

Outside the courthouse, there are cameras and news vans, people congregating on the stone steps in pristine outfits and perfect hair. Evyn is wearing a blouse from her gym bag that's only slightly wrinkled and a pair of tailored trousers Rachel loaned her. She had brushed her hair straight but her fingers were shaking too badly this morning to apply anything other than lipgloss. She ducks her head as the car turns through the gates.

Rachel is nervous, Evyn can tell by the way she keeps tucking a loose strand of hair behind her ear. But the social worker seems completely at ease, walking them across the car park and pointing out the usher waiting at the double doors of the building.

"Just this way," she says, as if directing them around a supermarket. The hallways seem to loom, ornate coving, huge curved windows, and people in dark suits with somber expressions. She follows the adults like she's in a dream.

Calver is waiting inside the courtroom, directly behind her seat. He doesn't say anything, just nods at her as if he's completely confident that she can manage this - like being charged with attempted murder is an everyday occurrence. Somehow, it's comforting.

She cracks her knuckles so incessantly that the lawyer she's never met before stares hard at her. He holds out his hand to shake hers, "Try to hold your hands by your sides, Miss Donovan," he says, straight-backed in his seat. Someone at the side of the courtroom calls out and everyone in the room stands at the same time. Evyn stands too, though her knees are weak and the crutches make everything awkward.

There's murmuring behind her that increases in volume until the whole room is filled with muttering and whispers. The judge looks up, scowling over his spectacles at the center aisle.

"Judge, could I address the court?"

"Mrs. Silva-Doyle, you may."

Evyn swings around, ignoring the twinge of pain that such a fast motion produces. Daire's mother stands in the center of the room, a few feet away from her. She has a folder in her hands, wearing a glacially-cut suit with her hair sharpened to points on either side of her jaw. She tilts her chin higher, staring at the judge.

"I'd like to advocate on Miss Donovan's behalf in relation to the attempted murder of my son, Daire Silva-Doyle."

Evyn can't breathe. She doesn't understand any of the words but Calver is leaning forward with a huge, relieved exhale.

"Mrs. Silva-Doyle, is there new evidence that I should be aware of in this case? Has your son recovered?"

"No, your honor," there is the slightest hint of a tremble in her voice, but she continues a moment later with the same steely tone, "But I do believe the charges are unfounded and I recommend they be dismissed."

The judge sits back in his seat. On the other side of the aisle, the two prosecuting lawyers talk fast and low. Behind them, in the audience, Officer Obasi is smiling at her and Evyn blinks back, unsure of what's happening.

"Having reviewed the charge sheet, I've already determined that the manslaughter charge should be dismissed due to the fact that Miss Donovan was under extreme duress at the time. But the testimony does point to the Accused's probable involvement in this case, given that her own statement was so easily found to be inaccurate."

"I believe those inaccuracies were caused by Miss Donovan's state of mind on the day of the events."

"How do you mean?"

"She had several injuries inflicted by her father, and she was, understandably, emotionally fraught. I don't believe Miss Donovan is lying about the phone call she says she received. I feel that, in her traumatized state, she may have..."

There's a buzzing sound. Evyn swipes at her ears as if it might be coming from outside herself, but she knows this feeling, this slip away inside herself instead of trying to hear what's happening around her.

If she could, she would set her head on the desk and close her eyes. It's too much. None of it makes sense. And no matter how she stares, Mrs. Silva-Doyle will not look at her. It's as if she doesn't exist at all, as if all the people around her, people who have her fate in their hands, barely even realize she is there in the room with them.

She wishes Daire were here, standing beside her.

EVERYONE IS MOVING, FILING out of the room. Calver pats her back and smiles wider than she's ever seen. Rachel leans over, cupping Evyn's stricken face with her hands.

"It's over," she tells her, "The prosecution dropped all charges."

The lawyer is packing up, stacking papers into a leather briefcase with monogrammed locks. "Take her out the back way if you want to avoid the press," he says. Rachel nods, still beaming and searching the crowd in the atrium behind them. Evyn looks too, searching for sharp, dark hair and a set of brown eyes that used to be soft. But Daire's mother is nowhere to be found.

"Let's get you out of here," Calver says. Evyn can only nod, awkwardly following them to the side of the courtroom where another usher holds open a door for them.

Calver and Rachel walk on either side of her, holding her elbows above the cast. They shuffle her into Rachel's car and Evyn is surprised when Calver gets into the driver's seat, his hand resting on the gear-stick next to Rachel's knee. She hopes for them, she really does. But their closeness also stings, and she looks away.

"Alright, let's get you home," Calver ducks his head to look at her in the rearview mirror. His face falls and he turns in his seat, twisting to look back at her with his eyebrows in a concerned upturned 'v' that lifts his hat slightly off his forehead, "Hey, it's alright, it's over now, Evyn."

She's crying, though she hadn't realised it. She's not even certain what the problem is until she opens her mouth and the words come tumbling out. "I don't want to go home," she says, the flash of the peeling peach paint of her crumbling house clear in her mind.

She can't see Rachel beyond the bulk of Calver's shoulder but she hears her say "Oh, sweetheart, no," like she's talking to a child instead of a newly-freed, teenaged murder suspect, "You don't ever have to go back there."

"Please can you take me to Daire? I need to see him," she asks, "Please?"

It's a pitiful cry and this is the youngest she has felt in so many years. Calver closes his eyes and turns back to look at Rachel.

"You've been through a lot this morning, Evyn. I think you need to rest," she says, not quite meeting Evyn's eyes, "Then, we'll talk to Daire's mother, okay?"

Evyn doesn't have the energy to argue. She sobs instead, and clicks her seat belt into the lock. Her body feels heavy, sore and unfamiliar, like she's been hollowed out and only her skin is holding her together.

And there's a part of her, growing and pulsing in her chest, that thinks she might never see Daire again.

It takes a long time to drive back to Blackditch, more than an hour of low murmuring chatter from the front seat, lulling her. She doesn't listen to them, the softness of their voices, the delicate thread they're holding like both of them are just as fearful to break it. It's calming, even though she can feel the thrum of some nervous tension from both of them.

It's so familiar; wanting, and not doing a single thing about it. She hopes they don't leave it until it's too late, like she had.

A T THE WELCOME SIGN for Blackditch, she asks Calver to take her back to her house.

"Evyn," he says, and all his disapproval snakes into her name, "You don't want to go back there. Rach has a room for you and you're going to need some support for the next—"

She cuts him off, raising a hand to stop him talking, "I just need a few things, that's all."

He shoots a concerned glance at Rachel but pulls the car in, rocking over the cattle-grid with a familiar, stomach-turning metallic ring. She tells them she's fine when she gets out of the car. She doesn't need anything but the key Calver hands her to her own childhood home.

Slowly, she makes her way to the front door. Graffiti is scrawled over it, 'Murderer' in artless red spray paint. Numb, she wonders who it was meant for. Evyn or her father? Her crutches rock the broken step so badly that Calver opens the car door.

"I'm fine!" she calls but her voice wobbles as she steps inside.

In the hallway, there's the stink of stale carpet, soaked with decades of cheap alcohol and the tang of old smokes stubbed in ashtrays and left to rot. How had she never smelled it so clearly before? The walls are bare, cracked and never repaired, fading slivers of wallpaper still stuck in spots and streaks. Deliberately, she steps on all the creaking floorboards.

She doesn't go into the living room or the kitchen, just shuffles to her sister's room and leans against the door frame.

Her yellow bedspread, tucked neatly into corners, as inviting as Evyn could make it. Her wall, covered with Evyn's drawings and sketches. The tiny set of drawers that contained every scrap of clothing she had, the top covered with cheap plastic jewelry and beach stones and dollar-store lip glosses. The ache in Evyn's chest is so bad she has to sit on the bed, breathing through her nose to stifle it.

"I know you can hear me," she says, though she's not sure of that at all, "And I want you to know that I love you, and I'm sorry, and it's okay now, Stella. I'll be okay. You can go."

She's crying again, despite her best efforts, but she doesn't let it twist her insides the way it had in the hospital. She takes a drawing from the wall, a mermaid she had drawn that Stella had colored with markers. She lifts and hugs Stella's half-unstitched teddy bear, and pockets a small bracelet with plastic hearts. Cradling her treasures to her chest, she turns her back on her own bedroom.

There's nothing she wants from it.

Rachel and Calver watch her lock the door, two sets of eyes on her as she tries to hold her items and make her way down the step. She crosses the uneven ground, taking in the piles of old farm machinery and molding pallets. Out beyond the yard, the fence is dull and rusted. The opening she so often squeezed through looks dangerous now, tetanus waiting to happen. The trees beyond sway calmly in a cool breeze.

"I'm ready," Evyn says, when she's seated in the back, holding her treasures in her lap. Rachel dabs at her cheeks with a tissue, a small downturn at the side of her mouth. Calver reaches across the handbrake as if to pat her knee, but pulls back at the last moment. He rests his arm on the back of her seat instead and twists to reverse back onto the road.

Evyn stays quiet for the rest of the drive. A short few minutes and they're outside Rachel's pretty home. White-painted wood and profusions of pink rhododendrons, roses in an arc over the tiny front porch and the bay glinting reflected light off the upstairs windows.

"Let's get you inside," Rachel says, slipping around the car to hold her elbow as if she might fall at any moment.

"Thank you, Rachel," Evyn says, and lets herself be helped.

TWENTY-NINE

now

INSIDE, RACHEL'S HOUSE IS clean and quiet with white painted walls, overstuffed furniture, and wicker baskets full of blankets and toys. There are photographs on every wall; Aimee smiling, laughing, hanging upside down from a willow tree that Evyn recognizes with a jolt. Rachel ushers her past a kitchen that smells like lemons and salty sea air from the open windows.

"Aimee's with her Nana," she tells Evyn, "She's home tomorrow. Her room is upstairs next to mine, and yours is here."

She frowns a little, maneuvering so both of them can fit through the hallway easily. Calver follows behind with her bag and Evyn feels awkward and exhausted all at once.

Her room is pure white, aside from one bare stone wall with a huge mirror resting heavily against it. The gauze curtains move lightly in the breeze and there's a small patio outside the old French doors with a quaint seating area, slanted light warm enough to curl up in.

"I can't afford this," Evyn says suddenly, stopping short in the doorway and staring at the snowy-white sheets, "I don't even know how long it will be till I can find a job and, with school, it will only be part-time so there's no way I can pay you back, Rachel."

Rachel tuts at her, urging her toward the bed and taking away the crutches as soon as she's sitting, as if she's afraid Evyn will run.

"Don't worry about any of that, Evyn. Just focus on getting better. I'm going to make you something to eat and then I'll make that call, like I promised."

She's gone before Evyn can even thank her, ponytail swinging behind her. Calver glances at her retreating back and abruptly drops the bag in the corner of the room. He takes a deep breath, so vast his whole upper body moves with it, and rubs absently at the scars on his face, pressing into the twisted skin as if he could smooth it out.

Evyn thinks of Daire, how he'd unfurled like a spring on the gallery roof, moving like some unstoppable thing had snapped inside him, hands touching everywhere all at once.

"Get some rest, kid," Calver says and follows Rachel down the long corridor. Her bedroom door swings shut and Evyn lays down on her bed, covering the corner of her smile with an embroidered pillowcase. She tries to rest. Tries for what feels like hours, until the sun is lower in the sky and the walls are tinted pink with it.

C ALVER'S HAND IS ON her shoulder, shaking her gently from the first dreamless sleep she's had in two years.

"Time to get up, Evyn," he says quietly as she turns over to squint at him. He looks disheveled, his cap is gone and his hair is mussed. The collar of his t-shirt is pulled lank and the usual straight line of his mouth is soft and curved. "Let's get you some breakfast and then I'll bring you to the hospital to see Daire, if you still want to go?"

She gasps and nods fast, trying to push herself upright with her undamaged hand until Calver reaches down to help her. Evyn cleans herself up as quickly as she can. It's not possible to shower with so many casts and bandages, but she washes everywhere she can reach and scrubs yesterday's make-up from her face. She swaps Rachel's tailored pants for a sundress that pulls easily over the cast and ties a chambray shirt in a knot at her waist. She does her makeup in the gilded mirror and twists her body to check how she looks at all angles, as if she's going on a date instead of visiting a comatose boy. She wants to curl her hair, but instead, Evyn makes her way slowly down the hallway to the kitchen.

Rachel is leaning over the wooden table, hair tumbling over her arm as she sets a bowl in the center. There's the comforting waft of freshly baked bread as Rachel turns back to the counter with a dreamy smile. Calver hands her three plates, his free hand sliding along the curve of her waist.

Evyn coughs into her elbow and they both turn to smile at her, not jumping apart the way she had expected them to.

"Evyn! You're awake!" Rachel smiles wide and motions her toward a seat, "It's just salami and cheeses for breakfast. I thought you'd want something quick."

Evyn can't remember the last time she had an appetite at all, certainly not at the hospital, where weeks of over-seasoned, unpalatable mush came pre-cut for her.

"Sounds delicious," she says. In the watery glow of the kitchen, all three of them are smiling. They eat in a tumult of soft murmuring and half sentences, as if they've done this a million times. Evyn feels like the courtroom yesterday was a nightmare, something she has woken from in a familiar, safe place. It's an odd sensation, not being afraid. She hopes it lasts.

Just as she starts to get restless, the front door opens and Aimee comes running in. She's like a different child, her hair streaming out behind her and her clothes pristine. An older woman with a French twist in her hair follows her inside, smiling after her. Aimee pulls to a stop in the kitchen doorway. For a moment, Evyn thinks this is where everything will end. The child will burst into tears, remember everything that happened to her, and Evyn will be sent away, to live somewhere else.

"Hi!" Aimee says, shyly twisting her foot.

"Hello," Evyn answers.

"My mom says you're going to teach me how to draw."

Rachel groans and holds out her hands so her daughter can run into them. "We said we might ask, *some day.*"

"I'd love that!" Evyn says, surprised by how much she means it. She sees herself sitting down at this table, papers and pencils spread everywhere, showing a shy little girl how to draw a mermaid or a pirate.

Calver stands, awkwardly tall in a kitchen filled with women.

"Mom, this is John Calver and Evyn Donovan," Rachel says. Calver reaches out to take the older woman's hand. She seems to drop it as quickly as she can, her short nod and zipped lips evidence of her disapproval. Evyn's wave goes unanswered. Calver is unfazed, as always. He takes his plate and leans down to murmur his thanks to Rachel, so close she must feel the movement of his mouth against her ear. Her cheeks were already pink, but the flush spreads wider and Evyn glances away,

"Okay," he says, once the plates are in the dishwasher, "Let's go see him."

Evyn's stomach jumps, rolls and topples over itself and, for a moment, she thinks she might be sick, but she stands tall and follows him to the car. He helps her into the car and Rachel stay behind, standing in the doorway, washed in gentle morning light. Calver strides back to kiss her goodbye. Once he's behind the steering wheel, pulling out of the driveway in awkward silence, Evyn smirks at her knees. "Rachel and Calver sitting in a tree," she sings to herself.

Calver frowns at her and says, "Thank you, Miss Donovan, that's enough," in a deep-dropped detective tone so familiar it makes them both grin.

AT THE HOSPITAL, HER crutches are spongy on the thick lino and the hallways seem miles long. By the time they reach Daire's ward, Evyn is panting lightly, trying to hide it. It's quiet. The few staff members on duty murmur low greetings and point them in the direction of Daire's room.

Through the glass panel in the door, a huge display of cards and flowers rests on a side table. She can see the edge of his bed, a familiar blanket draped over the edge, trailing to the floor. It's the one from his room, a soft grey and navy throw they had wrapped around their shoulders on his patio so many nights. Calver holds the door open for her and the room falls away.

Daire, a solid point of focus behind tubes and wires and ventilators. His arms are by his sides, limp fingers curled. His chest rises and falls steadily with the mechanical hiss of the machine he's hooked up to. The stark paleness of his face is shocking, light stubble in glinting patches, a profusion of tubes distending his taped mouth and lines running from his long, straight nose. His lashes are dark against the tinted blue beneath his eyes and his forehead has that shadowy line he used to get while studying, as if he's about to frown.

It's embarrassing, the sob that bubbles up, how it takes hold of her legs and makes them shake. Seeing him like this, so vulnerable and drained of his usual intense presence, feels irreversible. She can't hold her balance.

Calver catches her elbow.

"Steady," he whispers, "They say coma patients can hear you."

Evyn's never been so grateful for the reminder. She stands taller with a deep breath, and inches forward toward the empty chair.

There's a cough from the other side of Daire's bed and Evyn realises they are not alone. She'd been too focused on Daire to notice his parents, both of them sitting quietly in the dim area next to the curtain.

"Thank you," she tells them, because it's all she can think of to say. Her voice is barely above a whisper but Mrs. Silva-Doyle looks up and zeroes in on her with a sharpness that feels like a slap.

"When you found him, did he say anything?"

Evyn licks her lips and tries to make her voice audible above the hammering of her heart.

"Yes. He told me to run."

"But you didn't."

"No. I tried to help but..." Evyn doesn't know what else to say.

Mr. Doyle looks up, nods briefly, and then stands, holding out his hand to his wife. She's not finished though, and she lets his hand hover.

"If you hadn't found him, we would have been left searching. Just like you were, for Stella," she says and Evyn has to take another deep breath,

"So thank you, for calling the ambulance. For trying." She takes her husband's hand and lifts out of her seat. "We'll give you a few minutes."

"Going for a coffee if you want to join us, Detective," Mr. Doyle says. His voice is tired, but it still holds that parental tone that says 'let's leave the kids to it'.

"I will, thanks," Calver says, but he waits until Evyn is seated to follow them, a small squeeze to her shoulder before he walks away, and then she's alone with Daire.

She's grateful. She couldn't say what she came to tell him in front of anyone else. Though she's not sure if he can hear her, Evyn's cheeks redden and she twists her hands together. She's almost afraid to touch him, unsure of where it might hurt or whether she even should, given that he can't tell her if he doesn't want her to. She takes his hand in both of hers, quick, like diving off the pier before she can back out and run. He's warm, dry palms and slack fingers that open easily and curl back in to rest against her knuckles.

"I'm so sorry," she tells him, a short whisper like the trickle of a dam before it tears open. And then it's flooding from her, all the things she did wrong, all the things she wishes she could take back. "I'm so sorry I said those awful things. I didn't mean them. I'm sorry I didn't listen to you or let you help me but, most of all, I'm sorry I never told you how I feel."

She leans forward, pressing his wrist to her forehead. The contact isn't enough. She wants to feel his free hand in her hair, for him to turn on his side and shrug one lazy shoulder so she'll know everything will work out. She wants their bare knees under his coat and the scratch of chalky roof tiles on the backs of their thighs as they talk about nothing in a way that means everything.

Instead, she settles for laying her head on his chest, looking up at his closed eyes and placid face. It gets harder to speak, her throat burns and the sheet is dampening under her cheek. Evyn pushes through it, forces herself to tell him everything, because she knows that not all stories have a happy ending and sometimes, lost things don't ever get found, no matter how hard you look. She won't let that happen to him.

"You were right. About everything. I wish I'd listened."

She listens now to the steady thump of his heartbeat, watching for any signs of recognition. Just beyond him, on the small shelf over his bed filled with Get Well cards and photos of Daire with his friends, teammates, and family, is a small vase. The glass is thick and old, patterned, and Evyn can smell the flowers it holds, as familiar as air.

"I've been in love with you for so long, Daire. Please come back."

The light above the bed sparkles in the cut glass, flashing bright spots that catch in the compass around her neck. She reaches for it instinctively, places it over Daire's heart. Its broken needle points toward him, as it always has, and Evyn takes a deep breath and lets the lavender scent work to calm her pounding heart and her aching insides.

The needle swings slowly as she watches, swirling one way and then the other, and Evyn can feel the tug of it inside her, like a shifting in her chest, a weight she wasn't aware of until it wasn't there anymore. The lightness in its place is quivering, unfamiliar and strange, like hope.

The needle points North, steadies there, away from both of them, as if it had never been broken at all.

And Daire's fingers move against her thumb, the barest tremble, then stronger, holding on to her.

Thank you so much for reading Evyn and Daire's story.

Acknowledgements

"Fine. I'll do it myself."

Well, that was the thought... Turns out, in order to publish a book, you actually have to have a *massive* amount of help, or at least I did.

Firstly, to my wonderful husband, thank you for uprooting your entire life to give your family everything they need and so much more. Thank you for always finding ways to make me laugh, even when I'm about to blow a gasket, and for all the help with 'research' you so obligingly put up with. I will always love you more than cheesy potatoes.

To my gorgeous babies, all my wishes came true with you. This is just icing.

Mom, thank you for being my cheerleader. You were always proud, even when I was bringing home 'art' with jagged pieces of glass stuck in it. If I am even half the mother you are, I will be ecstatic. Also, thank you for your proofreading ninja skills! Dad, if I told you I wanted to be an astronaut, you would work out a plan to get me there. With this book, you gave me more details on legal procedure than a judge! Thank you for always having my back and pointing me in the right direction. My bro's,

Mark for his tech skills, and Owen for helping with the police details, thank you so much. I am one lucky girl to have such an amazing family.

My extended family, the Lynch's, thank you for defying all in-law jokes and being absolutely awesome support.

To Red and Loki, I am so grateful to know you both. You continue to be a source of pure joy that I carry around in my pocket. And all my Reylo pals, including Pen, Laura, Sadie, Xav, Nikki, Stef, Random, Becca, Carrots, Jen, Kal, Quam, Junk, Rach, Nixy, TBR, Mish, Patti, Grace, Hannah, Edda, Elle, Xyla, Ashley, Andrina, Liana and all the beautiful writers in the 123, Sin Bin, and Frussy Hussies servers - you all gave me a voice I never knew I had and unlocked more kinks than I will ever be comfortable with. I adore you. Also Thea, whose beautiful work I came across by accident and thus became my portal into a whole new landscape.

To Davena for showing this story so much love that it swelled from forty thousand words to eighty thousand. You are a true bestie. And to Barb, who edited so well that it quickly dropped back to seventy thousand, I am so grateful for your friendship, generosity and your pinpoint accurate advice. Our writers group, Thursday Night Writers will always be my fave drinking buddies.

My lifelong friends, Victoria, Jenny, Nicola, Grainne and Annie, when we are together, it always feels like I'm a teenager again. I hope we all end up as little old ladies in the same nursing home, wreaking havoc. I miss you and I love you.

The funding for this project was awarded by The Arts Council of Ireland. I am so appreciative of the essential work they do supporting Irish Artists. Thank you so much for seeing worth in my story.

Finally, Sarra Cannon gave me the knowledge and courage to try to make my dream happen and I cannot thank her enough. Her community of writers is such a beautiful place to be.

So, while I wanted to do it myself, turns out I have a whole raft of amazing people in my life and, without them, this manuscript would still be in my kitchen drawer giving me stink-eye. I am so very grateful.

www.ingramcontent.com/pod-product-compliance
Lightning Source LLC
Chambersburg PA
CBHW011034190726
48290CB00011B/2844